"The Sweetest Neighbor"

Three Sisters Cafe #3

By Laura Ann

This is a work of fiction. Similarities to real people, places, or events are entirely coincidental.

THE SWEETEST NEIGHBOR

First edition. June 14, 2022.

Copyright © 2022 Laura Ann.

Written by Laura Ann.

DEDICATION

To those who have gone before.
It's your shoulders we stand on,
and your victories that push us forward.
Thank you to all who made it possible.

ACKNOWLEDGEMENTS

No author works alone. Thank you, Tami.
You make it Christmas every time
I get a new cover. And thank you to my Beta Team.
Truly, your help with my stories is immeasurable.

NEWSLETTER

You can get a FREE book by joining my Reading Family!
Every week we share stories, sales and good old fun.
Go to lauraannbooks.com to sign up!

PROLOGUE

From the end of "The Sweetest Moment"

Maeve smiled and handed a plate full of cake to the next person coming down the table.

"It was a beautiful wedding, wasn't it?" the older woman said with a smile.

"It was," Maeve agreed. "Absolutely stunning." And it had been. Layla had been the perfect little flower girl, Harper had been a stunning bride and Mason, the big teddy bear, had been a handsome and doting groom. The event was everything fairy tales were made of.

She sighed, pushed up her glasses and continued to pass out cake. Maeve absolutely did not want to admit that she was jealous...but...she was jealous. She had felt the same way at Aspen's reception.

Maeve knew she was excellent at hiding it, but she was lonely. She spent her time behind a calculator and a set of glasses she didn't really need, trying to convince herself that they were all the company she needed, but each night when she went to sleep...the heavy need for more crushed her chest like a two ton weight.

"Oh my gosh, did you see him?"

Maeve frowned at her sister. "Who?"

Estelle sidled closer and dropped her voice. "Mason's brother...Crew." She shook her head slowly. "I think that might be the most handsome man I've ever met." She fanned herself playfully. "Too bad he doesn't live here."

Maeve nodded. "Yeah...Cali's a bit of a commute."

Estelle sighed longingly, her eyes still focused across the room. "Guess that just means I should make the most of tonight, right?"

Maeve knocked their shoulders together. "Right. Go get 'em, Tiger."

Estelle scowled in a teasing way before sauntering away.

Maeve deflated when her sister left. If only she had the excuse of a long commute...

Laughter caught Maeve's attention and she couldn't help but look. She knew she shouldn't...after all, she knew exactly who was having such a grand time...but as always, the sound of Ethan's voice drew her like a scientist to a boiling beaker.

Ethan was dancing on the small wooden floor that had been placed in the middle of the reception hall for that exact purpose. Layla was in his arms and the little flower girl was leaning back, while he spun them in a circle. Dark curls flew through the air and then Ethan would stop, pull the toddler in and together they would laugh.

Maeve's eyes roamed his face. She could have described it in her sleep. A strong, slightly square jaw that was clean shaven today, though he often left just enough scruff to be attractive. Straight, white teeth that he flashed around all the time, as if his smile wasn't enough to stop traffic. Medium brown hair that he kept just a little too long, which was perfect for showing off the surfing highlights he got every summer. Instead of large, bulky muscles like Mason had, Ethan was lean, but she'd seen him without his shirt on enough times to know there wasn't an ounce of fat on his body.

He was the exact type of man that made women flock to surfing competitions. And his easy-going personality caused those same flocks to stay.

Except when he leaves you.

Maeve jolted when she realized that Ethan had caught her. His hazel eyes were more green than brown today against his suit and when their gazes met, he paused, his smile drooping every so slightly.

Normally, Maeve looked away immediately, but today she felt caught. Like a tractor beam that refused to let go. It wasn't until

Ethan's face turned hopeful and he started to walk in her direction that Maeve was able to gain control.

"Would you like some cake?" she asked, forcing a smile at the next person in line. She studiously ignored the hard stare from the most handsome man she'd ever known, no offense to Mason's brother.

It didn't matter that she had known him since he was a young boy. It didn't matter that he ate dinner at their house three times a week. It didn't matter that at one point she'd worshiped the ground he walked on. He had lost her trust back when they were teenagers and Maeve didn't have the ability to give it back to him.

His choices that fateful day had nearly cost her her life and Maeve was determined not to let his current choices cost her anything else.

According to her family, Maeve was simply too serious for playful Ethan. She was irritated with his happy-go-lucky attitude and only wanted to spend her time crunching numbers.

Maeve did like numbers. They made sense. She always knew what she was going to get when she added or subtracted or ran formulas. There were never surprises, and numbers never left her behind with a laugh or almost killed her.

She pushed up her glasses again. Sometimes they drove her nuts. She didn't need them. Her vision was just fine, but as she'd gotten older and Ethan had refused to leave her alone, she'd adopted wearing them as a way to create a barrier between her and the persistent neighbor.

It hadn't worked as well as she'd hoped, but Maeve was too stubborn to admit it and stop wearing them.

"You should take a break and come dance."

Maeve jumped, nearly dropping the plate she was handing out. "Ethan," she scolded. "You nearly gave me a heart attack."

"So you *do* know my name," he said with a grin, stepping a little closer. He must have passed Layla off to someone else, since his arms were currently empty.

The soft scent of his cologne hit her and Maeve had to forcefully stop herself from leaning closer. Fate must have a daily laugh at her expense, causing Maeve to fall in love with the one man she couldn't trust. It was a cruel, cruel joke and Maeve wanted to be free of it.

If only she knew how.

She's been fighting her growing feelings for years and somehow, over time, they only became more solidified, despite the incident between them.

"Maeve?"

She blinked, coming out of her thoughts. "I'm busy," she said tersely, turning back to the table.

"I'm pretty sure all these lovely people can pick up their own plate," he whispered in her ear.

There was no stopping or hiding the shiver that ran down her spine from his closeness. She was completely positive that if she simply gave in, all her loneliness would vanish like one of Aspen's cakes.

"Why do you fight it so hard?" he asked, a note of pleading in his voice. "Maeve..."

She straightened and stepped away, his words the reminder she needed to snap back to reality. "I'm working, Ethan. Thank you for the invite, but I'm sure you can find someone else to accompany you."

He sighed and pushed a hand through his hair, messing up the styling job he'd been sporting. "I'll catch you another time," he said, turning away.

Someday he'll get tired of trying, a voice said in the back of her head. *And then where will you be?* "Satisfied," she whispered to herself, but the word rang false. The day Ethan moved on to someone more welcoming would be like a sword through her heart, but Maeve didn't know how to let it go.

She'd almost *died,* and he'd left, breaking her heart and her confidence in him. That wasn't something easily rebuilt and each time Maeve thought of forgiving, she broke out in a cold sweat, memories of her near drowning consuming her.

She wanted to be free, but she simply didn't know how.

CHAPTER 1

Maeve pushed her glasses up onto her head. As helpful of an accessory as they were, right now they were driving her crazy. The numbers in front of her began to swim and she squeezed her eyes shut, pinching the bridge of her nose to try and set things right again.

Blinking rapidly, she tried again, but the numbers still swirled. "Ugh." Reaching into her desk drawer, she pulled out some headache medicine and popped a couple of pills in her mouth, washing them down with a swig of warm water. "Bleh." Maeve scrunched her nose and stuck out her tongue.

No one had to tell her that she was too old for that kind of behavior, she was fully aware. But she was by herself in her office and there was no one but the computer screens to see her acting like a child.

"I think I need a nap," Maeve muttered, leaning back and closing her eyes. Her sleep lately had been less than peaceful. For some reason, her stress load felt extra heavy and Maeve's brain was refusing to relax even though what she needed most was a break.

"You look like you need a piece of cake."

Maeve cracked open one eye. "You've gotten sneaky. I didn't hear the door open."

Aspen smirked. "I had Austin grease the hinges."

Maeve smiled. "Niiiiice. Way to put the hubby to work."

Aspen plopped herself in a chair. "Eh. It keeps him close." She frowned. "I've gotten used to having him at the shop. I hate when he works from home."

"Spoiled," Maeve shot out.

"Blessed," Aspen retorted.

"Argumentative," Estelle said, entering the space. She put her hands on her hips.

As the oldest daughter, she sometimes was a little too mother-like for Maeve's tastes, but Maeve knew there was no one who had her back like Estelle did. Their oldest sister was the most trustworthy person Maeve knew...and since trust was something she struggled to give, that was saying a lot.

"Sisters," Maeve said, essentially ending the conversation. She leaned back in her office chair. "What did I do to earn visits from both of you at once?" Maeve frowned. "Who's running the front?"

Estelle sighed. "No one. It's been busy and I was coming back to tell Aspen we need more mint chocolate chip cookies." She raised an eyebrow at the baker. "But she was in here."

Aspen nodded. "I'll get right on that."

"Thanks." Estelle smiled. "I'll get back to duty." She pointed a finger at Maeve. "You have no idea how nice you have it back here."

Maeve rolled her eyes. "We can hire a teenager if you want a break," she said. "Our profit margin is enough to make that work."

Estelle pursed her lips. "I'll consider it. I'd really like to build the wedding cake side of our business. I've enjoyed decorating the last few we've done and having someone else in the front would give me more time for that."

"Just let me know and we'll get someone hired," Maeve said easily. "I think Michael said there were a couple of kids at the school looking for jobs." Michael, their cousin, was a middle school literature teacher, but their town was small enough that they only had one school campus. All grades, kindergarten through high school, were all on one piece of property, so Michael heard all the gossip whether he wanted to or not.

"I just might take you up on that," Estelle said before sweeping out of the room.

"Okay, one sister down," Maeve teased. "What brought you in here? Or was it only to scare me with your new silent door prowess?"

Aspen snorted in amusement. "As tempting as that is..."

Maeve shook her head.

"Actually…I wanted to see how you were doing."

Maeve waited, but Aspen didn't speak more. "How I'm doing with what?"

"How you're handling things with Dad being home." The words were quiet and filled with concern. Aspen and Maeve's parents had recently gotten home from a long trip to Italy to see their father's family. After being diagnosed with Parkinson's disease, Antony Harrison had quietly slipped from the limelight as a famous chocolate sculptor and focused on family. Knowing travel would be difficult in the future, he and his wife Emery had gone to visit those who lived too far away for him to visit when the disease progressed.

Now, however, they were home and Maeve and Estelle were adjusting not only to having them back, but how to help their father. He'd been gone nearly a year and the disease had progressed a lot during that time. His life was more difficult than ever and Maeve had to admit the adjustment hadn't been a fun one.

"We're making it," she said. Aspen had gotten married while their parents were gone and didn't live at home anymore, so she wasn't there for the day to day struggles. Maeve didn't blame Aspen for it, but she definitely felt the added weight from having one sister gone. One less set of shoulders to bear the weight was still one less set of shoulders.

"How bad is it?" Aspen asked.

Maeve shrugged. Her head hurt too much for this conversation. "He's struggling to do things like feed himself," she admitted. "And I think he fell while getting dressed two days ago, but he won't admit it."

"Do we need to build an addition on the main floor?" Aspen's dark brows were pulled together. She might not still live with them, but Maeve knew her sister cared.

"It's something to think about," Maeve murmured. Her brain began to run the numbers. If they hired a teenager, it might be a bit tight to do an addition, but the master bedroom was on the upper floor and those stairs wouldn't be manageable for much longer.

Maybe I can help out in the front for Estelle so we can save the money.

The thought made her shudder. She wasn't made for working with the masses.

Aspen snickered.

"What?"

"You were thinking about talking to people, weren't you?"

Maeve huffed and folded her arms over her chest. "How would you know that?"

Aspen mimicked the movement. "Because I know *you*, dear sister. Your mind immediately went to paying for the addition, which led you to realize you had just told Estelle we could afford a worker." She pushed on past Maeve's snort. "I'm guessing you decided paying for an addition *and* a worker might be too much." She held out her hand. "Which means you considered whether or not you could bring yourself to helping out front... Spoiler alert, you can't."

"You're unbelievable."

Aspen shrugged. "It was either that or you were thinking about Ethan."

Maeve stilled, then forced herself to relax. "I don't know what you're talking about."

Aspen stood, her grin a little too amused. "Said every person ever, who didn't want to talk about a certain subject."

"That many people are talking about Ethan?" Maeve gasped in mock astonishment. "I didn't realize he was famous."

Aspen shook her head. "Someday, you'll tell me why you dislike him so much."

"Yeah, well...someday is not today."

Aspen chuckled and slipped out, leaving Maeve to her rioting thoughts. Ethan was the last person Maeve wanted to think about, but once he was in her head, she struggled to get him out. She'd been struggling for nearly eight years, and yet the fight continued.

Someday she'd be strong enough to let it go, but like she'd said earlier...today was not that day.

*****

"Yes, sir..." Ethan pinched his lips together. "I understand. Thank you so much for calling. Uh-huh...we'll catch you next time." Ethan nodded even though the customer couldn't see him. "Yep. Right. Have a good time. Thanks." He pressed the button on his business cell and dropped the phone on the counter.

That was the third cancellation this week. The whole summer had been rough, but these last few weeks were the worst. The cold weather was moving in a little earlier than normal and it was driving people out of the water, making Ethan's surf lessons drop off several weeks earlier than normal.

He grabbed the mouse in front of him and woke up his computer screen. Maybe he had an online order or two to help offset this latest setback. He frowned. Traffic on his website was staying similar to other years, but orders had been low.

All in all, the year had not been one of his best. Just what he was going to do about it, however, remained to be seen. Fall should be one of his busiest times of year, not his slowest.

He glanced at the clock on the wall. He had a group lesson in an hour. That should help. It was a full class, which should definitely help keep him going even with the cancellations. Personal lessons were more money, but group lessons were more steady.

Grabbing his bar of wax, Ethan headed out to the pile of equipment. He'd get the boards ready for the group so they could get into the waves right away. His helper, Parker, would be showing up soon and together they would handle all the newbies.

Popping in his ear buds, Ethan jammed out to his favorite music, rubbing down the boards. It was one of his favorite things in the world. There was nothing like getting a board ready for a smooth run on the waves. This time of year was perfect for catching a clean wave without risking hypothermia just to be in the water.

A tap on his shoulder startled Ethan and he jerked out his ear-bud. "Geez, Parker," Ethan said with a laugh. "I didn't hear you arrive."

Parker grinned. "You were too busy dancing." He leaned in. "I know they say dance like nobody's watching, but..." He raised his eyebrows and pointedly tilted his head to the side.

Ethan turned and his face flushed, even though he laughed. A small crowd, more than likely his upcoming group, were standing around watching his antics. He rubbed the back of his hot neck. "I suppose I should have paid attention to the clock." He turned away when a teenage girl smiled and waved.

That was one of the downsides of his job. He definitely fit the stereotypical surfer look. His skin was brown, his hair bleached by the sun and Ethan was self aware enough to know that his looks didn't drive away people very often. He also was able to admit that he was attracted to younger women...or at least, a younger woman...and she wasn't sixteen like the girl in the bikini, waving at him right now.

A picture of dark hair and golden brown eyes, hidden behind fake glasses, flashed through his mind. The usual pain pinched his chest as Maeve's stunning face came into his mind's eye.

That woman had no idea how gone he was over her... She also didn't care. Of all the women in the world, she was the only one that frowned back when he smiled. Truth was, there were days that Ethan was sure Maeve hated his guts. It didn't make a lot of sense. She was a wonderful woman. She cared for her family, ran a successful accounting business, was a genius with numbers and would give a person the shirt off her back...all except him.

Back when they were teenagers, Ethan had made the worst mistake of his life and it had cost him the girl he was falling for. The problem was, he'd continued to fall even as she pulled away.

Now here he was, eight years later and still pining for the one thing he couldn't have. It was ridiculous and yet no other women had been able to turn his attention away from Maeve. He sort of wished it would happen. He prayed his heart would heal and he could find someone to be with, but time continued to pass and his heart stayed the same, and the chemistry between the two of them refused to dim.

"Welcome, folks!" Ethan said, pushing his signature wide smile on his face. He loved his work. Getting into it a few minutes early would help clear his thoughts where a certain difficult woman was concerned. "I'm so glad you're here today. I'm Ethan." He put a hand to his chest. "This is Parker, my assistant."

The young man waved and winked at the teenage girl who had been eyeing Ethan.

I'll have to remember to give him a bonus for that one.

"Let's get you set up with wetsuits and a board and then we'll begin our instructions."

It took twenty minutes to get everyone settled before Ethan was able to start giving instructions. "We're going to start by learning how to do a pop-up," Ethan said loudly.

They spent another twenty minutes practicing technique before they began to go into the water. Ethan walked over to a group with several young children. "How about I go out with you guys and get you started, okay?"

"That'd be great, thank you," the mother gushed. She looked a little nervous and Ethan kept them moving so her worries wouldn't stop the kids from having a good time. He'd seen it all before, but never once had anyone been hurt on his watch.

Except Maeve.

"Not now," he muttered under his breath. He had a job to do and letting Maeve invade his thoughts would hinder his ability to focus. He held out his hand to the youngest one. "Ready to ride a wave?"

He bit his bottom lip but nodded.

"Perfect. You're gonna rock it." Ethan picked up the boy's board and guided him to the water. They wouldn't go too deep for someone his age. Ethan's head wouldn't even go under the water. Just enough to catch a mild wave.

"That's it!" Ethan shouted as he pushed the boy off the front of the wave. "Now stand up!"

The little guy jumped to his knees and wobbled before putting his feet under him. Almost immediately he landed in the water, the board shooting off to the side.

Ethan ran as best as he could through the water, picking the kid up so he could get a good breath of air. "You were amazing!" Ethan cried, giving the boy a fist bump. "Good work."

"I fell," the boy grumbled, wiping the water out of his eyes.

"Dude, I've been surfing since I was three and I still fall sometimes." Ethan grinned. "You did awesome. Each time you do it, it'll get easier." He nodded toward deeper water. "Ready to try again?"

The boy smiled, a bit of eagerness flashing in his eyes, and nodded. "Yeah. Okay."

Ethan grabbed the board and out they went. This was why he loved his job. Surfing had been Ethan's passion since he was a little boy and sharing it with others was the most amazing feeling in the world.

The only thing that couldn't possibly be better would be having Maeve forgive him. Some dreams, however, were a little far out for anyone to believe they were attainable. And Maeve Harrison was one such dream.

CHAPTER 2

"Maeve! Would you please put this on the table?" Emory Harrison, Maeve's mother, held out a bowl of salad.

"Got it." Maeve grabbed the bowl and walked to the dining room, setting it down in the middle of the table. "Hey, Dad," Maeve said softly. Her father was sitting, waiting, in his usual seat at the table, but instead of his large presence taking up the room, his illness made him appear older and less...just less.

Antony Harrison smiled and raised a couple of shaky fingers. "Hello, my lovely daughter. How was the office today?"

Maeve shrugged. "Easier than dealing with the front desk," she said. "Numbers always behave the way they're supposed to."

He chuckled, just as intended. "People might not behave how you want, but that doesn't make their behavior wrong."

Maeve made a face. "Life would sure be easier if they all did what I wanted them to."

"Easier, yes. But then how would we learn and grow?"

Maeve turned back to the kitchen. This conversation was getting deep and she wasn't looking for a lecture at the moment. "I gotta help Mom. We'll have dinner on in a jiffy."

There was no answer behind her and Maeve felt the stirrings of guilt as she walked away. Her father wasn't well. Parkinson's was stealing him from them. If she was a good daughter, she would sit at his feet and soak up all the wisdom he was willing to impart. But Maeve was already feeling torn inside and the direction of their conversation would only make it worse.

No one in her family understood her struggles. Mostly because she'd never shared the truth with them. They didn't know about her near death experience. They didn't know that Ethan had broken his promise. They didn't know that her aloofness was all an act.

And they especially didn't know that she was still desperately in love with him and longed to let go of her anger and fear.

Then why don't you tell them?

Maeve shook off her inner conscience. What was she supposed to tell them? *Oh, by the way, eight years ago, I nearly drowned when Ethan was teaching me to surf and now I can't bring myself to trust him or even give into my attraction because when he broke my trust, he also broke my heart.*

"Yeah, that'd go over well," she muttered as she spooned mashed potatoes into a bowl.

"Let's eat!" Maeve's mother hollered.

Footsteps above their heads let Maeve know Estelle was on her way downstairs. Their family seemed to be getting smaller and smaller. It had all started a few years ago when Antonio, Maeve's older brother, had left for the military. Now Aspen was married and the table simply looked...empty.

Her heart pinched slightly. Life was changing, passing her by, and there were times when Maeve felt she had nothing to show for it. She had gone to college, she now had a career, but had she really lived?

"Shall we say grace?" Dad asked, reaching out his hands to his wife and Estelle, who was seated on his right.

Maeve took Estelle's other hand and closed her eyes while she waited for her father to say the blessing. Once done, they all began to grab dishes, though Maeve's appetite was far from hearty.

"How was the shop today?" Mom asked, raising her eyebrows to Estelle. Mom picked up an extra piece of chicken and began to cut it into small pieces on her plate before transferring it to her husband's.

The weight on Maeve's shoulders grew heavier at the gesture. The love between her parents was enviable and something Maeve craved. Aspen had found it, Maeve was positive Estelle would eventually find it as well, she was too beautiful not to...but Maeve knew if she couldn't get over this stupid infatuation with the next door neighbor, she'd never find it herself.

"Busy, as always," Estelle said easily, dishing potatoes onto their father's plate. "No one seems to be able to get enough of Aspen's cookies and cream cake lately. It's being sold as fast as she can make it."

Dad chuckled. "It's in her blood," he said with a nod. His wife fed him a bite and he gave her a grateful smile.

"What about your wedding cakes?" Mom pressed. "Any more orders?"

Estelle glanced at Maeve. "Actually, I was hoping to talk to Maeve about that." Turning more fully, she addressed her sister. "Can we go ahead and hire someone, then? I've got an opportunity to do three weddings this fall, but I can't unless I have help." Estelle quirked an eyebrow. "Unless you're willing to run the counter?"

Maeve put her hands in the air. "I think we can all agree that would *not* be a good idea." Maeve wasn't shy, but she definitely didn't like crowds. Dealing with large groups of people drained her energy faster than pulling the plug in a bath. Shy? No. But introverted? Absolutely.

Her dad chuckled again. "I think you missed the Italian genes," he teased. "No one in my family is as quiet as you."

Estelle snorted. "Except she looks more Italian than any of us," she said with a grin.

"Except for the curves," Maeve shot back, rolling her eyes. "Some people took those genetics and left the rest of us with nothing."

Estelle groaned. "Those people would gladly hand off some of those curves, just for the record."

Maeve leaned into her sister's shoulder, laughing lightly. "Deal. You can hand them over after dinner."

The family laughed, lightening the mood, which always seemed a little heavy these days. It seemed to Maeve that each meal was simply a reminder of things they were losing. Whether it was family members moving on with their life, or the ability of their father to take care of himself, it all seemed to be slipping through Mave's fingers and she didn't like it, not one bit.

"So?" Estelle pressed.

Maeve blinked herself back into the present. "What?"

"A helper? Can we get a teenager or something to come work in the afternoons so I can work on the wedding cakes?"

Maeve took a breath. She hated spending money, but it would make Estelle happy and in the end, could actually help the cafe make *more* money, so... "Yeah, sure. We can do that."

Estelle beamed. "Thanks." She turned back to their parents. "I'm so excited to take on those clients! Their wedding cakes are going to be stunning!"

Emory smiled proudly. "Just like the decorator," she said.

Maeve rolled her eyes. "Mooom, cheese doesn't go with the meal tonight."

"Jealous," Estelle said behind her hand as she pretended to cough. Once done, she batted her eyelashes at her sister. "Sorry. Had a tickle in my throat."

Maeve mock-glared. "I think you've been spending too much time with Aspen. That was totally something she would have done."

Estelle shrugged and went back to eating. "Maybe so, but you're half Italian. There's something you need to learn."

Maeve made a face. "And what's that?"

Estelle smiled sweetly. "Cheese goes with *every* meal."

*****

Ethan punched the numbers into his calculator for what seemed the tenth time. "Come on," he muttered. There had to be a mistake. Surely his bank account wasn't really that low. The numbers on the screen proved him wrong and he made a face.

Sighing, he scrubbed his hands over his face. The end of the season was coming up. In only a couple more months he would set aside his shop and step into the world of construction to get him through the winter when his paycheck from the surf shop was nonexistent, but with what he was seeing in front of him, he needed to make quite a bit of extra money this winter if he was going to be able to re-open the shop next spring. He had to have cash in reserve because the money from the shop always took a few weeks to start flowing in.

And right now, there was nothing in reserve. He was literally living from invoice to invoice. He could definitely feed himself this winter, but unless something changed very soon, he wouldn't be able to spend his morning cruising the waves and teaching others to enjoy the finer things in life.

He swiveled his chair, gazing out into the dark night. He couldn't see his beloved ocean, but Ethan could hear it. Even with the chilly night air, he had left the window open. The sound of the waves hitting the shoreline were like a siren call to him. He couldn't imagine his life without it.

The thought of working a nine-to-five job for the rest of his life nearly gave Ethan hives. He would die a slow death if he ended up stuck behind a desk for the rest of his life. He'd gone to college. He'd created a "back up plan" as his mom had called it, but nothing had ever called to Ethan the same way the salty spray of the Pacific did.

If he could figure out a way to make money during the winter, he wouldn't even bother with construction, but with Oregon's weather, the surf crowd during the colder months was only made up of the die-hards who didn't need rental equipment or lessons.

Ethan tapped his fingers against his desk. "Maybe I can build up my custom board business?" If he could get a few extra orders during the off season, then perhaps he could make up his deficit. Making custom boards was time-consuming and very lucrative, but few people actually wanted a custom board, making the trade difficult to break into. If he lived in California or Hawaii, he would have a better chance since that's where the competitions were, but he liked Seagull Cove. He lived in the house he was raised in and wasn't eager to leave.

His parents were both gone, and this was where Ethan's friends were...and this was also where Maeve was. Much as he wished he could move on, he couldn't bring himself to move away from the Italian beauty.

Standing from his desk, he began to gather his stuff. It was time to go home for the night. His brain needed a break and he needed to do something that would take his mind off Maeve. It never served him well to get caught up in the mystery of their relationship.

There were times when he was sure she felt the same pull that he did. It seemed as if the very air around them vibrated when they got close, warming him from the inside out, and at other times he was sure he got a cold just from being in the same room.

He knew he'd screwed up all those years ago, but he'd been a kid! It was so frustrating that she wasn't willing to give him any mercy on the subject. He was a teenage boy! His brain hadn't been fully developed yet! Why couldn't she understand that?

Shaking his head, Ethan got in his car and headed home. "This is useless," he grumbled. Maeve frustrated him and enticed him all at the same time and like the sucker he was, he kept coming back for more.

With that constant stress sitting on his shoulders and his worries about his business starting to weigh him down, he knew he needed to do something drastic. Making a turn at the last minute, he headed down to Main Street. A dark and cold home wasn't what he needed right now. He needed to be around people and let someone else's problems overcome his own.

A hit of Aspen's cookies or cakes would go a long way, but he knew the cafe would be closed at this time of night. But there was one place that never closed and Ethan just happened to know that the woman who ran it was always there past visiting hours.

Pulling into the animal shelter, Ethan threw the car in park and walked up to the front. He cupped his hands around his face and looked through the glass door. A light in the back let him know his hunch was correct. He knocked hard. "Riley! Are you there?"

A strawberry blonde head with her signature messy bun peeked around the corner. "Ethan?"

He grinned and shrugged before pointing to the locked handle. "Need some help?"

Riley laughed and shook her head. She came over and unlocked the door, letting him in. "What in the world are you doing here so late?"

Ethan slung an arm around Riley's neck. He'd known her for almost as many years as he'd known Maeve, yet the only pull he'd ever felt between them was one of sibling fondness. Riley was like the little sister Ethan never had. "I needed something to keep me busy tonight. Are you still cleaning out kennels?"

Riley elbowed him in the ribs. "You're the only person I know who asks to help clean out poopy cages."

He chuckled. "Then I suppose you should say, 'Why thank you, Ethan. You're the best big brother ever!'" He said the words in a high pitched tone, completely butchering Riley's soft soprano tone.

She covered her ears. "If I ever sound like that, someone please put me out of my misery."

His chuckle grew stronger.

Elbowing him one more time, Riley slipped out from under his arm and headed to the back. "Come on, Superman. I can certainly put you to work. We just had a couple of puppies be dropped off and I'm trying to settle them and get them to eat."

Ethan shook his head. "What happened?"

Riley shrugged. "Not sure. They're thin, but not starving. I'm guessing they were abandoned, but not too long ago."

"Can you tell what breed they are?"

She shook her head. "Nope. Mutts." She grinned. "But oh, so cute."

Ethan grinned. "You think all animals are cute."

Riley put her back to a swinging door and shrugged. "They are."

"No, they're not," Ethan corrected, following her through the door. "But that's an argument for another time." He followed Riley to a room, past all the barks and meows of the animals still waiting for someone to take them home. As usual, he wished he could be that person, but Ethan didn't feel like he had the time for a pet. In the future, when he had a wife and a family, maybe it would all work out, but right now? Right now he needed to focus on saving his business. Then he'd worry about saving a puppy.

"Here they are," Riley said in her soothing tone. She bent over and made cooing sounds at two tiny fluffballs who were curled into a corner. "Aren't they darling?"

Ethan stood still. He could barely tell one puppy from the other, but when a pair of light brown eyes met his...he knew he was in trouble.

Riley carefully walked to the corner and lifted one of the mutts up. She held it close to her chest and brought the wiggling bundle to Ethan. "Here. See if you can calm him down. Then we'll try to feed them together."

Ethan took the puppy and brought it close to his chest to help it feel secure. The puppy whined for a moment longer, then curled up and rested against him.

Riley's smile widened. "He likes you!"

Ethan couldn't seem to stop petting the tiny head. The soft hair slipped through his fingers like fine silk.

"Uh-oh," Riley sang.

Ethan jerked his head up. "Hm?"

She smiled and shook her head. "Oh…nothing…"

CHAPTER 3

Maeve sighed as she walked through the front door a couple nights later. She was exhausted. Today had been one of those days where too many reports had been due at once and she'd been scrambling to keep up with it all. The companies she did financial books for had all been in a hurry today, wanting their information and during the few minutes between calls, she'd been trying to interview teenagers to help Estelle out at the front desk.

Her feet ached, along with her backside from sitting at the computer too long. All she wanted was some dinner and a chance to soak in a bubble bath before she went to bed.

A thudding sound caught her attention and Maeve jerked her head up. "Dad?"

"Maeve!" her mother shouted. "Come help!"

Maeve ran up the stairs, her exhaustion forgotten as she rushed to her parents. "What happened?"

Her mom was kneeling next to her father. "His leg buckled," she whispered, tears in her eyes.

"I'm fine," Maeve's dad said, brushing them both off. "Just help me back to my feet and I'll be fine."

"Dad," Maeve scolded. "You're not fine. And Mom and I can't carry you down the stairs."

He scowled. "No one needs to carry me. I'll use the banister. This is just like what happened in Italy. My knee buckled, but get me back up and I'll be fine."

"Oh?" Maeve challenged. "Like when you fell and broke your wrist?" When her father's face fell, Maeve knew she shouldn't have said it, but this was serious! No one liked that this disease was stealing his strength, but they couldn't ignore it either. He already struggled to eat. Going down the stairs was just another problem in the long list that was headed their way. It broke Maeve's heart, but there was nothing she could do to stop it either. "I'm sorry," she said, forcing her tone to drop. "But I think we might need some help." Her smile was self deprecating. "Mom and I are the smallest of the bunch. We're too itty bitty to carry you down."

Her father tried to smile back, but it was as shaky as his hands. "I know," he assured her. "Maybe...maybe we need to move my bed?"

"Not without me, you don't," Maeve's mom said adamantly. "I won't have you sleeping on the couch or on a blow-up mattress. If you need to be downstairs, we'll need to build a room." Her lips pinched. "For both of us."

Her father sighed. "There isn't space for a room," he said softly. "And you shouldn't have to leave the place where we've spent all our married life."

Maeve backed up a little as her parents argued quietly back and forth. This wasn't getting them anywhere. First things first...they needed help getting their dad down the stairs.

Ethan.

As soon as she had the thought, Maeve paused. Yes, Ethan should be home this time of night and he was close enough to be easily accessible, but Estelle wasn't home to go get him. If someone was going to get him, it would have to be Maeve. "Um...maybe Ethan could come help us?" she asked, keeping her voice as even as possible.

A voice in the back of her mind begged her mother to say they didn't need help, but Maeve had no such luck.

"Oh, Ethan," her mother gushed. "Perfect, hon. Would you go get him, please? He's just the answer we need right now."

Fear immediately pushed through Maeve's system, but she forced it aside. *This is for Dad. I'd do anything for him.* She forced her own shaky knees into compliance and walked back down the stairs. As she walked out the door and across the yard, her breathing grew erratic and she nearly turned back three times.

How could she simply show up at his door and ask for help? Maeve had been ignoring, or trying to ignore Ethan for nearly eight years. She had no right to ask him for anything.

Not only that, but this meant she'd have to speak to him face to face. She'd not only have to humble herself, she'd have to address him in a way that gave every opportunity for her heart to get involved.

She wasn't cold to him by choice but necessity. Any chink in her armor meant that her feelings for Ethan came rushing to the forefront as if she hadn't spent years trying to hold it back. His ability to draw her attention and make her heart speed up was unlike anything she had ever known and was exactly why she had never been able to move on.

If another man ever came close to replicating those feelings, Maeve knew she'd be able to heal. But it had never happened. It had never even come close. Every other man was boring and tedious compared to Ethan and try as she might, Maeve had been unable to change that.

Taking a deep breath, she raised her hand. "For Dad," she whispered. Surely she could do this for her dad. Her feelings and emotions didn't matter nearly as much as getting him help...right?

Her knuckles hit the wood once...twice...three times before her hand dropped and Maeve intertwined her fingers to keep them from shaking.

"Coming!" There was shuffling from the other side before Ethan pulled the door open. "Maeve?" A quizzical smile broke across his handsome face. "What are you doing here?"

Maeve opened her mouth to speak, but she had to snap it shut again. Did he have to look so daringly delicious at this time of night? Shouldn't he be as ragged and worn as her? Why did his messy hair and five-o'clock shadow only make her enjoy looking more, rather than turning her off?

Ethan leaned forward a little. "Maeve?"

She cleared her throat. "We, uh...we need your help."

Ethan frowned and stepped outside, closing the door behind him. "What's going on?"

Maeve scrambled back, only to barely catch herself before falling down the porch steps. *Way to look smooth, idiot.* "Dad fell."

"What?" Ethan took off running before Maeve could explain any more. When he realized she wasn't with him, he came back and grabbed her hand. "Come on. Is he okay? Do we need an ambulance?"

Maeve couldn't speak. Her legs could barely keep up as he rushed them back across the two yards and her arm was on fire in a way that was so pleasant she was momentarily mute.

"Emory? Antony?" Ethan burst into the house, finally dropping Maeve's hand. "Where are you?"

"Upstairs, sweetie," Maeve's mom said calmly.

Maeve followed Ethan up the steps. He stood in front of her parents, his breathing heavier than normal. He glanced back at Maeve, then focused on her parents again. "Had to send the pipsqueak to get the muscle, huh?"

Maeve's face flamed hotter than her hand a moment ago, but this heat wasn't nearly as nice. Before she could snap a retort, however, her mother and father laughed.

"I suppose that's a good way to say it," Maeve's mom admitted. "Do you mind?"

*****

"Do I mind helping the prettiest mom in Seagull Cove get her husband downstairs? Who the heck would mind that?" Ethan said with a forced laugh. His heart had gone through a roller coaster of emotions in the last two minutes.

When Maeve had shown up at his door, looking like she wanted to devour him in one bite, he'd had a fleeting moment of hope that a miracle had occurred. Her next words, however, had brought him crashing down to Earth. Antony Harrison was one of the best men Ethan knew and the thought of him being hurt was enough to send Ethan racing over without really knowing what he was getting into.

He'd pulled Maeve along, not missing the opportunity to touch her at least a little bit, then had another heartbeat change when he'd realized that Antony wasn't hurt, just stuck.

"Flatterer," Emory said with a grin. She stood up and stepped back. "We're trying to go down to dinner. Can you give him a hand?"

"On it." Ethan stepped behind Antony and gripped around his chest. "Okay, up first. Then I'll shift and we'll move forward, alright?"

Antony nodded, looking weary. "Sounds good," he said weakly.

Ethan bit back the emotion trying to crowd his vision. He'd already lost his parents when he wasn't yet twenty. He wasn't ready to lose Antony as well. "On three. One...two...three!" Ethan stood, pulling the man who had always been larger than life up as if he were a young teenage boy. Ethan hadn't realized until this moment just how much weight Antony had lost. "Perfect," Ethan said with a wide, forced smile. "Now let me..." He shifted so he was beside Antony, his arm wrapped around the man's torso. "Nice and easy, okay?"

Antony nodded, then looked up. "You women go ahead. We'll be down soon," he said soothingly.

Ethan had to admire how much the man was trying to spare his family. From the tears in Emory and Maeve's eyes, he knew everyone was having the same realizations as he was. *Life is too short with the ones you love.*

He couldn't help but watch Maeve comfort her mother, walking Emory downstairs with murmured words. His heart ached for her. He wanted to take care of Maeve the same way she was taking care of her mother. He wanted the right to hug, hold, touch, and kiss away her fears and worries.

"Don't give up," Antony whispered as he began to walk, forcing Ethan to move with him.

"Of course not," Ethan said easily. "We'll get you downstairs with no troubles at all."

Antony gave Ethan a sidelong look, waiting for Ethan to figure it out.

"Oh. You mean…" Ethan pinched his lips and cleared his throat. "That transparent, huh?"

Antony shook his head as he gripped the stair rail, steadying himself as they worked their way down. "I'm her father, Ethan. I see more than most."

"Then you know she's not interested."

Antony chuckled. "No. I know she fights it." His dark eyes came back to Ethan. "So I say again, don't give up."

Don't say it…don't say it. "She doesn't trust me," Ethan finally admitted. He'd never discussed that fateful day with the Harrisons. Maeve had never brought it up and Ethan hadn't been too keen on it either. He wasn't quite sure what he'd done to earn her disdain, but it had to be bad and no one wanted to talk about their worst mistakes.

Antony shrugged as much as he could against Ethan's hold. "Show her she can."

Ethan chuckled sarcastically. "Easier said than done, Tony. I've been trying to do that for eight years."

They finally reached the bottom of the stairs and Antony was breathing heavily. "She's worth it," he whispered before straightening himself and walking toward the dining room. His steps were slightly uneven and Ethan didn't dare leave him by himself, but Ethan did stay back just enough to let Antony have some of his dignity.

Ethan couldn't imagine how it must hurt the man's pride to have built a worldwide reputation as a sculptor, only to lose it to a disease far earlier than anyone would be ready. Instead of choosing to be done, he'd been forced out, his tremors too hard to ignore.

Many times over the years, Antony had offered advice and helped guide Ethan. He'd been a second father since Ethan spent so much time at their house. But nothing rang through his mind with as much strength as what the man had just uttered.

She's worth it.

Antony was right. Maeve was worth it. Those who had her love and trust never had to question it. She'd give her life before she let someone else be hurt on her watch. And that was the problem. He was positive it was why he hadn't been able to move on and find someone else. Between their natural chemistry and the fact that he simply would never find someone as inherently good. Maeve Harrison stood out on every level and Ethan couldn't look away.

"You're joining us for dinner?" Emory said as the men entered the dining room. She wiped her hands on a towel, raising her eyebrows at Ethan in expectation.

Ethan smiled. "That's alright. You don't need to do that."

Emory frowned. "Ethan. I know better. Now sit." She pointed to a chair, which just happened to be next to Maeve.

There was no helping the slow smile that crept across his face when Maeve blushed deep enough for her tanned skin to flush pink. "Thanks, Mama Em," he said with a wink. "I haven't had a home cooked meal in a while. And I worked up an extra appetite tonight."

Emery tsked her tongue. "You used to come over all the time. We'll have to see that happen more often again. Your parents are probably rolling over in their graves at our neglect of you."

They all sat down and Ethan tried to ignore Maeve's stiff shoulders. Try as he might, though, he couldn't help pushing his seat just a *little* bit closer when he pulled it forward to sit down.

The look Maeve gave him said she hadn't missed the move.

"How was the office today?" Ethan asked, trying to keep her from stabbing him with a fork. He nodded at Emory in thanks when she passed him a bowl of peas.

Maeve shrugged. "Same as always." She stabbed at her salmon, breaking it into tiny pieces.

"It's already dead," Ethan whispered close to her ear. Man...she smelled good.

Maeve jumped, then cleared her throat as if to play off the moment. "I'm aware, thank you."

He kept his smile inside, but it was hard. Sometimes her determination to avoid him was hilarious, though other times it smarted like a jellyfish sting. "This is delicious, Mama Em. Thank you."

Emory beamed, her eyes darting between Ethan and Maeve. It occurred to Ethan that Antony wasn't the only one pushing for something more between the two. "Tell us about the shop, Ethan. Are you running it year round yet?"

Ethan's fork dropped as a topic he wasn't ready to address came up. "Uh...nope," he said with false cheer. "Not yet." *As if I wasn't already enough of a loser in Maeve's eyes. Let's just show her that I can't keep a business afloat.*

"Oh?" Emory asked, her eyes wide. "What's going on? You sound a little upset."

Crud. This wasn't what he signed up for.

CHAPTER 4

Maeve tried to subtly move her body a little further away from Ethan while he was distracted. It was clear he didn't want to talk about his surf shop, though she wasn't sure why. Normally, he would be willing to talk about his passion with anyone and everyone. Still...Maeve's biggest struggle was with him sitting so close. She could smell the ocean on him and it was as enticing as it had always been, which meant her girly side was screaming at her to get over her grudge and snuggle up.

Stop it!

"I ran a business for a long time," Maeve's dad said in a low tone. "Maybe we can help."

Ethan scratched under his chin, scrunching his face. "Well..." His beautiful hazel eyes darted her way before going back to her father. "I just didn't have the best season this year..." He looked at his plate, poking at the food. "Reservations were low, cancellations were high and unless something shifts, I'm not sure I'll have enough to reopen next summer."

Maeve'e heart fell to her stomach. She might not want to have a relationship with Ethan, but she also didn't want him hurt. Losing his surf shop would break him. He'd been a surfer since he was a little kid, having learned at his dad's feet. Truthfully, she'd never quite understood why he hadn't packed up and headed down to warmer weather so he could surf all day every day.

Her father leaned back and narrowed his eyes. "That bad, huh?"

Ethan nodded. "That bad."

"What would it take to turn it around?"

Ethan ticked his head back and forth. "I'm not sure. A dozen custom boards? A slew of lesson reservations in the next month before I close? A really good winter in construction?"

Maeve's mom perked up. "I forgot you did construction." She smiled. "We were just talking about adding an addition to the house so we can have a master bedroom downstairs."

Ethan smiled, but Maeve could tell it wasn't his true one. "I'm just a laborer, Em. You'd have to hire a regular company."

She waved a hand. "There's no reason why you can't work for us with that. We can hire individual contractors with you doing the bulk of the building."

Ethan sighed and set down his fork. "Mama Em...you know I love you, but I'm not taking a handout. That's not how I was raised."

Maeve kept her mouth shut. She could totally understand where Ethan was coming from, but she also kind of wanted to shake him and tell him that saving his shop was more important than his pride.

"It's not a handout if you're doing the work," her father said softly.

"Come on, Tony. You know you wouldn't be willing to do it either."

Maeve's father nodded. "I understand, but I also don't think there's anything wrong with taking the opportunities handed to you."

Ethan shook his head. "I probably just need to go over my books again. I'm sure if I budget right, I'll get it all figured out."

The words were said with finality, Ethan obviously believing the conversation was over, but Maeve's mom wasn't done.

"Maeve can help you with that!"

Maeve nearly spit out her water. As it was, she choked on the liquid and it took several seconds of coughing before she could pull in enough air to speak. "Excuse me?" she finally managed.

Ethan chuckled, looking a little too pleased with the situation for a guy who was turning down help just a moment before. "What's the matter, Maeve? You not up to the challenge?"

She knew...she *knew* he was trying to prick her ego. Dang if it didn't work. She sat up straighter. "Are you saying I can't turn your accounts around?"

Ethan shook his head, his eyes wide. "I didn't say that at all. If anyone knows how to push the buttons of a calculator in order to save a business, it would definitely be you." He leaned in, that far-too-attractive smirk on his face. "After all, those numbers are your favorite armor."

Maeve sputtered. "Excuse me?"

"You already said that, sweetie," her mother said with a grin. She looked flat out delighted at Maeve's discomfort. "You'd be willing to help him out, wouldn't you? Especially after Ethan has been so helpful with your father?" Maeve's mom rested a hand on her husband's and gave her daughter an imploring look.

Maeve knew she looked like a fish as her jaw hung open, her head twisting back and forth between her parents. Didn't they understand how impossible it would be for her to handle working in close proximity with Ethan? Didn't they care at all for their daughter's well being? Maeve knew her family loved Ethan, but they didn't have to bring her into it. Why couldn't she just sit on the sidelines and let them work it out themselves? A little distance was key to keeping her heart and mind intact.

"See?" her mom said, turning to Ethan. "It won't be a big deal at all." Maeve's mother stood. "Are you sticking around for dessert? I'm sure we have some of Aspen's cookies around here somewhere."

Ethan shook his head. "Nope. I gotta get home, but thanks anyway." He stood, patting his flat stomach, which Maeve tried not to watch.

She knew from personal experience there was a six pack under that sweatshirt. *Stop it!* she scolded again.

"Maeve," her mother said, her tone brooking no chance at an argument. "Why don't you walk Ethan out?"

Maeve stubbornly refused to move, but when her father cleared his throat and gave her *the* look, she sighed. "Come on, Ethan. Apparently, my parents think you might get lost somewhere between here and next door." She ignored the delicious chuckle and the fact that she was bound for a scolding when she got back and marched toward the front door. Better to do this quickly and if she was lucky, she could disabuse him of the notion that she would be spending any time with him. He didn't need help with his books. He needed to just accept her parents' help and build the stupid addition. She could avoid him, he would get paid, and everyone would be happy.

*****

Maeve's stiff back and shoulders told Ethan everything he needed to know about what their conversation would be when they got outside. She was pricklier than a rooster protecting his flock and Ethan was fighting between amusement and offense.

The night air was chilly when they stepped through the door and it felt good on Ethan's heated skin. Turning down the Harrisons' charity had embarrassed him, which was a feeling Ethan didn't experience very often.

Maeve walked ahead of him a little, then spun around.

Here it comes...

"Look. If you'll send me the link to your spreadsheets, I'll take a look at them tomorrow," she said in a tightly controlled voice. "I know my mom was trying to force us to spend time together, but we both know that doesn't have to happen in order for me to settle your budget."

Ethan had caught the not-so-subtle push, but now that Maeve was fighting it, he had a mind to fight back. Folding his arms over his chest, he tilted his head. "Actually, I don't think that would work. It would be better if we looked over them together. That way we could discuss strategies and go over what I might have been doing wrong."

"I can send you an email," she said wryly.

"I prefer in-person conversations."

Maeve let her head fall back. "Of course, you do."

Ethan took the opportunity to step close enough to allow the pull between them to hum to life. His skin, which had been cooling, became warm again and his fingers twitched. Her skin was flawless in the moonlight and her wide eyes made him want to leap in and never leave. "Some of us like the company of others," he whispered. There was no hiding the fact that his eyes had dropped to her lips. They drew his attention far too much to be healthy and yet not once had he had the opportunity to kiss them.

"And some of us prefer to be alone." She said the words, but there was no heat behind them. She could feel it. He was sure of it. Why couldn't she let go of something that happened when they were simply kids? It was eating him up inside and making both of them miserable.

"No..." Ethan slowly shook his head. "Some of us are just really good at holding onto the past."

Maeve jerked and winced at his words.

He knew he should feel bad about them, but they were the truth and were far less harsh than what she had lobbied at him over the years.

"Some of us have good reason to."

She was about to run. Ethan was as sure of that as he was that she would fit perfectly in his arms. He racked his brain for something...anything to keep this going. It was the most she had spoken to him in years and he had a sudden spurt of panic that if he didn't push this chance, he'd never get another one. "How about a trade?"

Maeve frowned. "What?"

"How about we trade services?"

She put her hands on her hips. "What are you talking about?"

"Your dad," Ethan stated, moving closer once more. "He's not going to be able to handle those stairs much longer."

Her lips thinned in anger. "I know that," she said tightly. "We're working on it."

"Your mom said she trusted me to manage the addition."

"Yeah, but you said you weren't one to take charity," Maeve shot back.

"A trade of services isn't charity." Ethan clenched his fist to keep from tucking a stray chunk of hair out of her face. It caressed along her cheekbone in a way that had him simmering in envy. *Why can't I be in love with someone easier than this?* he asked himself for the millionth time.

"So...what?" Maeve took care of the hair herself. "You'll take care of the addition and I'll take care of your books? It sounds like I get the better end of the deal. It's a much smaller job."

Ethan shook his head and risked moving toe to toe. "No. I'll manage the addition and you work with me *personally* on my finances and budgeting for the shop." He hurried on before she could react. "I'm talking about going over the books together, and making a plan for the future. You help me save my business and I'll help with your father." There was absolutely no need to tell her that he'd help with Tony for free if it came down to it. He had planned to address that later with Mama Em, but Tony had said not to give up. This was Ethan fighting for what he wanted.

Maeve swallowed hard.

Ethan could practically see the wheels turning in her head. This was exactly why he couldn't quite bring himself to give up hope for the two of them. She wasn't nearly as cold as she wanted people to believe. He knew her well enough to know that behind her nervousness, she was just as affected as he was. Longing mixed with wariness in those caramel golden eyes and Ethan wanted nothing more than to answer the call.

"You'll help my dad?" she whispered hoarsely.

Ethan nodded solemnly. "With everything, not just the addition." He let a small smile pull at his lips. "I'm guessing that with Antonio still gone, you could use a set of muscles around to help on occasion." He flexed and winked, rejoicing when her lips twitched. "I happen to be pretty good at being muscles."

"Lots of practice, huh?" she asked sarcastically.

"Not enough to put it on my resume, but..." He smiled and leaned in ever so slightly. "Well? Do we have a deal?"

The world paused in that moment as Ethan waited for a response. He was positive that even if he tried to breathe, his lungs wouldn't have worked. The very wind seemed to be holding its breath in anticipation of Maeve's answer.

"Okay."

When he got home, Ethan had every intention of doing a touchdown dance, but it would only occur behind a closed door. Instead, he allowed himself to breathe again and held out his hand. "Deal."

When Maeve reached out to seal the agreement, Ethan jumped right in. He pulled her hand up and kissed the back of it, eliciting a gasp from his beautiful neighbor. He wouldn't be able to waste a single moment in this situation or he'd lose her, he was sure of it.

"I'll see you in the morning," he said, knowing she could hear the promise in his voice. Giving her one last wink, he walked across the lawns, whistling as he went. He had work to do and this time, it had nothing to do with saving his business. This time it was about saving his heart.

CHAPTER 5

Maeve didn't bother going to see her parents again when she walked back inside from her agreement with Ethan. She might possibly have just committed to the stupidest mistake of her entire life.

"No," she whispered. "That was going surfing with him in the first place." *But this is a close second.*

She had no idea how she was going to work on a personal basis with him for days on end. She could easily go over his finances and point out any places that needed tweaking. Maybe he spent too much in deductions. Maybe he'd indulged in some extra expensive materials and he could cut a few corners without sacrificing quality. "Maybe he just can't add," Maeve muttered, then snapped her mouth shut.

She sighed when guilt flooded her system. Ethan was an intelligent man. She knew that whatever was bothering his business wasn't because of his own neglect or lack of understanding. He more than likely really had had a bad year and needed help keeping things alive. She might have to get creative in order to help save his shop, and despite her worry about spending time with him...Maeve knew she had to save his business.

She might not like surfing, she might have nightmares about drowning, she might not trust another surfer ever again...but none of that changed her feelings for Ethan, welcome or not. She loved him and she knew it would break him to lose his shop.

Upon reaching her room, Maeve quickly changed into her pajamas. She needed some downtime if she was going to be strong enough to handle working with Ethan for the next while. Reading a good book and shutting out the world would go a long way in helping her shore up her resolve.

No sooner had she wrapped herself in blankets and cracked the spine of her favorite novel than a knock came on her door.

Maeve almost ignored it, but the worry that her mother needed help with her father had her answering. "Yeah? Come in."

Estelle poked her head in. "Hey..."

I need to install one of those cameras so I know when I should pretend to be asleep. "Hey."

Estelle eased herself the rest of the way inside and closed the door. She paused, leaning back against it. "So...Mom mentioned that Ethan ate with you guys..."

Maeve rolled her eyes. "Stelle, just ask what you want to ask."

Estelle laughed softly and came farther in, sitting down on the edge of Maeve's bed. "Sorry. I thought I was supposed to be sneaky about it."

"No. You're the oldest. You're supposed to be blunt. Aspen's supposed to be the sneaky one."

Estelle nodded sagely. "I'll remember that for the future."

Despite the reason why her sister was there, Maeve laughed a little. They might fight once in a while, but she adored her family. Even when they poked their noses into her business.

"So, what's up with you and Ethan?"

Maeve nodded, her eyebrows high. "Well done. Very blunt."

Estelle dropped her chin, acknowledging the compliment. "I've been practicing."

"Apparently not, since you didn't even know it was your role."

"Maeve." Estelle groaned. "Just answer the question."

Maeve sighed and burrowed further into the blankets. "Well, since I'm the youngest, I get to be the most angsty and I don't want to answer it."

"Don't you think this has gone on long enough?"

Estelle's soft question caught Maeve off guard. Maeve thought no one knew about her true feelings, but Estelle certainly sounded a little suspicious. "What do you mean?"

This time Estelle rolled her eyes. "Maeve...not all of us are fooled by your 'I hate you' act."

Panic began to trickle down Maeve's spine and she sunk even lower into the blankets.

Estelle reached forward and tugged on the covers. "Maeve," she scolded. "You have to tell me what's going on."

"I don't give in to nosey people."

"And I don't suffer liars."

Maeve sighed and buried her face in her hands. "Estelle, it doesn't matter anymore." It mattered. It very much mattered. But admitting that out loud would just prove what a weak idiot she was. Maeve wasn't supposed to be weak. She was the logical one, the one who was good with numbers, the one who never dropped the ball and could always be counted on for help. There was no room in her life to be weak.

"It obviously does or you wouldn't still be hurting," Estelle said firmly.

"Maybe a little less blunt," Maeve said, her voice going up like a question at the end.

"Or maybe a little more pushing is in order." Estelle raised one eyebrow in a perfect imitation of their mother.

"You're not my mom," Maeve said automatically. Unfortunately, it was a line she and Aspen had used all too much during their childhood.

"Thank heavens for that," Estelle shot back. "And it looks like you're choosing the toddler route. Classic deflection. Want to stomp your foot for emphasis?"

Maeve groaned and sat up enough to mostly emerge from her cocoon. "I don't have anything I want to share."

Estelle shook her head. "Mae...then why are you so unhappy?" She leaned in. "You used to adore Ethan. I was positive you had a crush on him when we were teenagers. That day he took you surfing…" Estelle paused.

Apparently, the change from that day hadn't gone completely unnoticed.

"I was sure that that day was going to be the first of many dates," Estelle continued, though much more softly. She paused as if waiting, but Maeve didn't respond. "What really happened?"

Maeve pinched her lips together. She hated the fact that she wanted to tell her sister everything. Eight years of holding back was growing too heavy. Instead of getting easier, the whole situation was getting harder and her feelings toward Ethan were far from simple. She found him attractive and attentive. He was generally happy and loved to laugh. He had a stress-free way of looking at the world that enticed Maeve to no end. He was talented and intelligent, though he was far from a show off. And seeing him help her dad tonight had almost been more than Maeve could handle.

But none of that mattered because despite all his wonderful qualities…Maeve simply couldn't trust him. At least not with herself. He'd made her a promise and when it had really mattered…when her *life* had depended on it…he hadn't been there.

"I…can't," Maeve whispered.

Estelle watched her a moment longer, then leaned forward and wrapped Maeve in a tight hug. "I'm here when you want to talk."

Maeve nodded against her sister's shoulder. Maybe someday she wouldn't be such a coward and she could share it all, but bringing the story up when she was still struggling with it would only make it all the harder. She needed to conquer those feelings. Be in control. Have a firm handle on her heart before she could share the story without breaking down.

And the next few days or weeks would give her plenty of practice. If she could manage to spend time with Ethan and come out as intact as she went in...then Maeve knew she'd be able to handle anything. Even telling her sister how she lost the love of her life.

*****

Ethan was a mix of nerves and excitement by the time he made it back to his house. Maeve had agreed. She had *agreed*. He'd been positive that she would see through his plan and call him on it.

Really, the situation was a win-win for him. Sort of. At the least, he'd get help with his business from someone who knew numbers and marketing like the back of her hand. At the most, he'd be able to save his business and possibly rebuild the relationship between himself and Maeve. He was hoping for the second option.

Turning on the lights in his dark house, Ethan grabbed his phone, knowing he was going to need a little help to fulfill his side of the bargain with that addition. He wasn't lying when he'd told Emory that he didn't have the experience necessary to run such a venture, but now he was committed and he wasn't about to let Maeve down...again.

"Hey, Matt," Ethan said when his call was picked up.

"Ethan! It's a bit early to be hearing from you," the middle aged man said with a laugh. "Are you ready to come work for me full-time?"

Ethan grinned. His part-time boss was a nice guy and Ethan was lucky to work with him. Not a lot of men would hire the same worker for only half the year, every year. "Not yet," Ethan admitted. "But I do have a project I've been asked to work on and I was looking for a little advice."

"Shoot," Matt said automatically.

"Do you know the Harrisons? Their daughters own the bakery on Main."

Matt laughed. "I think everyone knows who they are by now, even my family that live in Texas. That thing with the baker and that guy who reviewed food was enough to put even our tiny town on the map."

Ethan nodded, though Matt couldn't see it. "True enough. Anyway, their dad is having trouble getting up and down the stairs. They'd like to have me build an addition to the main level they can use as a master."

Matt whistled. "That's gonna be a big project."

"Which is why I called you," Ethan insisted.

Matt was quiet for a moment. "Okay, well, I think it might be best for me to see the house. After that we can talk about the best place for such a room and start looking into plans."

"I don't want to put you out," Ethan said. "And I have no idea what kind of budget they're working with, though I can probably find out tomorrow."

"That'll work," Matt agreed. "As long as I know before something starts being drafted, then I'd say we're good to go." He chuckled. "I told you I'd make a builder out of you yet."

Ethan laughed. "Not as long as there are waves in the ocean," he shot back. They'd had this conversation too many times to count. Ethan knew it had nothing to do with the fact that he was some great worker, but he was steady and dependable and every boss he'd ever worked for had been grateful for it. Unfortunately, it seemed to be a dying art in the world today.

"Well, maybe global warming'll take care of that too, someday," Matt retorted. He chuckled at his own joke. "Let me know what you find out and we'll get it on the calendar."

"Sounds good. Thanks, boss."

"Anytime." The phone went silent and Ethan dropped it from his ear.

He sat still, letting his mind wander over the conversation he had had with Maeve. He had a lot of work ahead of him. What could he do to show her that he'd changed? That he deserved a second chance? That he wouldn't break a promise to her again?

"What would catch Maeve's attention?"

His phone buzzed.

Ethan opened the screen and grinned.

Isn't he cute?

Riley had texted a picture of the puppy Ethan had played with yesterday. She was right. The runt was adorable, though Ethan would never say that in public. He had a reputation to uphold, after all. But that puffball had curled up and gone right to sleep and Ethan had had a hard time putting him down.

"You're not in the market for a dog," he muttered to himself.

Still can't take care of him. Ethan texted back.

Another picture came through, this one a close up of the puppy's eyes.

Who can say no to this face?

Ethan rolled his own. **Ri...how would I take care of a dog?**

A knock on his door had him jerking in shock. Frowning, Ethan hurried over. Maybe Tony needed help again. Had he fallen and actually gotten hurt? "Riley." Ethan groaned after opening the door.

Riley grinned and held up the exact puffball she'd been texting about. "Come on...you can't tell me you don't want to say yes!"

Ethan folded his arms over his chest. "He's cute," he admitted. "But I live alone. And I can't take him to work. What happens when he starts marking all the surfboards or chews all the ankle straps?"

Riley gave him a look. "That's what training is for." She held up a hand to stop him from retorting. "But! If you don't want a long term commitment, what about fostering him? You just take him on until I can find a home. That's all."

"And how long will that be?"

Riley shrugged. "Years?" She laughed. "Just kidding. He's really cute, so I don't expect it to take long, but sometimes I have to reach outside town, since our population isn't exactly booming." She gave him a sheepish grin. "It's not like I can hit up the same household for twenty cats, you know. City ordinances being what they are..."

Ethan chuckled with her. "I don't have any supplies."

Riley squealed and handed the startled pup over. "I've totally got you covered!" Running down the steps, she went to the driveway and the back of her car. Her arms were laden with dog supplies by the time she stumbled back up his porch.

"Why do I have a feeling that I've been had?" Ethan muttered when she pushed past him.

"Whatever," Riley shot back. "It's not my fault you're a pushover." She looked up from where she was setting stuff on the coffee table. "Or that you bonded with the little guy."

Ethan held out the puppy, getting a close look at his pitiful face. "She's trying to manipulate us," he told the dog.

"Good thing it's working!" Riley sang.

Ethan shook his head and brought the puppy back to his chest. "Does he have a name?"

Riley straightened and shook her head. "Nope. You can be as creative as you want."

"Fido it is," Ethan said automatically.

"Don't you dare," Riley threatened.

Ethan cracked a grin, then pursed his lips consideringly. He hadn't named a pet since he was a little kid. What could he possibly call a tiny guy like this? "Tox."

Riley made a face. "Tox?"

Ethan nodded, tucking the puppy under his arm. "Yep. I'll call him Tox." Maybe someday he would explain to Riley that the idea had come from his next door neighbor. That Maeve's name meant "The Intoxicating One", which he found to be more than appropriate, and that Tox was a short reminder of the woman who had all his attention.

Or maybe not.

But nonetheless, in a small, weird way, Ethan had just named the puppy staying with him after the woman he loved. Maybe he'd get lucky and it would eventually be a point in his favor. It certainly couldn't hurt.

CHAPTER 6

Maeve ate her breakfast unusually slow the next morning. She was supposed to drive over to Ethan's shop to go through his books and she wasn't looking forward to it in the least.

You're going to get hurt.

He can't be trusted.

You owe him this for helping with your dad.

This is for Dad. It's just business.

The back and forth in her head refused to budge and at times Maeve felt as if she was going to go crazy. She'd never been much of an actress, but she was going to have to learn...and quick.

"Are you coming in today?" Estelle asked as she rushed around, packing a lunch.

Maeve shook her head. "No. I'm meeting with Ethan at the shop."

Estelle paused, her head slowly coming out of the fridge. "What?"

Maeve kept her eyes on her plate of scrambled eggs. The longer she sat there, the less they tasted appetizing. "I'm helping him with his books." She shrugged. "He said his business is having a rough year." Daring to glance up from under her lashes, she defended herself. "Ethan agreed to help us get together what we needed for an addition for Dad downstairs."

Estelle nodded slowly. "Right. That sounds like a fair trade."

"It is." Maeve stood and took her plate to the sink, ignoring the fact that she'd wasted her mother's good cooking.

"Good luck," Estelle called out as Maeve turned away and left.

Not bothering to answer, Maeve raced up the stairs two at a time, brushing her teeth and making sure her hair was pulled back in a tight bun. As she walked out of the bathroom, she grabbed her fake glasses from her nightstand and plopped them on her nose. Today she needed all the protection she could get.

The drive to his shop took much less time than she wanted, since her heart was still beating out of control and she felt overly warm, though the morning was quite chilly. Jerking her keys out of the ignition, she marched up to the shop, forcing her trembling knees into compliance and pushing her glasses up higher on her nose.

Maeve hesitated in the doorway when something resembling a stuffed animal scuttled across the floor. "What in the world?"

"TOX!" came a deep voice from the back of the shop.

Maeve watched, wide eyed as Ethan stormed from the backroom, looming over what she could now see was a dog. A very tiny, very fluffy...dog.

"You can't chew on my ropes," Ethan scolded, holding up a shredded length of cord as evidence.

Tox whimpered and stepped back, away from Ethan.

Ethan's shoulders immediately slumped. "Don't look at me like that." He moaned, bending down to pick up the tiny creature. Cuddling the puppy to his chest, Ethan calmly explained the situation again, but this time with a lot less frustration. "You're gonna get sick," Ethan continued. "Plus, I can't afford to keep buying new supplies just because you're teething."

"I didn't know you were such a softie." Maeve could have bit her tongue in half. Seeing big, strong Ethan speak to the dog so gently was doing funny things to her stomach and causing her to forget that she was supposed to be keeping her distance.

Ethan's head jerked up and Maeve could have sworn his cheek flushed pink. "Oh, hey, Maeve." He scratched his stubbly chin. "I didn't realize you were coming in quite so early."

Maeve raised an eyebrow, putting up her protective shield once more. "I thought it best to get this done as quickly as possible."

He gave her a smirk. "Of course you did."

Maeve nodded toward the dog. "Since when do you have a pet?"

Ethan chuckled and walked over. "Since Riley was desperate for someone to foster the little guy." He held out the wriggling bundle.

"Oh!" Maeve quickly grabbed the puppy and settled him into herself. "You're fostering him?" She stroked his silky head and giggled when the puppy reached up, trying to lick her chin. "No face," Maeve said, though she couldn't help but smile.

Ethan's grin was exactly the type that made all the ladies swoon around him. Lazy and handsome with just a hint of mischief. "If I'd known a dog would have gotten your attention, I'd have done that ages ago."

Maeve's smile dropped. She needed to remember why she was here and it wasn't to hold a cute puppy. "Why don't you show me the books?"

Ethan gave her a salute. "Yes, ma'am. Right back this way."

Maeve rolled her eyes at Ethan's back. She carried Tox with her as they headed to Ethan's office. It was a simple room with a desk, computer, filing cabinet and a couple of bookcases. To her surprise, the shelves were actually full of books, not surfing nicknacks like she would have expected.

"Believe it or not, I do read," Ethan teased as he pulled a second chair around to the computer side of the desk.

Maeve scowled. "I didn't say anything."

"You didn't have to." He grinned. "Your face said it all."

This time she rolled her eyes where he could see it. "You don't need a second chair," she said. "I'm sure you have classes and customers to help. If you'll just pull up your financial documents, I'll get started."

Ethan huffed. "Already going back on your word, huh?"

The words were sharp...and a little ironic, since the trust issues went the other direction. "I didn't say that."

"No. But you're trying not to have to spend time with me."

Maeve sighed. "Look. We both know this really isn't a good idea, but I'm willing to help. Believe it or not, I don't want you to lose your business and we really do need help with Dad. With Antonio gone, we're all kind of at a loss."

Ethan nodded. "Believe it or not, I'm perfectly willing to help your dad and would have been happy to do so without you looking at my books." He leaned forward. "But you're wrong if you think this isn't a good idea. I know you've got it in your head that I'm untrustworthy and you've held a grudge since we were kids, but I've changed, Maeve. Like most people, I grew up. I'm not the same lanky teenager who first took you surfing and accidentally hurt you."

Maeve stiffened. This was exactly the conversation she was hoping to avoid. She hated talking about it. Absolutely hated it. She set down Tox, who was whining and wiggling. She used the few moments of broken eye contact to refocus herself. She was here for her dad. That's all. She took in a deep breath when she stood. "I'm here to help with the books, Ethan. Nothing else."

Slowly he shook his head and walked back around the desk.

Her heart beat in double time with every step he took.

"You might use that as an excuse," he said in a low tone, stopping when he was toe to toe with her. He reached out and tapped the side of her glasses. "And you might put plastic between us, but I'm not going anywhere, Maeve. Not until you give me a fair chance."

Maeve tried to swallow, but there wasn't enough moisture in her throat. "What exactly do you want?" she rasped.

He leaned in just a hair more, sending her pulse into warp speed. "I want to show you who I am now. And I want to explore this pull between us." He held up a finger. "Don't even try to deny it. No one, not even Tox, will believe you." He waited, but Maeve had no words.

What could she say to such a proposal? It went against everything she'd worked for these last eight years and yet it offered something she wasn't sure she'd ever have again.

Closure.

Closure that would give her freedom from her feelings of fear and anger and would allow her to finally drop the facade she held onto so tightly. The deal wasn't that she had to date him or even do more than spend a little time with him. He just wanted her to stop pushing him away.

"Well? Can you do that?"

Her mind was screaming in two different directions and after several seconds of indecision, she spoke honestly. "I don't know."

He gave her a small smile. "That's good enough for now."

*****

Ethan knew he had pushed as far as he could...for now. He hadn't really planned to lay it all out so clearly, but the conversation had been right for him to state his intentions and if he was going to earn her trust, he was going to be as brutally honest as necessary...even if it meant he told her how much he wanted to be with her.

He tapped the computer chair. "Have a seat. I'll pull up the documents and be back in twenty minutes or so, and we can start to chat." He tapped a few keys on the keyboard and stepped back, giving her breathing space. "Tox!" Shaking his head, Ethan grabbed the puppy, who was playing What Else Can I Chew? with a pair of his flip flops.

The soft laughter coming from Maeve, however, made losing his shoes so worth it. She didn't relax enough to laugh around him very often and the sound was enticing.

Ethan glanced over his shoulder. "You'll only encourage him."

Maeve shrugged. "Isn't that the best part about not owning a pet? I can spoil other people's and never have to deal with the consequences."

Ethan laughed as he scooped up the miscreant. "Remind me to never leave him alone with you."

Maeve only grinned and Ethan nearly ran into the wall because he couldn't make himself look away in time to walk out without losing his dignity. Grunting at his own stupidity, he walked back out to the front of the shop. It was much too early in the morning for his normal customers to come around. Only the die-hards seemed to hit the early waves. Vacationers liked to sleep in and often came when the weather was warmer during the afternoon.

Walking around, he kept an eye on Tox while doing any last minute cleaning that his helper had failed to do yesterday. Who'd have thought that teenage boys wouldn't dust as often as they were supposed to?

When a family unexpectedly walked in, Ethan found himself caught up at the front desk for the next couple of hours, much longer than he wanted to be away from Maeve, but it couldn't be helped. She had planned this on purpose, knowing he'd need to work out front and it would let her do the work without him being there.

Grumbling under his breath, he realized with a start that it was almost lunch time. "Perfect." Changing the sign at the front of the shop, Ethan walked to the back, feeling much more confident than he had earlier. "Lunch time!" he hollered, then felt bad when Maeve almost jumped out of her seat. Trying to act casual, he took Tox to his kennel and locked him inside.

"Oh my gosh," Maeve snapped. "What the heck was that for?" She had a hand over her heart and Ethan chuckled.

"Were you seriously that caught up in the numbers?" He made a face. "Or is my bookkeeping really that bad?"

Maeve sighed and shook her head. "Actually, your financials are in surprisingly good order, though there are a couple places we can shift some expenditures around. But you're right...things are unusually tight this year."

Ethan nodded, then tilted his head toward the door. "Why don't you tell me about it as I treat you to some food?"

Maeve leaned back in her seat. "Uh...shouldn't I be treating you to lunch?" She looked pointedly at the computer screen. "I just saw your savings account."

"If twenty bucks for a couple of sandwiches is going to break me, then I don't deserve to be running this shop." Holding out his hand, Ethan let his invitation sit between them. He couldn't hurry her. He knew better. But she knew where he stood and he would keep offering until she accepted.

The fact that she'd been unable to flat out say "no" earlier gave him hope. The chemistry between them was tangible and he had no idea how she'd been putting it off for so long, so this time together was going to be his chance of breaking down that wall once for all.

All he was asking was a chance. A chance to prove himself and a chance to see if their pull was because of their past or something that could be cultivated for their future. Ethan had his suspicions, but he would let Maeve make up her own mind. To do any less would completely go against what he was trying to show her.

Maeve stood, shut down the computer and walked around the desk. She hesitated, but didn't actually take his hand. Instead, she simply nodded and walked past him.

Progress, he thought. She wouldn't have even acknowledged him before. He followed right behind her as they walked out to the parking lot. "I'll drive," he said, opening and holding the door to the passenger seat. Again, Maeve hesitated, but this time she actually gave in.

"I don't know why I'm doing this," she muttered so he could hear as she sat down.

Ethan paused before closing the car door. "Because you're just as curious as I am," he whispered.

Maeve looked up. She didn't look happy, but she also didn't look mad. In fact, if Ethan had to name the look on her face, he would call it...lost. It pulled at him, but he forced himself to keep at least a little distance.

Maeve wasn't a little girl and she wasn't ready for him to jump in with both feet. He was an adult now as well. He could keep a pace that would be comfortable for them both... He'd have to.

Ethan pulled into a small cafe that was known for their sandwich wraps and they walked inside side by side. Ethan could practically feel the heat of her skin and he had to remind himself a dozen times not to take her hand yet.

"Thank you," he murmured to the hostess when she showed them to a table. Ethan pulled back Maeve's chair and couldn't hold back a grin when she gave him a side eye. "I'm sorry. Is it wrong to be a gentleman?"

"You're treating this like a date," she accused after sitting down.

Ethan sat and shrugged. "And that bothers you?"

"We're not on a date."

"Okay."

Maeve frowned. "Okay? That's all you have to say?"

"What do you want me to say? You don't want this to be a date. Fine. It's not a date. But that doesn't mean I won't treat you well or with respect." Ethan held his breath as she studied him. She was trying to figure out if he was serious and he wasn't going to give her any clues that he wasn't.

He'd waited years just for the opportunity to have a conversation with her. No way was he blowing it now.

After they'd ordered, the table grew quiet and Ethan tapped his fingers in a rhythm. "So...tell me what all's going on with your dad."

Maeve raised her eyebrows. "You don't want to talk about your books?"

Ethan shook his head. "We'll get to that." He folded his hands together and leaned onto the table. "Estelle told me he has Parkinson's, right?"

Maeve nodded, all the wariness leaving her face. Though the sadness that replaced it wasn't necessarily any better. "Yeah. He got the diagnosis several years ago. He held onto it for a time, but when his hands began to shake too much in his work, he couldn't keep going."

Ethan whistled low. "So he didn't tell you kids until after he retired?"

Maeve shrugged one shoulder. "We knew right before he retired, but still...yeah...he and Mom knew a long time before we did."

Ethan ran a hand through his hair. "That had to have been tough."

She grunted quietly. "You could say that."

"And the trip to Italy?"

"It was to see family before he got too bad to travel."

"How long are they expecting him to live?" Ethan asked softly. His chest ached with the question. Tony Harrison wasn't just a neighbor to him, he was like a second father figure. And loving Maeve and knowing she was hurting only made Ethan's pain feel twice as heavy.

Maeve took a deep breath. "Dad was younger than most when he developed it, but most patients live ten to twenty years after their diagnosis." She hesitated. "But his has been developing rapidly, so we don't really know..." Her voice trailed off and she couldn't seem to look him in the eye.

Taking a chance, Ethan reached over and covered her hands, which were picking at her napkin. "Hey..." He waited until she looked up. "You're dad's a champ. Have faith."

She blinked, her eyes slightly watery. "Thanks," she said, wiping at the side of her eye.

"For what?"

"For not offering a bunch of overused platitudes that aren't true."

Ethan smiled. "I'll always be upfront with you, Maeve." He squeezed her fingers one last time before reluctantly letting go. "And I'll always be here."

CHAPTER 7

Maeve pulled her hair back in another ponytail. It was day two of working with Ethan and Maeve had been scolding herself for nearly twenty-four hours. She'd let down her guard yesterday. She'd gone to lunch with him, let him touch her hand, and hadn't turned him down when he said he wanted to use this time to give each other a chance.

It had all sounded wonderful. Frightening but wonderful and in the heat of the moment, Maeve had been unable to come up with a good excuse for why she wanted to keep some space between them. That is, until she went to bed last night. She'd had *the dream* again. The one where she was drowning and all her insecurities and worries about Ethan had come flooding back like the ocean water that had nearly taken her life all those years ago.

Maeve had woken in a cold sweat with her heart beating an abnormal rhythm and she'd known she couldn't do it. She couldn't give in. It didn't matter how handsome his smile was, or how much she wanted to run her fingers along the stubble on his chin. His windblown hair wasn't enough and neither was his soft spot for orphaned puppies.

Her heart might be struggling, but Maeve's mind knew exactly what was going on and it had warned her last night not to give in.

She tightened her ponytail until she winced with the pain. *Good,* she thought glumly. *Maybe that'll knock some sense into you.* Glaring at her own reflection, Maeve marched downstairs and out the door. She didn't even bother with breakfast today, it would only slow her down. The sooner she got to the shop, the faster she could get out of there and leave Ethan behind.

By the time Maeve got to the surf shop, her heart had practically run a marathon. It was still beating hard against her rib cage and

Maeve was struggling to calm it down. Leaning her head back against the seat rest, she closed her eyes and practiced her slow breathing.

In...out...in...out...

A timid knock on the window caused Maeve to squeal in shock and undid the good her breathing had just accomplished. "Ethan!" she scolded, pushing the door open and jumping out of the car. "Seriously! You're going to give me a heart attack!"

Ethan gave her a sheepish smile and held up his hands. "I just wanted to check that you were alright. You look pale and you're here extra early." His hands fell to his side and his brows furrowed. "Now that you're out of the car, you look even more tired. Are you alright?" He reached out as if to touch her face but stopped when Maeve ducked away.

"I'm fine," she snipped, marching toward the front door. "Can we just get started for the day?"

"Is your dad alright?" Ethan persisted as he followed after her. Tox was whining and tugging on the leash he was attached to and Ethan bent down to scoop the puppy up.

Maeve paused, realizing she had been in such a hurry to get started she'd completely forgotten to check in with her dad this morning. She usually tried to make sure he had slept well and see what he needed before she headed out. *I'm the world's worst daughter,* she thought to herself.

"Maeve?" Ethan's eyebrows were raised in question now.

Maeve sighed and shook her head. "I...didn't see him this morning."

Ethan opened his mouth, then shut it, as if figuring it wasn't worth pushing her about. Finally, he smiled. "Well, I'm sure you can call or text when we get inside, right? Someone ought to be awake by now." Putting his back to her, he opened the door and Maeve slowly padded inside.

She had never felt so low. First she'd been shrewish with Ethan and now she'd realized how terrible she'd been to her parents as well. "Eeks?" she whispered, not realizing she had used his childhood nickname.

Ethan stopped mid stride, then slowly turned. "Yeah?"

"I'm sorry."

His grin was slow and understanding. "I guess you had a rough night, huh?"

Maeve rubbed at her eyes. Good thing she hadn't put on mascara today. Makeup had been yet another luxury sacrificed on the "get this over with" altar. "You could say that, I suppose," she hedged. It wasn't like she could tell him about the dream. The situation might have been his fault, but the fact that she couldn't get over it was her own.

"Anything you want to talk about?"

Maeve shook her head. "Nah. I'll get over it." She took in a cleansing breath. "Now...shall we take a look at the books?"

Ethan nodded and scratched behind Tox's ears. "Yep. And since I don't open for an hour, we can talk about what you're seeing."

Maeve nodded, feeling overwhelmingly weary. The weight of the fear and strength to keep holding herself back from Ethan was becoming too much. She wanted freedom. But how? Nights like last night reminded her just how *un*free she was. It was like being caught in a rip tide. No matter how hard she swam, she simply couldn't get herself out.

Ethan pulled out her chair again and Maeve gave him a weak smile. "Thanks."

"Here." He plopped Tox in her lap. "Puppies make everyone feel better."

Maeve laughed a little before scratching the wiggling pup.

"That's what I was looking for," Ethan said softly.

Maeve looked up. "What?"

"Your smile."

Heat rushed up her neck. Why in the world did he have to be so charming? It made her life so much harder. *Or easier, if you think about it.* But Maeve didn't want to think about it. She just wanted life to go back to the way it was. Before she'd almost died. Before her dad got sick. Before she'd pushed Ethan so far away she wasn't sure how to let him back again. "You're a flirt," she responded.

"Only with you," he shot back. Then he nodded at the computer. "Alrighty. Tell me what's going on."

Maeve took in a long breath through her nose and held onto the dog with one hand, grabbing the mouse with the other. "Like I said, your math is just fine. You don't have any major discrepancies or anything." She pursed her lips. "Really, other than switching a few expenses into different categories, I don't see what you can change other than to drum up more business." She turned to look at him. "How's the online shop going? You have a website, right? Where people can order custom boards or other equipment?"

Ethan nodded. "Yeah...but I don't see a lot of traction there. Most of the time people wanting custom aren't surfing the net." He grinned at his joke and Maeve rolled her eyes. "They usually go where they surf. If I was in California or Hawaii, I'd get a lot more move-ment, but people up here are already set up with boards for the most part."

Maeve nodded. "What kind of social media presence do you have?"

Ethan scrunched his nose. "None?"

Maeve shook her head. "Okay. Well, let's start with that since it's free to set up an account." She tapped the desk. "We can have Austin help us out there. I mean...I can certainly get you an account set up, but Austin will be quicker and more efficient. Plus, he'll have a better idea of graphics and what to say in order to get people interested in what you're doing."

*****

Ethan found himself watching Maeve's lips as she spoke, entranced by how soft and pink they looked. One part of his brain warned him that he was going to get in trouble if he didn't pay attention, but who could concentrate when the mouth he'd wanted to kiss since he was a teenager was so close?

"Does that sound okay?"

Ethan shook himself back to the present. "Yep. Sounds good." *What the heck did I just agree to?*

Maeve nodded and handed him Tox. "Here. Let me call Austin and we'll get started."

Oh, yeah...Austin...social media. He eyed the wall clock. "Is the newlywed going to be awake at this hour?"

Maeve groaned and set her cell back down. "I obviously left my brain at home today," she grumbled. Her stomach got in on the action and Maeve covered it with her hand, her cheeks turning pink.

"Sounds like you left your breakfast at home as well," Ethan said with a grin. He stood and held out his hand. "Come on. We've got time to grab something."

Maeve shook her head. "I can't. You paid for lunch yesterday."

"Then we'll just run back to the house," he said easily. As long as he spent time with Maeve, he wasn't going to complain where it was happening. She had looked so tired when she'd arrived this morning. He'd known immediately something was wrong. He was just glad it wasn't her father. If Tony continued to go downhill, there would be nothing Ethan could do. As it was, he'd already called his boss again, begging for him to move up the date for the house inspection. There was an urgency sitting in the back of Ethan's head and he felt compelled to really jump on the project without delay.

Maeve groaned but stood up and followed him, the puppy still in her arms. She didn't take Ethan's hand, but she did come, and he would count that as a win for now.

"I'll drive," he said as they went back outside.

"You drove yesterday," she pointed out.

"Your hands are full," he said triumphantly. His grin widened when she glared. Why was it so fun to ruffle her feathers a bit? He didn't actually want to make her mad, but he did enjoy a little banter and right now this was as close as he got.

He opened her door and got her settled before jumping into the driver's seat and taking them home. "Okay...I've got eggs, cheese and veggies," he said as they walked inside. "How about an omelet?"

"That sounds wonderful," she replied, sitting down at one of the tables.

Ethan got to work. He liked having Maeve in his home. She hadn't been over for more than a few minutes since they were younger and it felt right having her at his table once more. Of course, his house was a little less full than it was back then, but that wasn't worth dwelling on.

The room was comfortably silent for several minutes, all except for Tox's panting when Maeve spoke up.

"Do you miss them?"

Apparently she'd noticed how alone they were as well. Ethan turned and gave her a sad smile. "Every day."

She broke their eye contact and looked down at the snoozing dog. "How did you do it?"

Ethan took a moment to think before answering. There wasn't one answer to such a question. He'd been just out of high school when his parents had been killed. Although he'd been an adult, he'd still been young and it had been the shock of his life. Instead of getting to live it up as a freshman, he'd been in lawyer's offices, trying to settle wills.

He finally shrugged. "A day at a time." He turned off the stove and spun around, folding his arms over his chest and leaning against the counter. "If I'm being completely honest, the only reason I made it was because of your parents."

Maeve nodded slowly. "They're pretty amazing, huh?'

"They are."

She looked up from under her lashes. "Yours were too."

"Thank you."

"I'm not sure I ever said how sorry I was that they passed."

He shrugged one shoulder. "It's all in the past now. No big deal." He had no idea why that line bothered Maeve so much, but she seemed to grow even paler. Not quite knowing how to handle it, he decided his best bet was food. He turned and picked up the skillet, then walked to the cabinet with the plates in it. "Ready to eat?"

She didn't respond, but Ethan just kept going. Someday...*some-day*...she would trust him again, enough to confide what was going on. Was he sad today wasn't that day? Yes. But he'd known this was going to take time. She'd held him off for a long time and in the last two days, she'd spoken to him, commiserated with him, laughed with him and simply spent time in his company. That was more progress in forty-eight hours than he'd had in eight years.

It's enough.

He slid the plate in front of her. "Don't let the pup eat any," he teased. "Not unless you want to clean up the puke."

Maeve shook her head. "Ugh. No thanks." She picked up her fork, careful not to disturb the sleeping animal while she cut off her first bite.

"Mind if we say grace first?" Ethan asked.

"Oh, gosh," Maeve said. "I really did leave my brain at home." She straightened. "Yes, sorry."

Ethan chuckled. "It's fine." He quickly said a blessing over their food and then they dug in. That little momentary reset seemed to do Maeve some good since she ate with gusto.

"I didn't remember you being such a chef," she said as she polished off her plate.

"I'm a single guy," Ethan reminded her. "It was either learn to cook, or starve."

"You could always just buy frozen stuff," Maeve pointed out. "Or eat takeout every night."

"I could, but frozen sounds gross and takeout sounds expensive."

Maeve laughed. "You sound like my mom." She tilted her head. "And Aspen."

"Somehow I'm guessing your dad would fit that category too."

"True," Maeve mused. "But he doesn't cook. He baked, so he didn't have a lot of room to talk."

Ethan grabbed both their plates. "Ready to try the office again? I open in fifteen, so we should probably get back."

"Oh, gosh, yes." Maeve scrambled to her feet. "So sorry, baby," she cooed to Tox, who wasn't exactly happy to be woken from his nap.

"You'll spoil him," Ethan warned as he led her outside and into the car.

Maeve grinned. It was so full of impish delight that Ethan had a hard time keeping his scolding face on. "That's my job." She waggled her eyebrows at him. "He's not mine, so I can spoil him rotten and then let you deal with the consequences."

Ethan paused before closing her door and leaned in until they were practically nose to nose. "I'm not sure how yet, but that's going to come back to bite you in the tush..." He grinned. "And I'm gonna laugh when it does."

Maeve's eyebrow made a perfect arch. "I look forward to proving you wrong," she said in an airy tone.

Ethan could barely hold back his laughter and from the twitching of Maeve's pursed lips, she was feeling the same way. "Let the best man win."

CHAPTER 8

Maeve yawned and stretched her arms to the sky, arching her back. "What time is it?" she murmured, finally looking at the corner of the computer screen. She nearly jumped out of her seat when she realized she'd been in Ethan's office almost the entire day.

She knew lunch had come and gone since he'd brought her a peanut butter sandwich and some chips, but she'd been so caught up in working with Austin to get all the social media up and the graphics put together that Maeve had completely lost the day.

"It's amazing you're still alive," Ethan teased from the doorway.

Maeve groaned and let her head fall back against the seat. "Sometimes I'm a little...hyper focused."

"I can see that."

Maeve cracked open one eye and glared at him. "This is for your business, bub. Be nice."

Ethan put his hands in the air. "I'm not complaining. I'm honestly amazed. I don't think my brain could handle what you just did."

Maeve rubbed her aching forehead. "I don't think mine handled it well either." A hand appeared in her vision with a bottle of pain pills. Maeve's heart fluttered. Why was he so darn nice? "Thank you," she said softly, her fingers brushing his. The heat that ran up her arm wasn't nearly as unwelcome as it had been earlier. In fact, it gave her a small jolt of energy that felt wonderful after her work day. "Is the shop closed?" she asked, throwing a couple pills in her mouth and washing them down.

Ethan nodded. "Yep. It's just me, you and a sleeping dog." He tilted his head toward the corner where Tox was snoring.

Maeve grinned. "My dad would probably love to meet him. He always wanted a dog, but Mom didn't want one in the house."

"Then it's a good thing I was supposed to come over tonight anyway," Ethan said, walking over to his charge. He picked the little guy up, tucking Tox under his arm and waving toward the door. "Your chariot awaits, m'lady."

Maeve smiled and laughed under her breath. "But I'm driving this time."

"Probably best," Ethan admitted as he locked doors behind them. "You'll want your own vehicle come morning."

Maeve was surprised when he still came up and opened her door for her. "Thank you," she said, knowing her surprise was heard in her tone.

"I told you," Ethan said. "We don't have to be dating for me to treat you like the princess you are."

Maeve paused before sitting down. "I'm not a princess."

Ethan stepped closer. "Yes, you are."

She smiled self-deprecatingly. "No. That honor goes to Estelle. She's the—"

Ethan stepped even closer, cutting Maeve's words off. "No. This isn't about Estelle...or anyone else." His eyes grew serious. "It's about you, Maeve, and only you. *You* are special. *You* are worthwhile. *You* are the one I want to spend my time with." His intense look softened, allowing Maeve to breathe a little. "I love your family like my own, but it's not your sisters I've been chasing after for the past eight years."

Her lungs weren't working properly and Maeve couldn't seem to get her legs to move. She couldn't run and she didn't know how to respond. There wasn't the tiniest lick of deceit or teasing in his demeanor. Any stranger would be able to see how serious he was...and it was all about her.

"I..." Maeve took a shuddering breath and tried to swallow. "I'm broken," she said softly, thinking of her dream this morning. "You should move on."

Ethan slowly shook his head. "I've been patient for a long time," he whispered. Reaching out with his free hand, he brushed the back of his fingers down her cheek. "I can wait a little longer." He finally moved away enough for her to get control of herself.

Maeve sat down and then looked up. "I don't know how to respond to that."

Ethan smiled. "You don't have to. I'm a big boy, I can make my own decisions." He hesitated, but then whispered, "And you're worth waiting for."

Maeve blinked rapidly, but she still felt the sting of tears. The door closed. Ethan once again doing his gentleman thing and she put the key in the ignition by rote memory. Starting the car was enough to get her brain back where it belonged, but the whole ten minute ride home, Maeve was completely lost in her thoughts.

She meant it when she said she was broken. Something wasn't quite right and she wasn't sure how to fix it. She'd come to realize, especially recently, that it wasn't really about Ethan anymore. Yes, he'd broken her trust, but any normal adult should have gotten over that by now.

He was working overtime to show her that he was responsible and that she could let down her guard around him, but the idea still terrified her. Why? Why was she so scared? And why did he think she was worth sticking around for?

Being the youngest of three sisters hadn't been easy on Maeve's ego. Her oldest sister was perfect. Gorgeous, curvy, responsible and so intimidating to men that very few managed the courage to ask her out. It was like asking out a supermodel with a brain.

Aspen was driven and loud and fun and could bake like nobody's business. Her artistic side was so stereotypically Italian that it had been a joke for most of their growing up years. She was passionate and excited and drove Maeve crazy...in a good way.

Then there was Maeve. She'd always been quiet, even as a teenager. Where Aspen could talk someone's ear off, Maeve was more of a listener. Maybe that's why she'd gotten along so well with Ethan. His laid back way of handling life had appealed to her. He was cool and cute and his smile made her heart flutter. And since he was an only child, he had been over at their house a lot, since he spent time with Maeve's older brother, Antonio.

But that one summer...the one that had changed every-thing...Maeve had finally stepped out of her shell. She'd gotten the courage to talk to the cute boy next door as something more than her brother's friend. To laugh at his jokes and smile when he flirted with her. When he'd offered to take her surfing for the first time, Maeve had thought she'd won the lottery. What girl in their school wouldn't have traded her right arm to be in that position?

Maeve shut off the engine and closed her eyes. One moment. One terrifying, terrible moment had changed it all. She'd retreated back into her shell, she'd lost her trust in Ethan and life in general, and had stopped living.

"You're a coward, Maeve Linlee Harrison. An absolute coward." How long had it taken her to finally realize Ethan was never the problem? Yes...he'd broken a promise. But was anyone perfect? Plus, they'd been kids. Kids! How could she hold him so responsible for something he did eight years ago?

"And more importantly," she murmured to the dark car, "why are you so willing to trust him with your father...but not yourself?" There was no good answer to the question. If she was willing to trust him with her family, Maeve knew that deep down, somewhere inside the frightened little girl that still ruled her...she wanted to change. She *wanted* to trust him.

Headlights pulled in behind her.

"And he's giving you every opportunity," she continued. She wasn't sure why she was speaking out loud, except that there was something more convincing when the words were given tangibility. "Maybe it's time you took him up on it."

Nervous, but also intrigued, Maeve gripped the door handle. The first fissures of doubt were starting to shake her foundation and this time...she wasn't going to fight back.

*****

Tox's hind end was just about to come out of socket with the way he was wiggling. It was funny how quickly the puppy had adjusted to being around people again. Only a few days ago he'd been scared to death at the shelter and now he couldn't seem to stop moving, licking and tasting everything in sight. "Is Mama Em gonna skin me for bringing a pup by?" Ethan asked as they walked up the front steps together.

Maeve laughed. She looked a little less weary than she had this morning, though Ethan couldn't figure out why. She had to be dead on her feet after spending so much time trying to give him an online presence. He'd have to make her a nice breakfast tomorrow as a thank you. "No. If it makes my dad happy, she'll be all for it."

Maeve pushed open the door. She hadn't said anything more about their little chat outside the shop and Ethan decided it was best to wait and watch. He'd played most of his hand and she'd said something that gave him hope, but worried him too. Why did she think she was broken? Had their situation when they were teenagers been so horrible that she was still traumatized? All this time he thought she was simply mad, but maybe there was more to it. Or had something else happened that made things worse?

Too many questions and not enough answers, he thought as they walked inside.

"Maeve? Is that you?" Mama Em called from deeper in the house.

"Yep," Maeve hollered back.

A dark head appeared around the corner. "Oh! Ethan, I'm so glad you..." She trailed off, then put her hands on her hips. "What in the world is that?"

Ethan grinned, then set the puppy on the floor. Tox's little legs immediately propelled him to the new person and he began sniffing Mama Em's bare feet.

"Is it even real?" she asked with a laugh.

"Oh, he's real," Maeve teased. "Ethan's chewed up ankle cords are in the garbage to prove it."

Maeve's mother bent down and picked up the fluffball. "Aren't you just the cutest thing?" she cooed. She brought the puppy to her chest. "When did you get a dog, Ethan?"

Ethan shrugged. "I'm only fostering him, but Riley talked me into it."

Mama Em rolled her eyes. "I should have known. We'd have a zoo here if that girl had her way." She waved them back. "Come on. Dad will want to see the little guy." She paused. "What's his name?"

"Tox." Everytime Ethan had to say the name, he felt his neck heat up. Maeve hadn't given him a hard time about it, but someone was eventually going to push for an explanation and he didn't want to give one. Who named a dog after their crush? Teenage girls?

"Tox? Hm?" She looked down at the dog. "Interesting name. Is that like a surf brand or something?"

"Or something," Ethan muttered.

Mama Em laughed. "Well, come on." She led the way to the family room where Tony was sitting in front of the television. "You have a visitor, sweetie." Mama Em leaned over the back of the couch and deposited the puppy in Tony's lap, then kissed his cheek.

Ethan couldn't help it. A surge of jealousy reared its ugly head and it took him a few moments to push it away. Their interaction made him miss his own parents and long for that kind of connection again in his life. His eyes darted to Maeve, who was watching her parents with an adoring look. If only he could skip through time to see if his investment in this relationship was worth it. Was she ever going to let him in?

"Who's this?" Tony asked, chuckling as Tox began licking everything in sight. Tony's hands shook, but he began scratching behind the dog's ears, much to Tox's delight.

"This is Tox, Daddy," Maeve said, moving around the couch to sit by her father. She pet the puppy's head. "Ethan is fostering him for Riley and I convinced him to come visit."

Tony looked over his shoulder, found Ethan and winked.

Ethan winked back.

"I always wanted a dog," Tony said to his daughter in a deliberately loud whisper. "But your mother is a stick in the mud."

"I heard that!" Mama Em shouted from the kitchen.

Tony made a face, then he and Maeve laughed.

Ethan watched, enjoying every minute of Maeve's light heartedness. This was why he kept doing what he was doing. This was why he didn't give up hope. She had such *goodness* inside her, but she hid it, especially from him.

"Think we can feed him dinner for bringing a dog?" Tony asked his daughter.

"Eh," Maeve teased, glancing at Ethan over her shoulder. "I doubt he's hungry. Ethan's never hungry."

Ethan chuckled and it was for more than just her teasing. *I do believe she's flirting with me*, he thought with a mental grin.

"Is that right?" Tony asked. He made a face. "That's not what I remember from being young."

Maeve leaned over and rested her head against her father's thinning shoulder. "You're still young," she whispered.

Ethan's grin grew slightly smaller. He wasn't sure what was worse. Watching a parent waste away slowly from a disease or having them suddenly be gone overnight. His protective instincts were screaming for him to somehow save Maeve from this pain. To help her manage it in a way that would save her heart, but he knew from first hand experience, he couldn't. He couldn't save her, he could only choose to be there. And if he played his cards right, then hopefully she would learn to turn to him when it grew difficult.

"Dinner!" Mama Em called out. "You too, young man," she said, pointing to Ethan. "You don't eat enough."

"I don't know about that," Maeve said with a laugh as she helped her father off the couch. "He fed me an omelet this morning, so I saw exactly what he eats during the day and it's far from insubstantial."

Ethan pinched his lips together when Mama Em froze.

"He fed you breakfast?" she asked.

Ethan looked over to see Maeve turning bright red even with her darker skin. "Uh...yes?" she squeaked.

Mama Em looked at him. "At your house?"

Ethan nodded. "She came to work with a stomach growling so loudly she couldn't crunch her numbers." He shrugged. "So I ran us home and had her crunch vegetables instead."

Mama Em tsked her tongue and Ethan let out a breath. Maeve had almost gotten them in trouble and from her blush, she knew exactly what she'd done. "There's always time for a good breakfast," she scolded her daughter. "Come on. Let's at least feed you dinner before you both blow away."

Maeve didn't meet Ethan's eye as she hurried past him and into the kitchen, but when Tony walked up, he held out a fist and Ethan smirked as they bumped knuckles.

"She's worth it," Tony whispered.

Ethan nodded. "Yes, sir."

CHAPTER 9

The heat in Maeve's cheeks took *forever* to calm down. She hadn't meant to tell her parents about eating breakfast with Ethan. She was afraid of giving anyone the wrong idea... Instead, she'd *really* given everyone the wrong idea.

I need a guardian angel to slap a hand over my mouth sometimes, she lamented.

"He's coming over in about a half hour," Ethan said, his fork resting in his hand. "Is that alright?"

"Who's coming over?" Maeve blurted out before she could think better of it.

The whole table turned to look at her.

ANGEL! she screamed internally. *Where in the world are you?*

"My boss from the construction crew," Ethan answered calmly, though his lips were twitching in amusement. "He's gonna look at the house with me so we can figure out the best plan for an addition."

Maeve nodded. "Oh, yeah. I forgot."

Her parents went back to their dinners and Maeve released a breath, until Ethan leaned into her ear.

"Whatcha daydreaming about over there, Little Mae?" he whispered.

The goosebumps running over her skin couldn't be helped, though Maeve prayed Ethan couldn't see them. Had she just recently decided she wanted to give him a chance? How could she do that when she couldn't even control herself around him? She wasn't ready to jump into a relationship with both feet. Right now all she wanted was to test the waters with her toe...but if he didn't stop being so...Ethan...she wasn't going to be able to help herself.

Maeve feigned indifference, though she knew she wasn't fooling anybody. "Sorry. I was going over shop numbers in my head."

"Really?" Ethan continued. His finger trailed up her arm where it was hidden under the table, keeping her parents in the dark about their little conversation. "The redness in your cheeks says otherwise."

Maeve jerked her arm away, bumping the table and making the blush on her face triple. She groaned and covered her face with her hands when her parents gave her another quizzable look.

"Are you alright, sweetie?" her mother asked. "You look flushed."

"Fine, Mom," Maeve said, kicking Ethan's foot when she realized he was chuckling. "Just embarrassed about hitting the table." When another voice of soft laughter joined Ethan's, Maeve peeked between her fingers to glare at her father.

Her dad immediately stopped and widened his dark brown eyes. "What?" he asked.

Maeve narrowed her gaze even more. "Traitor," she mouthed.

"I think I'm ready for dessert," her father announced, completely ignoring Maeve's distress.

"You've hardly eaten dinner!" Maeve's mom scolded.

Her dad shrugged and grabbed his wife's hand. "Life's short," he said, kissing the back of her fingers. "It's a night to eat dessert first. Besides..." He gave her a look that kept the heat in Maeve's cheeks even longer. "Who wouldn't want to be fed something sweet by a beautiful woman?"

Maeve couldn't look...but she also couldn't not look. Her head was ducked, but somehow her eyes just kept going back to her parents. Why was it so sweet and so disgusting all at the same time?

Her mother's cheeks heated, the same way Maeve's were and she shook her head in a scold. "You're a flatterer. You've always been a flatterer."

Her dad shrugged. "It got me you. Why change my ways now?"

Her mother giggled. *Giggled!* Maeve didn't know whether to join in or gag a little. A hushed chuckling came from beside her and she turned to glare at Ethan for interrupting her voyeurism.

"Think you can handle that?" her dad asked.

Maeve's head jerked back. "What?" After a beat she realized he was talking to Ethan.

Ethan coughed. "Excuse me?"

Maeve's dad's eyebrow rose high. "Always pay attention to those who have conquered before," he said with a smirk. "You'll learn something."

When Maeve finally realized what her father was saying, all the blood drained from her head and her jaw followed. "Dad!" she screeched. "Are you kidding me?"

"Are we kidding who?" Estelle asked as she walked inside. "Whew!" She plopped in the seat next to their mother. "I'm exhausted." Either Maeve's older sister was oblivious to the tension in the room, or she simply didn't care because she began filling an empty plate high with food.

"Ethan?" her father pressed.

Maeve groaned and covered her face again. Why was her family so embarrassing?

"Got it, sir," Ethan said. Even without looking, Maeve could tell he was laughing. How he could laugh at a time like this was beyond her.

Maeve wanted to melt into a puddle on the floor. This was beyond embarrassing and she had no way of fixing it. And how did she scold her father? Not only was Ethan still sitting right next to her, but her dad was sick! How do you scold a sick man?

Life isn't fair...

"Come on, Little Mae," Ethan said, teasing her with her childhood nickname again. "I think your parents are great."

"I don't have parents," she said, though the words were muffled behind her hands. "I'm an orphan."

Laughter grew around the table.

"Apparently, I missed something," Estelle inserted. "What's going on?"

"Oh, nothing," their mother sang. "Just your father sticking his nose where it doesn't belong." She smiled at Maeve.

"She's my daughter, and she inherited her nose from my side of the family. Apparently, it does belong there."

"Why doesn't the earth just swallow us when we want it to?" Maeve asked no one in particular. "That would be a really useful skill to have right now."

"If you had that power, you'd be a superhero and I wouldn't have the pleasure of sitting next to you," Ethan offered.

"Very good!" Maeve's dad said in triumph. "Soon the student will be the master."

"Oh my gosh..." Maeve scooted her chair back and stood up. "Excuse me, I have a date with a calculator."

Ethan grabbed her hand and stood up as well. "Actually...I was hoping—" The doorbell rang, cutting off his words. He grinned. "I'm guessing that's Matt. Want to walk the house with us? That way you can keep us within budget."

Maeve sighed, trying to push her embarrassment to the side, but it refused to budge. She'd never been so humiliated in her life and to have it happen with her parents and the guy she loved? Life was about as low as it got at the moment. "Fine," she huffed, not wanting to admit just how much she wanted to stay close to Ethan.

His grin said he knew. "Great. Let's go let him in." He took her hand and led Maeve toward the front door.

Maeve tried not to grin as she tripped in his wake, but there was nothing for it. Her hormones had completely taken over and if she wasn't careful, she'd be drowning in all things Ethan Markle by this time tomorrow.

*****

"Hey, Matt!" Ethan said as he pulled open the front door. "Glad you could make it." Ethan tried to pretend like holding Maeve's hand wasn't a big deal, but he had never been so conscious of another person's touch before. His skin burned, in the best way possible, from her palm resting against his.

The situation at the table a few minutes ago had been as funny as it had been humiliating, but there was no denying just how open the door had become in letting him pursue Maeve. He had parental permission and everything. Now all he needed was Maeve's.

From the fact that she's not pulling away...I'm gonna guess I'm making progress on that too.

"Good to see ya, son," Matt boomed. He grinned at Maeve. "Ms. Harrison." He nodded in greeting. "Now which sister are you? Are you the one that makes all those amazing cakes?"

Maeve smiled shyly and shook her head. "Nope. That's my sister, Aspen. She's married and doesn't live here anymore." Maeve shrugged. "I'm the youngest."

Matt's eyes darted to their combined hands. "Doesn't seem to be deterring you any," he teased.

"Okay!" Ethan said a little louder than necessary. The last thing he needed was a stranger teasing Maeve and causing her to pull back. Her family had done that well enough. "Where do you want to start?"

Matt immediately went into work mode. "How about a tour? And I'd like to meet Mr. Harrison. That way we can see what new-fangled things are on the market to help someone with his needs."

Ethan nodded. "Right." He nodded toward the dining room. "The family's in here. Let's go there first." He led the way, Maeve being pulled behind him. "Mama Em, Tony, Estelle...this is Matt. He's my boss during the cold months and one of the finest men I know."

Matt laughed loudly, but walked over to shake Tony's hand. "Nice to meet you, Mr. Harrison, Mrs. Harrison. I understand we're going to help fix up a place for you to take it easy?"

Tony smiled. "I've always enjoyed being catered to. Thought I might push my luck a little."

Ethan saw Maeve's face fall. He couldn't exactly blame her, though he thought Tony was taking the whole thing in commendable stride. Not many men would be okay admitting that they couldn't handle certain tasks anymore. Physical therapy clinics were a testament to the fact that people always seemed to underestimate their capabilities. He squeezed her fingers and tugged her in a little closer. "Let him have his pride," Ethan whispered next to her ear.

He knew he didn't need to get quite that close, but who could blame him? When he drew her in to whisper, he could smell her sweet shampoo and enjoyed when he saw goosebumps run down the side of her neck. She couldn't hide her reaction and it only strengthened his determination.

"Ethan?"

He jerked away from Maeve's neck. "Hm?" Tony's smirk made Ethan feel like a kid caught with his hand in the cookie jar. Good thing he knew Maeve's dad *wanted* Ethan to make a move.

"You're comfortable showing Mr. Peters around?"

Ethan nodded. "Yep. Plus, Maeve's gonna keep us in line, right?" He looked down.

Maeve rolled her eyes. "If I must."

"Oh, you must," Estelle said, rising to her feet and walking quickly toward the kitchen. "If we're not careful, Ethan'll have Mr. Peters build one of the land surfing machines in the back of the house."

Everyone laughed, but Ethan made a considering face. "Now that you gave me the idea..."

"Ugh!" Maeve groaned. "Come on, let's get this party started."

"Wow...I hadn't planned on it being that big of a celebration," Ethan teased. "Do I get cake afterwards?"

The table laughed again and Ethan grinned as he and Maeve walked out of the dining room, Matt following in their wake.

The next forty five minutes were spent going over dimensions, accessibility, cost and working with the foundational structure of the house. Ethan was positive that it was boring Maeve out of her mind, but the way she listened, then jumped in with intelligent questions...a person would never tell.

"I'm meeting with the architect tomorrow," Matt boomed. "If I need to bring him by, is there a time that's best for that?"

Ethan turned the question over to Maeve.

Maeve shrugged. "Unless Dad has a doctor's appointment, they're usually here all day. If you want to send a warning text, I can make sure someone's here to let you in."

"Perfect." Matt grabbed the doorknob. "I'll get your number from Ethan when we talk tomorrow." He nodded. "Night, folks!"

Ethan turned to Maeve now that they were alone in the entryway. "What do you think?"

"I think you can hear that guy from one end of a football field to the other," Maeve said with a laugh.

Ethan chuckled. "Probably. He did play football when he was younger. Was on the second string in college, I think."

Maeve nodded. "I believe it."

"But about the house?"

Maeve grew serious. "I think it's a lot," she said more softly. "But I also think Dad's worth it."

Ethan hesitated only a moment before pulling her into his chest. When she wrapped her arms around him and burrowed in, he knew he'd made the right choice. Her dad's illness was eating her up inside. "Tony's tough," Ethan said into her hair. "Don't give up on him just yet."

Maeve nodded. "I know. But it's so hard." She sniffed and Ethan rubbed his hand up and down her back.

He'd been longing to comfort her for so long. What a tragedy that it took a terminal illness to make it happen.

"I know who he used to be," she continued. "And this isn't the man I remember."

Ethan had no words for that. It was going to be hard and odds were, it would only get harder. Instead of speaking, he just pulled her tighter. "Will you go to dinner with me?"

Well, that hadn't exactly been how he'd planned to ask her out, but now that the words were out there...

Maeve stepped back, breaking their connection.

Or perhaps I should have waited for better timing.

"You're really serious about this, aren't you?" she whispered.

Ethan nodded. "I am."

"And you don't care that I've been pushing you away all this time?"

That's a loaded question. He reached out, letting his fingers trail along her jawline. "Do I care? Of course, I do. It's been horrible. But answer me honestly." He stepped a little closer. "Has your pull to me waned at all during that time? Even though you didn't want anything to do with me?" His voice was low and husky, though he hadn't meant for it to be. Still...it only added to the tension brewing between them.

He kept his eyes on hers. He wanted a *real* answer. Not her default when she was trying to weasel away from her feelings. Her eyes told him exactly what he needed to know, but he wanted to hear her say it.

Her chest began to rise erratically and her breathing became audible, the longer they looked into each other's eyes. Finally, after Ethan thought he might explode with waiting, her head began to slowly shake. "No."

A slow smile pulled on his lips. Someday, he was going to kiss that mouth, but tonight...he'd simply let the anticipation build. "Then I'll pick you up tomorrow at seven." He bent just slightly closer. "Wear something nice."

CHAPTER 10

Maeve couldn't sit still. Her foot bounced, she jabbed her glasses up on her nose so many times, she was sure the skin was gone, she'd redone her ponytail until her head screamed in protest, and still...she felt like she needed to move.

"What is *with* you today?" Estelle asked, leaning her shoulder against the doorframe of Maeve's office.

Since she'd spent several days in a row at Ethan's, Maeve had taken a break to come back to her own office in order to get caught up on the cafe's numbers and a few other businesses that she worked with. The plan was to let the social media for Ethan percolate for a few days, then she'd check back in and see where things stood.

"Even when we were getting ready for work this morning, you were twitchy...like you drank a bunch of caffeine or something." Estelle narrowed her eyes. "What's going on?"

"I don't know what you're talking about," Maeve said, sticking her nose in the air.

"You do realize that every time someone says that, there really is something going on, right?" Aspen said from behind Estelle's shoulder. She pushed her taller sister aside. "Let me in on the gossip."

Maeve rolled her eyes. "There's no gossiping here. Only an accountant working the books, and they aren't as nice as I'd like them to be."

"Puh-lease." Aspen groaned, throwing herself in one of the chairs across from the desk. "The books are fine." She grinned. "Nice try, though."

Maeve huffed and folded her arms over her chest.

"Denial," Estelle said, nodding. "Classic denial." She pointed between herself and Aspen. "But we're the older sisters. We invented that technique."

Maeve threw her arms in the air. "What do you want from me?"

"The truth," Estelle said simply. She sat down in the other chair.

"Don't you have customers to be helping?"

Estelle grinned. "Anna is working on her own for a few minutes." Her grin grew wider. "I love having a helper. I haven't had a break from that counter in too long."

Maeve shook her head, pushed up her glasses and went back to the computer. "I have work to do," she muttered. She didn't. She was so good at keeping up with the books that it had only taken a couple of hours this morning to catch back up, but her sisters didn't need to know that.

"Liar."

Maeve's head whipped around. "What did you call me?"

"Maeve," Estelle said in a soothing tone, sending Aspen a glare. "Come on. We're your *sisters*. Tell us what's going on."

"How is you being my sisters supposed to help this conversation?" Maeve argued. "Maybe that makes you the least likely people to be told what's going on?"

"Ah-ha!" Aspen shouted. "There is something going on." She leaned forward excitedly. "Okay...spill."

Maeve took off her glasses and pinched the bridge of her nose. "You two are impossible."

"We're not the ones holding back something juicy," Aspen accused.

"I'm not holding back something juicy." Maeve made a face. "Ew. That just sounds wrong."

Aspen shrugged. "Doesn't bother me."

Estelle waved Aspen off. "Come on, Mae. You're obviously worked up about something. Is it good? Bad? Can we help? Is it about Dad?"

Maeve sighed and fell back against her seat. "It's not about Dad," she said softly. "And I guess I don't know if it's good or bad." She wanted to talk to them...sort of. She wanted to talk to *someone*, but in her quiet, introverted life...Maeve didn't have a lot of choices. Riley would probably spill the beans to Ethan, since they were close. Harper was busy with her new daughter and store. Jayden, their cousin, would only tease and cause a ruckus. Michael, another cousin, wouldn't care at all. He probably wouldn't even listen to what Maeve was saying.

But she was nervous about telling Aspen and Estelle because...well, because...she'd spent so many years pushing Ethan away, Maeve was worried they would give her a hard time about it. She was already really good at giving herself a hard time, she didn't want it from someone else.

She looked over at Estelle and Aspen's expectant faces and the words came bubbling out before Maeve could stop them.

"Ethan asked me on a date and I couldn't say no."

The room was quiet. Much quieter than any space with three females had a right to be. Maeve found herself holding her breath, unsure what was going to happen next. She bit her lips between her teeth and her eyes went back and forth between Aspen's wide ones and Estelle's astute ones.

"It's about time," Estelle finally said with a soft smile. "I'm so proud of you."

That had not been what Maeve was expecting.

Aspen jumped to her feet and did a little dance. "I knew it! I *knew* it! You've liked him for soooo long!"

That *had* been what Maeve was expecting.

"Aspen," Estelle ordered. "Sit down."

Aspen obeyed, but the wild delight in her eyes never dimmed. She clasped her hands and leaned in. "Tell us everything."

Maeve shrugged. "There's nothing to tell."

"Has he kissed you?"

Heat, which Maeve was starting to get used to, rushed up her neck and into her cheeks. "No," she said succinctly. *And if he ever does, I certainly won't be sharing it with you.* Aspen would tell everyone everything and Maeve preferred her life be kept a little more private.

"Bummer." Aspen groaned. "I'll bet Ethan's a good kisser."

"Aspen!" Estelle scolded. "You're married!"

Aspen rolled her eyes. "I didn't say he would be better than Austin." She grinned. "But Ethan's always been a cute kid. Even you, Ms. Stoic Older Sister, have to admit that."

"So, what? Cute means he has to kiss well?"

Aspen shrugged. "Why not? I don't look at less attractive people and think they'd be fun to kiss."

Maeve slapped her forehead. "This is why I didn't want to tell you."

Aspen laughed and stood up. She walked over and leaned in to give Maeve a kiss on the cheek. "Hang in there, Little Mae. Good things are ahead." She straightened, having no idea that her use of Maeve's nickname brought Ethan immediately to Maeve's mind. "I'll leave you to the considerate sister. She's better at these types of things." With a wink, Aspen disappeared back into her sanctuary.

Estelle took a deep breath and pinned Maeve in place. "Okay...now that the Aspen shenanigans are out of the way...why don't you tell me everything." She hurried to add, "From the beginning."

Maeve blinked hard. Why was she suddenly so emotional? Estelle had no idea what that really meant...to start from the beginning. Why dredge it all up now? Would it help to talk about it? Maeve had held it all in for so long, she wasn't sure how she felt about saying the words out loud. "I...don't know if I can."

Estelle nodded encouragingly. "One word at a time. Let's get it off your shoulders."

Maeve returned the nod. "Okay." She took a fortifying breath. Maybe it was time. Maybe it would help. Maybe...she'd finally heal.

*****

Ethan ran a hand through his hair, ruining all his hard work only a half hour before. "Idiot," he muttered into the cool evening. He'd stood on this porch a million times during his twenty-plus years of life. So why was he freaking out now?

His hand went through his hair once again, but this time Ethan didn't even care. His heart was about to come out of his chest and sweat was trickling down his spine. He was going to show up for his first real date with the girl he was in love with looking like he had come straight from the gym. Awesome. Just what every girl wanted in a date.

He tugged on his collar. Why had he worn a collared shirt? He probably looked like a dork. He was a T-shirt and board shorts kind of guy. Collared shirts were for the accountants she probably should be dating.

Before Ethan could turn tail and run, the front door opened. "Oh, hey Ethan." Estelle stood there smirking, a little too smugly.

Ethan gave her an unimpressed look. "What?"

She shook her head, looking him over. "You look like you're all dressed up. What's the occasion? Going to a funeral?"

Ethan spun around. "That's it. I'm outta here."

Estelle laughed. "Come on, come on," she said. "I'm only teasing. It's what older sisters do."

Ethan glared while walking over the threshold. "You're not my sister," he muttered.

"Yet," Estelle quipped.

Ethan hung his head back and moaned.

Still laughing, Estelle waved him off. "Hang on. I'll go get her."

"I'm here," Maeve said. She gave her sister a look and walked up to Ethan. "If we hurry, we might be able to avoid her taking pictures like it's senior prom or something."

Ethan couldn't move. Maeve had always been beautiful to him, though she wasn't one to dress herself up very much. She wore very little make-up and was simple in her clothing choices. She always looked put together, just in a very natural way.

Tonight, however, she had taken a new step. Her lashes looked about a mile long now that there was mascara on them and they weren't hidden behind those fake glasses she wore. Her hair was down and soft instead of pulled out of her way and the large glossy curls made Ethan's fingers twitch with the need to touch. And the lipstick she had on her lips? It was going to make it extremely difficult for Ethan to wait to kiss her like he planned.

It had taken so long to get to this point that he didn't want to press his luck and scare her off, so he'd determined that he wouldn't kiss her on their first date. Date number two, however...she might just have to brace herself... He'd been waiting a *long* time for this and if she willingly spent more time with him, then all bets were off.

He jerked when a very sharp elbow landed in his rib cage. Turning, he found the amused eyes of Estelle.

"You've got something," she whispered, pointing to the corner of her mouth. "I think I've got napkins in the kitchen."

"And on that note," Maeve announced loudly, "we're out of here." She grabbed Ethan's arm and practically dragged him out of the house. Once they were outside, she let go and bent over, breathing heavily. "I don't ever want to do that again."

"What? Agree to a date with me? Or have me pick you up at your house?" Finally his tongue was working, but it was a little late.

"Next time I'm just walking across the lawn," Maeve said firmly. She stood. "Families are the worst."

The ice finally broke and Ethan grinned, taking her hand. *She said there'd be a next time. Those kissing fantasies will yet come true.* "Families are the best *and* the worst. Yours is pretty nice most of the time."

"Most of the time is right," Maeve said, following behind him. "Estelle, however, enjoyed that a little too much."

Ethan opened the passenger door. "It would have been worse if she'd made us wait so your dad could come to the door with a shotgun."

Maeve groaned and plopped unceremoniously into her seat.

He chuckled. The move was much more like the normal Maeve.

"Hurry. We're not safe until the house is out of sight."

Still laughing, Ethan walked around to his side of the car and got into the driver's seat. "We're going to take a little drive. That okay?" He had wanted tonight to be special and in their tiny town, there was very little that could easily be seen as special. At least not to two people who grew up there.

Maeve gave him the side eye. "What did you have in mind?"

Knowing he was pushing his luck, Ethan reached over and took her hand, bringing the back of it to his mouth. Her skin was just as soft as he thought it would be as he left a light kiss near her knuckles. "Did I tell you how stunning you look tonight?"

Maeve cleared her throat and tugged her hand back. "Can't say that you did," she said airily, looking out the window.

Ethan grinned. He hadn't missed the emotion in her voice. He knew she was probably still embarrassed from the situation at the house and the bridge between them was still delicate and new, but knowing she was affected gave him hope. "Well, you do. Estelle was right. I was practically drooling right in your front entryway."

She laughed softly. "You were not."

"I was," he said dramatically. "You've always been beautiful, but tonight you took things to the next level and I'm going to be the luckiest man at The Point tonight."

She whipped around. "You're taking me to The Point!"

Ethan nodded. "Is that alright? I know it's mostly seafood, but I was pretty sure you liked fish."

Maeve glowered. "Ethan. You're supposed to be watching your budget. You're trying to save your business!"

He gave her a look. "Maeve, the day I can't take a beautiful woman to a nice restaurant is the day I officially give up." He took her hand again, this time entwining their fingers so she couldn't get away as easily. "I've been waiting eight years for tonight. I missed prom for at least two years of high school, I missed countless Friday nights spent eating hot dogs on the pier or licking ice cream from our fingers on the boardwalk. I didn't get to take you to any anniversary dinners or splurge and buy you fake jewelry. All in all, one night at The Point is far cheaper than the last eight years would've been."

He waited, but she didn't respond. Glancing over, Ethan's face softened. He had probably gotten a little carried away in his response, but from the tears in her eyes, he hoped she understood.

"Okay," she said hoarsely.

Ethan raised his eyebrows. "Okay? No more fighting me about budgeting?"

Maeve wasn't looking at him, though he could still see the moisture in her eyes. She shook her head. "No more troubles from me...this time."

He squeezed her hand. "Thank you," he said sincerely. He wanted tonight to be perfect and if she was going to worry about him spending money, then she wouldn't soften enough to enjoy herself. Her capitulation was just what he needed. Yeah...she was right...he probably couldn't afford to do this a bunch of times unless business picked up, but tonight? Tonight he was pulling out all the stops because he had a sinking feeling it might be the only time she truly gave him the chance he'd been angling for for so long.

CHAPTER 11

"Thank you," Maeve murmured as Ethan pulled out her seat for her. Her head was completely spinning tonight. Ethan was dressed up and handsome in his collared shirt and fitted slacks...all except his hair, that is. His hair was just as wild as usual and Maeve loved it.

His cologne was messing with her senses and the fact that he couldn't seem to stop touching her had her skin buzzing like she was attached to some kind of live wire. What chance did a woman have of keeping her balance when a man worked so hard to keep sweeping her off her feet?

It's time, she reminded herself. *You've held him off for a long time. The only way to get rid of the fear and shame is to forgive and move on. It's weighed you down for too long.*

Estelle had helped Maeve come up with that little mantra, after the two of them had had a heart to heart at the office earlier today. It had felt so freeing to share it all with her older sister. Holding the story of her near death inside and the subsequent betrayal by Ethan had only become heavier during the time Maeve had kept it all inside. Instead of fading away and moving on, she'd become lonely, bitter and ached for reconciliation.

She still wasn't sure if everything would work out between her and Ethan, but the more he pushed, the more she wanted to try, if only to let herself finally rise above the dark emotions that had been keeping her stuck for the past eight years.

"What looks good?" Ethan asked, breaking into Maeve's churning thoughts.

She forced her eyes to focus on the menu. "I, uh, think maybe the salmon? Or halibut?"

Ethan nodded. "Both solid choices." He folded his men and set it down.

"What about you?"

"I'll get whichever you don't so you can try them both," he said with a smile.

"Ethan," Maeve scolded. "That's not how it works."

"Why not?" He frowned. "I like both fish. So either one will be perfect and if I get to watch you share it as well, then it's even more perfect."

"More perfect?" Maeve asked. "I don't think that's possible. Something's either perfect, or it's not." She couldn't stop her cheeks from flushing red again. The dim light in the restaurant was hopefully enough to cover the color, but Ethan's ability to fluster her and make her feel special was insane. How did he always know just what to say to make her heart flutter?

He reached out and ran the tip of his finger down her cheek. "Warm?" he teased.

Maeve smacked his hand, causing Ethan to chuckle. "You do that on purpose."

Ethan shrugged. "I told you earlier. I've been saving up for a lot of years."

Maeve sighed. She wished he'd stop bringing that up. If they kept going out, they would probably have to talk about the whole...past...but his casual remarks about it made her feel guilty.

You should.

"Stop," Ethan whispered in a firm tone.

Maeve met his gaze and frowned. "What?"

"Whatever's going on in that pretty little head of yours." He reached over and smoothed the wrinkle between her brows. "Stop. If it's not a happy thought, you're not allowed to have it tonight."

Maeve just watched him. There was no way this guy was real. Somewhere, she must have fallen and hit her head and her subconscious was creating this date with the man she'd been dreaming about for most of her life. There was no other explanation.

"So you're just going to monitor every thought I have tonight?" Maeve asked.

Ethan took her hand and began to play with her fingers, all while holding eye contact. "I'm going to make sure every thought you have tonight is about me," he said in a husky tone.

Maeve was going to faint. She was sure she was going to faint. Her lungs wouldn't move and Ethan would have to revive her using mouth to mouth. Her thoughts came to a screeching halt.

Actually, that might not be so bad...

One side of his mouth quirked up. "And we know if you're thinking about me, then there'll only be good thoughts."

The air that had been hiding in her lungs burst out in a bark of laughter that was much too loud for the restaurant venue they were in. Maeve covered her mouth, having to pull away from Ethan to do so, but she couldn't contain the laughter any other way. "Stop," she said through her fingers, still laughing. "I can't believe you're saying all that."

Ethan's smug smile was exactly the smile she had fallen for so many years ago when they were teens. "Hey, can I help it if I know my worth?"

Maeve reached over and slapped his arm in a flirting gesture. "You're horrible."

"Uh, uh, uh..." He put up a finger. "That's not a happy thought."

Maeve smiled and shook her head. "I can't believe you talked me into coming on a date with you tonight. I'm starting to think you'd prefer your own company instead."

"Never," he said, growing serious. "I'm not nearly as pretty to look at as you are."

That dang blush was back even though she knew he was just teasing her.

"How did I miss the fact that you blush so easily?" Ethan murmured, his eyes softening as he studied her face. "I don't remember that from when we were kids."

Maeve shrugged and looked away. "I didn't really have much trouble with it when I was younger. I suppose the older I get, the more embarrassed I get."

"Then you're worrying too much about what other people think," Ethan told her. Their waiter interrupted at the moment and true to his word, Ethan ordered the halibut so she could order the salmon.

The gesture was small but so sweet and exactly the kind of thing to break down the last bits of Maeve's wall that she was stubbornly holding onto. She could practically feel another brick fall victim to his charm and knew it wouldn't take much more work before all her inhibitions would completely jump ship.

A fleeting fear that she was heading for troubled waters tried to invade Maeve's mind, but Ethan's flattering and undivided attention was making it hard to focus on anything but him.

"Tell me about Antonio," Ethan said, his voice growing solemn. "I haven't heard anything about him for a while."

Maeve sighed. "He hasn't been as good about writing lately," she admitted. "Mom's worried, though she's trying to play it off. She already has her hands full with Dad, so I keep hoping Antonio will get his tush off his cot and let her know what's going on."

"When did you last hear from him?" Ethan pressed.

"About a month ago."

Ethan nodded. "Must be hard."

"Speaking of hard..." Maeve bit her lip. She wasn't sure she had the right to ask him this question, but despite the fact that they grew up next to each other and used to be very close, she had missed a lot of his life during those years she'd turned her back on him.

"Ask me," Ethan urged. "Ask me anything."

Maeve tried to build her courage. If she was truly going to give them any kind of a chance, she needed to know Ethan. Not just the flirty Ethan who was teasing her tonight, and not just the teenage Ethan she still remembered all too vividly in her mind...she needed to know the real Ethan. The one behind the smile, the one behind the carefree surfer attitude. She wanted to know Ethan the man.

"Tell me about when your parents died."

*****

She's not pulling any punches.

Ethan coughed a little. He was being sincere when he said "ask anything," but he certainly hadn't expected Maeve to go straight for the jugular. And honestly, he didn't know why she was asking. His parents had been gone several years. Why was she just now asking about them?

Maeve tentatively reached across the table and touched the back of his hand. "I missed that time of your life," she said softly. "And I'm sorry for that. So I guess I'm kind of asking for forgiveness and an update all at the same time."

Were grown men allowed to cry? Because Ethan felt like he might. He wasn't a really emotional guy. He rolled through life without much trouble, but right here, right now, Maeve was putting him in a different place and Ethan wasn't sure if it was a good thing or not.

He cleared his throat. "Well, you know they died in a car accident?"

Maeve nodded.

Ethan shrugged. "There's not really a lot to tell. I had just started as a freshman at college. School hasn't really been my thing anyway, so once the call came, I packed up, came home and began to fend for myself. Though I did finish a degree, a back up plan, my mother used to call it, but it was all online." He grinned ruefully. "Your dad was instrumental in making sure I got my business started and your mother made sure I didn't starve, so, you know…they're pretty much honorary parents at this point."

Maeve's smile was soft. "I know. I missed a lot of family dinners because of you."

She started to pull back and Ethan grabbed her hand before she could. While they were on serious topics, they might as well get it all out. "Why don't you tell me your side of things?" he urged.

"My side?" Maeve shook her head. "I don't understand."

"Why did you walk away from me, Little Mae?" Ethan tilted his head. "Why did you walk off that beach and take eight years to talk to me again?"

Maeve's eyes dropped and looked anywhere but at him. "Do we have to do this tonight?" she whispered.

"I suppose not, but don't you think it's time?" He leaned in. "Aren't you tired of being mad at me?"

She huffed. "I'm tired of everything."

"Everything?"

She looked back and her eyes were misty, tugging at Ethan's heart. "Tired of being angry, tired of being scared, tired of being lonely…" Her voice dropped. "Tired of carrying it all myself."

"Then don't. Tell me." He cradled her hand between his. "I thought that date was going to be the start of our future." His lips twitched. "You were so cute, so eager. I was sure that you liked me as much as I liked you and I was totally willing to listen to Antonio's smack talk just for the chance to take you out."

Maeve laughed softly, helping break the tension between them. "I was young and naive," she stated.

"Young and hopeful."

She shrugged. "You were right. I liked you…a lot." She looked up from under her lashes. "At least as much as a teenage girl could. I thought the sun and moon moved at your whim."

"They did," Ethan quipped, enjoying her laugh. "Go on," he urged when she quieted down.

"You made me a promise that morning, when we left... Do you remember?"

Ethan nodded, dread starting to pool in his stomach. "I said I would be there the whole time. That nothing bad would happen because I would protect you."

Maeve nodded and took in a long breath. "When I caught that wave, the one that pulled me away from you..." She swallowed.

This is it. Ethan could feel that this moment would be a defining one for them. Whatever happened next would make or break them as a couple.

"I...didn't last very long," she said thickly.

Ethan nodded. "Most first-time surfers don't. I was so proud of you for getting up at all."

"When I was pulled under..." Maeve closed her eyes and hung her head. Sweat beaded out of her forehead just along her hairline and Ethan began to panic.

"Maeve?" He reached over and took her hand. "What is it?"

"When I fell in the water, I got caught in the current," she whispered hoarsely. When she opened her eyes, there was such a stark fear in them that Ethan felt the shock to his core. "I couldn't get a breath. I couldn't reach the top of the water. I..."

Like the light bulb they used in cartoons, it all hit Ethan. "You were drowning..." he said slowly. "And I wasn't there."

Maeve pinched her lips together and nodded.

"And then I rode past on the next wave as if nothing was wrong while you were struggling."

Her nod was jerky, but still conveyed her answer.

"Aw, Maeve. Why didn't you tell me?" Ethan asked. "I was a young kid. A teenager who thought he ruled the world and was showing off for the girl he liked. Why didn't you say something?"

She shook her head. "What was I supposed to say?" she asked. "I've never enjoyed fighting. I'm not as aggressive as Aspen and not as authoritative as Estelle. They would both have reamed you up one side and down the other, but me?"

"You were the quiet one," Ethan finished for her. "Little Mae, who watched life with bright gold eyes and saw more than she was supposed to, but rarely got involved." He leaned back, guilt making his stomach churn. Their fancy meal suddenly didn't sound nearly as tempting as it had only moments before. "I'm sorry," he said softly. "I wish I could go back and see it all again with better eyesight, but...I'm sorry." He scoffed at himself and pushed both hands through his hair. "It's no wonder you wanted nothing to do with me. I convinced you to do something wild and dangerous, only to let you fight for your life by yourself." He shook his head in disgust. What was wrong with him? How did he not see her struggling? He'd ridden past on his board, assuming she would paddle in to shore and they'd celebrate her two seconds of surfing together. Instead, she'd crawled up the sand gasping for air and glaring at him as if he'd killed her favorite pet.

Her face had been red and her hair a mess, but Ethan hadn't taken it for anything other than the simplest explanation. She'd fallen off her board. Of course she'd look a little worse for wear.

He'd been stunned when she threw her board down and stormed off without a backward glance. For weeks he'd tried to talk to her, only to be given the cold shoulder, and eventually getting her notice had become a game. How far could he push before she'd finally talk to him again? Maeve was practically family already and though Ethan had worried about her, he'd kept swimming through life, assuming they'd eventually get over whatever imagined tiff the teenage girl had built up in her head.

Weeks had turned to months, and months to years, and Maeve had grown up in her quiet shell that Ethan had been unable to penetrate, but his crush had never wavered. Despite the icy attitude she often put on in public, he'd seen the real her. He'd seen her with family and customers, he'd seen her covered in dust while they built the cafe, he'd seen her on the ground with children and cleaning poop out of cages at Riley's shelter. He'd seen her mourn when her father's diagnosis became public and he'd watched her quietly support her loved ones as they went through very public trials.

How could he let go of his feelings when he knew who she really was?

She's everything I want...and everything I don't deserve.

CHAPTER 12

Maeve could see the guilt seeping in. She could see it because she'd experienced it herself. "Ethan," she said. "It wasn't your fault."

He gave her a look. "It wasn't my fault?" he asked, slightly louder than was polite. "You nearly died and it wasn't my fault? I was right there, Maeve." He shook his head. "I was *right there* and instead of seeing what was going on and keeping my promise, I rode by on a wave like I was some celebrity or something."

Maeve bit her lip and paused the words that wanted to gush out. The waiter was back with their meals, and the timing was uncomfortable to say the least.

"Can I get you anything else?" he asked, looking a little hesitant.

"No. We're fine," Maeve answered, keeping an eye on Ethan's glower.

The waiter nodded, then scurried away, probably assuming his tip had just disappeared.

"Ethan," she said softly, drawing his attention. Once again, Maeve initiated a touch and reached for his arm. "Can we please try to set this aside for a moment? You've treated us both to a wonderful meal and while we should hash this out, maybe let's wait until we're out of here?" She begged him with her eyes, pleading for him to understand that she didn't want their talk to be public.

Ethan finally softened. "Okay," he whispered. "Eat up. Then we can walk the Boardwalk if you still want to have anything to do with me."

"Thank you," Maeve replied. Her fish was probably delicious, but Maeve wouldn't know. She was too caught up in watching the emotions play over Ethan's face and dreading the upcoming conversation.

It's already started, she told herself. *It's time to finish it. You said yourself that it needed to happen. Who cares if it came earlier than you thought?*

"Freedom," she whispered to herself as a reminder. Estelle had helped her see that's what she was truly fighting for here. The freedom to choose. To choose to be with Ethan, or not. To choose to love him, or not. To choose to be afraid, or not.

You can't experience anything until you've experienced its opposite, Estelle had counseled. *In order to understand your right to be free, you have to know what it's like to be caged. You caught yourself in a trap of hurt and pain and have been stuck ever since. If you'd let yourself feel just a little deeper, then you'd find yourself on the way to being free.*

"What was that?" Ethan asked. He hadn't eaten much either, merely moved his food around his plate.

"Nothing," Maeve murmured. "Just reminding myself of something."

Ethan threw down his fork. "I can't eat."

Maeve nodded. "Come on." She stood and found their waiter, slipping her credit card into his hand. "We need to go ASAP. Can you get us checked out quickly please?"

The young man nodded quickly. "Right away, ma'am."

Ethan's eyebrows were practically touching by the time Maeve got back to the table. "I saw that."

"I'll let you pay when we actually eat the meal," she said firmly. "I don't want to waste my big date on a night where I ruined our appetites."

"Miss?"

Maeve turned and took her card and the receipt. "Thank you," she said. "We'll be gone in just a moment."

The waiter nodded and disappeared again.

Maeve bent over, signed on a generous tip and then took Ethan's hand. "Let's go. We'll both feel better when we figure this out."

To his credit, Ethan didn't fight her, just followed her out the doors. She tugged him down the sidewalk a little ways before slowing their pace. "I have some more to say and I need you to hear it before you argue with me."

Ethan sighed. "Of course."

Maeve's heart was about to break through her chest; it was beating so hard. She needed to be able to tell him what had happened without hurting him further, but she wasn't sure how to do that. "I was hurt," she stated.

Ethan snorted, but Maeve continued on.

"I was hurt because I *chose* to be hurt," she emphasized. "I had a hard time emotionally from the near death experience and instead of dealing with it, I let it consume me. I wallowed in the fear and what I felt was betrayal and it's...it's cost me a lot of my life," she finished softly.

"Maeve," Ethan whispered. He stopped their forward progress and pulled on her hand until she turned to face him. "This is my fault, not yours. I should have noticed you were in distress. I should have been there. I said I would and I wasn't."

Maeve shook her head. "You're not God, Ethan. You aren't perfect and neither am I. The fact that you didn't notice I was having trouble wasn't your fault and I should never have blamed you." She put a hand on her chest. "I can't tell you that I'm not still struggling, because that would be a complete lie. I'm still terrified of the ocean and haven't been in over my knees since the incident, but..." She tried to fill her stiff lungs and moved forward until they were toe to toe. "But I'm tired of living the way I've been living. I'm surrounded by people, but still alone. I'm scared of water like a little child, and like that same toddler, I put the blame of the situation somewhere it didn't belong." She shook her head. "Just because you were there didn't mean you were to blame. An inexperienced surfer in rough waters was to blame, and I'm ...I'm sorry."

"Mae," Ethan said again. "This isn't on you."

"It is," she insisted. "Estelle is helping me see that. And I had started to come to the understanding on my own, but her tough love has made it easier," Maeve said with a little laugh. She turned away. "The problem was never you…you were just convenient and I'm mortified that it's taken me eight years to understand that." She looked back, but his face was blurry with her tears. "I'm so sorry, Ethan. I'm sorry I turned you away. I'm sorry for all the rude things I said. I'm sorry I wasn't there when you were hurting and when your parents passed away…I'm just…sorry." Her voice broke at the end and a sob climbed through her throat.

"Mae," Ethan croaked. He pulled her into his chest and Maeve buried her face against his sternum. "You're killing me. Don't you know what a woman's tears do to a man?"

"Not really," Maeve said through a tight chuckle. She wrapped her arms around his chest and clung like a barnacle. "Antonio wasn't exactly the touchy feely type."

Ethan's arms tightened. "That's because he's a wimp," Ethan teased.

Maeve smiled before becoming serious again. "I'm serious though, Ethan. I really am sorry. I've been so childish."

"I'm sorry too," he whispered, his face buried in her hair. "I'm sorry I didn't work harder to find out what was wrong. I'm sorry I didn't see you were hurting. I'm sorry I took you out there to begin with."

Maeve let herself simply rest in his embrace for a few more moments. The evening was cool, but his arms were warm and Maeve had never felt so safe as she did in that moment. "Where do we go from here?" she finally whispered.

Ethan leaned back and cupped her cheeks, forcing Maeve to look up. "If you'll let me," he said carefully, "I'm hoping we move forward." His thumbs rubbed over her cheek bones. "I've missed so much time with you and I don't want to waste another second."

She watched carefully, but as far as Maeve could tell, his request was completely sincere. Somehow, this amazing man was willing to let go of eight years of hurt and pain as if it never existed. *It's time to reciprocate.* "I'd like that," she said. The tension between them tightened and Maeve found herself leaning slightly forward.

Emotionally spent, her heart and brain were now caught on only one thing, and it involved a set of lips resting only a few inches from her own.

*****

*You were going to wait. You were going to wait...*Ethan needed someone to knock some sense into him. He was supposed to be taking this slow. Showing her he could be trusted. The truth had been so much worse than he'd ever expected and now he knew he didn't deserve her on top of it all, yet here she was, her eyes half closed, attention on his mouth. The pull between them felt like a siren's call and he was trying to figure out whether or not he should be a gentleman.

His hands flexed against her waist. Could he? Should he? This was everything he'd been waiting for...

Maeve pulled back slightly, a wounded expression in her eyes, mixed with embarrassment. He'd seen that high color on her cheeks enough to know what it meant. She turned slightly sideways, tucking a piece of hair behind her ear in a shaky gesture.

You caused that.

Guilt swamped his belly and Ethan knew it was now or never. "Gentlemen are overrated," he muttered, jerking Maeve forward and planting his mouth on hers.

She squeaked slightly in surprise, but quickly settled in.

If an angel came down from heaven and began playing a trumpet in his ear, Ethan was positive he wouldn't notice. Maeve's hands slipped up his chest and linked behind his neck, pulling him slightly lower, closer to her level.

Wrapping his own arms tighter, he pulled her farther up until he knew she was on her tiptoes trying to keep up with him. Over and over, with near frantic movements, he tried to show her how he felt. This moment had been far too long in the making and Ethan was having a hard time reining himself in. He wanted her...all of her. He wanted her forgiveness, her time, her attention, her kisses...her love.

Slowly, his desperation began to subside and their ardor began to slow. With one final lingering press of his lips, Ethan pulled back just enough to speak. "If that's how it goes, I think everyone should wait eight years before they kiss," he said in a husky tone.

Maeve laughed lightly and shook her head. "No. Because it means I could have already had eight years worth of kisses in my Ethan bank."

He leaned back a little farther, unable to help the smirk. "Ethan bank?" he asked, his eyebrows rising high. "I like the sound of that."

Maeve gave him a flirty smile and ran her fingers over the back of his neck. "Yeah? I just invented it."

"And what do you plan to keep in it?"

She rose up again until their mouths were barely not touching. "Kisses. Lots and lots of kisses."

"Let me help you with that," he whispered before bringing them together again. These kisses were much more under control, but for some reason, Ethan found that they touched him on a deeper level. This wasn't a burst of hormones that had been bound for too long, this was two people who had feelings for each other that were deeper than simply physical attraction and were acknowledging that in a way only couples could.

There was no way to know how long they'd been holding onto each other by the time Ethan forced himself to pull back. "I should probably get you home," he said when she shivered in his arms.

Maeve tucked her forehead into his neck and burrowed into his chest. "It's not supposed to be this cold yet."

He let his arms surround her. "If I had my way, we'd never have winter."

"I'm guessing that's the surfer side of you speaking."

Ethan shrugged. "Something like that. I surf in the winter though."

Maeve pulled back. "Yeah...because you're crazy."

Ethan grinned and kissed the tip of her nose. "Crazy for you."

Maeve rolled her eyes. "That was cheesy."

"And yet you loved it." Ethan stepped back and took her hand, walking them back to the car.

"Are you sure about that?" Maeve asked archly.

"Yep." Ethan opened the door for her. "Don't forget how long I've known you, Little Mae. I've had enough time watching from the sidelines to know exactly what type of humor you enjoy."

Her smile fell. "I really am sorry," she said softly.

Ethan stepped around the door and crowded her against the side of the car. "No more," he said, shaking his head. "I owe you more apologies than I can ever repay and if you're willing to forgive me, then how can I do anything but the same?" He leaned down until their foreheads were touching. "I never held a grudge," he whispered thickly, then cleared his throat. "I knew there had to be something I had missed, I just didn't know what." He sighed. "I could never have imagined how bad it was."

Her hand came up to cup his cheek and she pushed until he leaned back enough for them to look into each other's eyes. "I didn't want anyone to know," she admitted. "I..." Maeve shook her head. "I don't even know. I was so scared that I just kept it all to myself." With a sigh she dropped her hand and turned to the side. "But now I'm beginning to understand that if I had simply talked about it, I could have avoided so much heartache...for both of us."

"Enough," he said firmly. "We're starting over. Yes, we have a past, but it doesn't have to define our future." He gave her a look. "And there will be a future for us. We owe it to ourselves to have one...a good one."

She smiled. "Okay." She gave him one last little peck before slipping into her seat.

Ethan shut the door and walked around to the driver's side. After starting the car, he pulled out. Once settled on the highway, he reached over and took Maeve's hand, feeling ridiculously proud that for the first time, he actually had the right to do so. He'd grabbed her hands many times over the years, but it was always to push her boundaries, to try and get her attention... Tthis time it was simply because he wanted to touch her, and because he could touch her.

The ride was quiet, but not uncomfortable. They'd said enough for the evening and he loved that she was just as content to sit and enjoy each other's company as he was. Their entwined fingers sat on his thigh and Ethan could have died a happy man. Instead of dying, however, he found his mind drawn back to his business.

He'd meant it when he told Maeve they deserved a future and in his mind, he already knew he wanted this to be a long term one. There was no way his feelings had been this strong for this long if it didn't mean the two of them were meant to be together forever. Ethan wanted what his parents had while they were alive and what her parents still had now. The love, the family, the teasing...all of it.

Now that Maeve was willing to forgive and move forward, he hoped he would have all that with her.

But you have to be able to make a living first.

And there was the hold up. He couldn't plan for a future with Maeve if he had no way to support her. It didn't matter if Maeve worked after they were married, Ethan was determined to bring home enough money to take care of her and any children they might be blessed with. The pressure to save his surf shop grew a little heavier on his shoulders.

Surfing was what he knew and he really wanted to keep doing it if at all possible. *I'm just gonna have to work harder,* he decided. There was nothing else for it. He'd have to really dig in and drum up the business he needed. He'd already failed Maeve once. He wasn't going to do it again.

CHAPTER 13

Maeve stuffed her laptop into her bag and scrambled for her water bottle .She had slept in this morning and was now running late for work. "Stupid boys and their kisses," she grumbled when she nearly dropped her water bottle. She sighed. "Okay...not stupid. Entirely too dreamy might be a better description."

She and Ethan had arrived home late the night of their date, and for the whole weekend, Maeve had barely been able to sleep. She kept replaying his kiss over and over and over again. She was well past her teen years. Maeve knew what a man's kiss felt like. But nothing had prepared her for what *Ethan's* kiss would feel like.

She'd been pining for him from afar for years and yet she had never once come close to imagining the euphoria his touch would be. Apparently, she had a terrible imagination because real life was much better than her dreams.

"Are you going to eat breakfast?" her mother called as Maeve ran down the stairs. She poked her head out of the kitchen.

Maeve shook her head. "Nope. Sorry, Mom. I'm late."

Mom tsked her tongue. "Maeve. You need to eat. You'll waste away."

Maeve laughed. "I don't think I have any fears about that." She slapped her thigh. "Have you seen these lately?"

"Yes," Mom snapped. "And they're entirely too thin."

Maeve rolled her eyes, but smiled good naturedly. She walked over and kissed her mom on the cheek. "I'll be fine. Thanks, though."

"Where can I get me one of those?" her father asked, shuffling through the kitchen doorway.

Maeve wanted to smile wider and cry at the same time. She hated how this disease was deteriorating his body. Pushing aside her concerns, she walked over and kissed his cheek as well. "Happy?"

Dad shrugged. "A kiss from a beautiful woman? Who wouldn't be?" He stepped closer to Mom and wrapped an arm around her waist. "Unless it's the *right* woman."

Mom flushed. "Flirt."

"Beautiful," he shot back.

"And on that, I'm off!" Maeve put her hands in the air in surrender. She loved her parents' relationship, but like every dutiful child, she made sure to behave as disgusted by the display of love as possible.

Not bothering to hide her grin, Maeve made her way outside and got into her mist-covered car. "Brrr..." The air was wet and cold and she wished she'd remembered to grab a jacket before leaving the house. "Good thing the bakery has a heater," she muttered.

As Maeve got out onto the street, she had a thought and ended up turning left instead of right. Maybe...it would be a good idea to stop by the surf shop and make sure everything was doing okay. Just for...you know...just to be safe.

Her heart was beating against her chest as she pulled into a parking spot. She hadn't seen Ethan since Friday night when they went on their date, despite the fact that he lived next door. They had decided they would give their feelings a go, but other than some texting and a phone call for the last forty-eight hours, Ethan had been MIA. He claimed to have been busy but would see her soon and Maeve had taken him at his word. Besides, if she was being honest, she was slightly nervous about seeing him. How did you approach the person you made out with just a few days prior? She'd never gotten that far in a relationship before and now Maeve wasn't quite sure how to react.

"Just do it," she told herself as she walked up to the front door. Her fingers were shaking slightly as she pushed the door open, but the familiar smell of saltwater and wax met her senses and Maeve found herself unwittingly relaxing a little. "Ethan?" she asked as she walked inside. The space was empty. "Ethan?"

There was a bang from the back room and Ethan came running to the employee door. "Maeve!" he shouted. His smile was so wide it nearly split his face and he rushed her, grabbing her in a bear hug.

"Oof!" Maeve had the air squeezed out of her as she landed against his chest. "Eeks." She gasped.

His mouth landed against her neck. "You're so amazing," he said in a low tone, causing rippling goosebumps against her skin.

Maeve laughed a little, still kind of shocked from his greeting. She wasn't exactly complaining, but she was a little curious as to what had caused such a dramatic reaction. "Well, sure, but what did I do?"

Ethan pulled back a little, finally easing up on his grip, and Maeve sucked in a deep breath. "I got it," he whispered excitedly, his hazel eyes sparkling with joy.

Maeve blinked. "Got what?"

"The contract!" Ethan pulled back and began dragging her toward the office. "I came in to check out the social media you and Austin worked on last week, right?"

"Right," Maeve agreed.

"And I went to the website, checking to see if I had any emails, or whatnot." He sat down in the chair behind his desk and pulled Maeve into his lap.

Maeve was trying to keep from laughing. Ethan was acting just like a little kid, but she was enjoying being pulled along for the ride even if she had no idea what he was doing.

"There was a bunch of junk," Ethan continued, leaning around her so he could pull up something on the screen. "But then..." He clicked on an email and leaned back. "I found this."

Maeve read the email. "Oh my gosh, Eeks!" Maeve gushed. She twisted and threw her arms around his neck. "Your very first order!"

Ethan's arms banded around her even as he laughed. "It's not just that," he said. "Look at who it's for."

Maeve looked back. "Ollie Walker?" she read. She turned to look at Ethan. "Should I know who that is?"

Ethan groaned and dropped his head back. "He's the biggest up and coming surfer on the West Coast!"

"Oh!" Maeve said with a slow nod. "Well, cool! That's really awesome!"

Ethan shook his head, still smiling. "You still don't get it, do you?"

Maeve shrugged. "Well, from a strictly business side of things, I'm guessing that if he likes your board, he'll come back to you again and again."

"Sweetheart, if he likes my board, we can get him to endorse it and that could mean everything is about to change."

Maeve threw her arms around his neck. "Are you saying this might be everything you need to save your business?"

"That's what I'm saying," he said in a softer tone. His eyes had dropped to her lips. "And it's all thanks to you and Austin."

"Hmm..." Maeve leaned in until their lips were only a few centimeters apart. "How would you like to say thank you?" she teased.

"Well, I plan on kissing you until you don't know what way is up," Ethan said with a smirk. "But I'll probably just shake Austin's hand."

"I don't think anyone will have a problem with that," she breathed.

"Good," Ethan responded. "Because there's nothing you can do to stop it."

*****

He was never going to let her go. All weekend Ethan had been ruminating over what he could do to build his business. What sacrifices would he need to make? Where was he missing out on advertising that might be the push he needed to get up and rolling again? He'd come up with almost nothing.

So when he'd checked his messages this morning, the email from Ollie had been like an answer to prayer. This was exactly the boost he needed. If Ollie liked his board, it would be the miracle Ethan needed. He'd met the kid once, when his family had driven through Oregon and had stopped to surf along the way. The teenager was impressive and was catching the eye of the surfing world as he began to climb the charts at the surfing competitions.

And now the future for his business looked hopeful and Ethan had the woman he loved in his arms... There was nothing that could be better.

It had only been a couple of days since their date, but Ethan had missed Maeve. He'd missed her beautiful face and now that he knew what her kiss was like, he'd missed that as well. How it was possible to crave something he'd only tasted once, Ethan didn't quite understand, but it had happened anyway.

"I'm so happy for you," Maeve said breathlessly, her hands running through his hair.

"And I'm grateful for you," Ethan said, turning his attention to her jawline. It was such a perfect jaw. The skin was so soft. He could spend all day examining and enjoying every inch of her, but his mind was still spinning with ideas over the surfboard and how he could make sure it was everything it needed to be in order to launch the future of his shop. After all...Ethan had big plans for the woman in his arms and he needed this job to go well.

The bell from the front door rang and Maeve pulled back, breathing heavily. "You have a customer," she whispered.

"I don't really care," he said against her mouth. "But I suppose I'll have to pretend to."

Maeve grinned and pulled out his arms.

Ethan hated to admit how cold that made him. He wanted to hold Maeve forever, but she was right. He had a job to do. He couldn't have her if she couldn't trust him to take care of his work. Ethan stood up and cleared his throat. "Right. Back to work." For the first time ever, that didn't excite him. Maeve was much more interesting than surfing and even during his years of pining, that had never been the case.

Funny what a few kisses can do.

"I'm just going to glance at your stuff and then I need to get to the bakery," Maeve said, taking the chair he emptied.

"Sounds good." He leaned down for one last peck. "I'll see you after work?"

Maeve nodded. "Come over for dinner. Dad has questions about the new room."

"Done." Ethan walked to the front and smiled. "Hi! How can I help you today?"

The day went slowly, though it was busy with customers, and Ethan found his mind drifting all day long. He'd said goodbye to Maeve and helped people all day, but every free moment he had, Ethan had been drawing out the board. He not only wanted it to meet all of Ollie's specifications, but Ethan wanted to put his own touch on it. Something to make it extra special, so it would stand out against the crowd. This was going to be his masterpiece and Ethan was eager for the challenge.

Finally, the clock struck six and he was able to close down. Locking the door, Ethan turned the sign to 'Closed' and headed straight to his office. He would only work for a half hour before forcing himself to stop.

Maeve had invited him to dinner and he planned to go, but he also needed a little time to get started on the design for the surfboard. Sitting at his desk, he pulled out his sketchbook and began to mess with designs. He tried everything from skulls to flowers, but nothing stood out to him.

Tapping his lips with his pencil, Ethan wracked his brain for something that had never been seen before, but he was coming up blank. Setting down the pencil, he woke up his computer and began to pull up board pictures. "There has to be something interesting," Ethan muttered, his eyes glued to the screen. He scrolled for a while before finally closing his eyes and rubbing them. His eyes felt tired and gritty and Ethan leaned back in his seat, sighing. His eyes happened to wander to his cell phone and he cursed.

"Ten messages? What?" Ethan grabbed the phone, his keys and ran out of the shop. How in the world had he spent nearly two hours studying boards? It had felt like no time at all!

He punched in Maeve's number and put it on the Bluetooth as he pulled out of the parking lot. "Maeve?" he asked when she picked up.

"Ethan? Are you okay? You haven't been answering your phone." Her tone was worried and Ethan called himself a dozen names for not keeping better track of the time.

"I'm fine," he assured her. "Sorry. I got caught up at work and totally lost track of time."

"Wow. You must have had a busy day."

"It was," Ethan replied. "But I'm done now. I'm sure you had dinner forever ago. Does your dad still have questions? Should I stop by?" *Please say yes...* Even if dinner was off the table, he had every intention of getting a good night kiss.

"Come on over," she told him. "Dad would love to chat and we can totally warm you up a plate."

"You don't have to do that," Ethan said, even as his stomach growled.

"Eeks," Maeve drawled. "Do you know my mother?"

"Are you saying Mama Em is giving orders?"

"She's right over my shoulder demanding that you stop by. Aspen brought a new cake flavor by and Mom said she'll gain twenty pounds if other people don't come and eat it with her."

Ethan chuckled. "Well, I don't want to be a difficult neighbor, so I suppose I can take one for the team."

Maeve laughed. "Wonderful. I'm so glad you're willing to sacrifice to save us all."

"Be there in three minutes."

"I'll look forward to it."

Ethan hung up the phone and the wide smile he'd had on earlier couldn't be held back. For a moment there, he thought he'd hurt his chances with her before they'd really gotten started, but it was all going to be okay.

He'd get his goodnight kiss, he had some ideas for the board and he would continue to help push things for Tony's new master suite. Today had turned out to be about as good as life got.

CHAPTER 14

"You made it," Maeve said breathlessly. She had run to the front door when Ethan had knocked. She hated to admit how much she had worried when she hadn't been able to get a hold of him, but hearing that he'd been working made her feel like a fool and she was glad she hadn't voiced her concerns.

Paranoid much?

Ethan bent down for a quick peck. "Thanks so much for being willing to feed me." He grinned. "I wasn't looking forward to warming up old pizza."

Maeve scrunched her nose and shook her head. "Eww...no. That's just wrong."

Ethan chuckled and rubbed his hands together before blowing on them. "Geez. It's getting cold out there."

Maeve took his hand. "Yikes. Let's warm you up." She led him to the kitchen. "Mom! Ethan's here."

Mom's head popped up over the couch. "Ethan! You made it!"

Maeve rolled her eyes. "That's what I said."

Ethan was still smiling. "Sorry, Mama Em. I got held up."

Mom waved off his concerns. "It's fine. Your plate's in the oven."

"I'll get it," Maeve assured her parent. "Stay with Dad."

"When you're done eating, come over here," Dad called out. "I have a few questions about the addition."

"You got it, Tony," Ethan answered.

Maeve got an oven mitt and pulled out the hot plate. "Have a seat," she said softly. "I'll get you a glass and some silverware."

Ethan sat down and leaned back in his seat. "I could get used to this," he teased when she set down the plate.

Maeve glared playfully. "Don't count on it. You're an adult, I don't always spoil."

Ethan caught her hand before she got too far. Pulling her back, he tugged her down until their mouths were close together. "Then I'll count myself special," he whispered.

Maeve felt hot all over. Man...she loved this. She loved his playfulness and was beginning to wonder how she'd ever held it off for so long. She had never been so happy as she was now that they were dating.

Ethan pulled a little farther and gave her a soft, lingering kiss. "Boyfriend privileges are amazing," he teased.

Maeve huffed and softly smacked his shoulder. "Incorrigible."

"Whipped," he shot back.

Maeve shook her head, but there was no stopping the smile on her face. It stayed in place while she got him a glass of water, a napkin and silverware. Finally, she sat back down, handing him everything he needed. "Eat up."

"Thanks," he said. "You're amazing."

"I wish I could take credit," Maeve said with a sigh. "But it was all Mom's doing."

He stuffed a large bite in his mouth. "True. You definitely don't spend a lot of time in the kitchen."

She frowned. "How do you know that?"

Ethan raised a challenging eyebrow. "Just because you weren't speaking to me doesn't mean I wasn't watching."

Meave shrugged. "I guess the genes just passed me over. Estelle cooks like Mom and learned all of Dad's Italian recipes. Aspen, as you know, can bake like nobody's business. Me?" She made a face. "There were no culinary genes left by that point."

"Antonio wasn't much of a chef either, if I remember correctly," Ethan said as he wiped his mouth.

Maeve shook her head. "Actually, he had a knack for it, but he didn't have the patience. Always said it was easier to just toss something in the microwave."

"Ah. Guess I missed that one."

"See? You don't know all my family secrets," Maeve teased.

"I said I was watching you," Ethan corrected her. "Not your brother."

Maeve laughed. "I thought the two of you were friends."

Ethan shrugged as he took another bite. "Doesn't mean he was my first priority."

Maeve felt a little bit of the shame from the previous years begin to creep in. "Ethan...I'm so sorry."

He shook his head. "Nope. We already went over this, remember? We both made mistakes. We're both moving on. No more sorries."

She nodded, drawing a random design on the table. "Still. I feel like such an idiot for hanging onto those feelings for so long."

Ethan set down his fork and cupped her cheek. "Sweetheart, you were traumatized. I don't blame you one bit." He sighed. "I blame myself for not realizing something had happened. You stormed out of that water and out of my life and it never once occurred to my teenage brain that something had happened in the water. I thought you were angry that you'd fallen or something like that and just kept expecting you to get over it." He made a face. "Guess I learned better."

"Still..." She shook her head. "I'm still sorry. I've made us both miserable for too long."

He kissed her cheek. "No more," he whispered against her skin.

"Okay," she whispered back.

"Maeve? Are you going to share that boy? Or do I have to come break it up over there?"

Ethan chuckled as Maeve turned bright red. "Be there in a minute, Tony. I'm just finishing up."

"Well, tell Maeve to let you eat and then you'll actually finish."

"Leave them alone," Mom scolded. "You can talk to Ethan any time."

"Apparently not," Dad shot back. "He's too busy eating or kissing my daughter to bother talking to me."

Ethan choked on a bite and Maeve groaned, putting her face in her hands. "I think maybe it's time I moved out," she muttered.

"Now see what you've done?" Mom said loudly. "You're making my children leave!"

"How is that my fault? They grew up and you threw them a party when they graduated and became adults!" Dad argued back. "If you wanted them to stay, don't be so excited when they become adults."

"They all came back," Mom said with a sniff. "Probably because I *did* throw the party. They came back for my food."

"Or my chocolate."

Even from the kitchen table, Maeve could see her mother's eyes roll. "Nobody eats your chocolate," she said with a laugh. "It's just for looking at."

Dad's thinning arms went around his wife. "Good thing you're not chocolate, then, huh?"

Ethan choked again.

"Daaad!" Maeve shouted. "If I don't get to kiss, neither do you!"

"It's my house!" he shouted.

"And they're my eyes," Maeve retorted. "I'm going blind watching you two smooch."

"It's been happening since before you were born," he said breezily, not the least bit concerned with her disgust. "I'm not stopping any time soon. Learn to turn away."

Maeve smiled at Ethan and shook her head. "They're terrible," she mouthed.

Ethan put his arm on the back of her chair. "They're perfect."

*****

Ethan's eyes were stinging from too much time on the computer, but he wasn't ready to go home yet. He couldn't seem to stop laughing at Mama Em and Tony. They were hilarious and exactly the type of couple he hoped he and Maeve would be someday.

The ache that never seemed to fully heal from the loss of his parents grew a little stronger as Ethan watched the two adults bicker like young children, but in some ways it was good. It meant he loved his parents. It meant he'd had a good relationship with them. And it meant he came from a family and now he was looking forward to working toward his own.

His arm that was looped around Maeve's shoulders tightened slightly, pulling her into his side just a bit more. It seemed insane that he had spent so much time watching her from afar and now had the right to hold and to touch whenever he wanted. He sort of wanted to ask Maeve to punch him to make sure he was awake, but there was a small part of him that was afraid she'd actually take him up on the offer.

"Where's that little puppy of yours?" Mama Em asked as she stood from the couch and walked toward the kitchen.

Ethan stiffened. "Aw, crud."

Maeve straightened, pulling out of his arms. "What? Where is he?"

Ethan slapped his face. "At my house. He was being such a punk today at the shop that I ended up taking him home and putting him in his kennel."

Maeve grinned. "Let me guess. He's still there."

Ethan leapt to his feet. "Yes. And who knows how nasty that thing is."

Maeve stood up and walked with him toward the door. "Why not just kennel him at the shop?"

Ethan groaned. "Because every little kid who comes in opens it up and lets him out."

Her laughter grew. "I think Tox might be a bigger troublemaker than you are."

Ethan glared playfully at her. "Oh, yeah? Are you challenging me to see how much trouble I can get into?"

Maeve's jaw dropped when her father shouted.

"Yes, she is! Have her walk you home and give her a little show of what you're capable of."

"Antony Harrison!" Mama Em scolded. "Will you leave them alone? No one wants their dad interfering in their dating life."

"It's the Italian in him." Maeve groaned. "Please ignore everything he says."

"Actually, I think it's a fine idea." Before she could protest, Ethan grabbed Maeve's hand and began to drag her out the door. "She'll be back soon!" he called to Tony, who laughed when Mama Em screeched in outrage.

"It's a good thing they like you," Maeve said as he dragged her across the lawn.

"The question is, do you like me?" Ethan asked. He skipped up the front steps, nearly losing his hold on Maeve as a result. To his consternation, he couldn't open the front door without dropping her hand, but he grabbed it back as soon as possible. "Tox?"

The kennel shook and the puppy whined pitifully.

"Oh, you sweet thing," Maeve said, rushing over and opening the door. Tox burst out, his body dancing so much he could hardly stand on his feet. He kept slipping on the hardwood, his tail flicking back and forth like a whip.

"Oh...no, no, no!" Maeve grabbed him and ran back across the room, leaving a trail of liquid in her wake. "Grab the paper towels!" she called to Ethan.

Ethan flipped on the lights and eyed the mess. "And this is why Mom never wanted a dog," he grumbled. Muttering under his breath, he headed to the kitchen to find cleaning supplies. He slowly worked his way to the front door, grateful he didn't have carpet in the front room, making the clean-up much easier. Once done, he noticed Maeve was still sitting on the porch steps. "What're you doing?"

Maeve looked over her shoulder and smiled. "I think Tox needed a little space to burn off some energy."

Ethan walked up and looked out on the grass where the puppy was fighting some imaginary foe. First he'd run in circles, then he'd bend down, attacking a random patch of green before running again. "Hopefully he burns enough that he'll sleep tonight." Ethan rubbed the back of his head. "I might have saved myself some trouble at the shop but created more at home."

Maeve patted the wood next to her and Ethan sat down. "He's a social puppy. He might do better if you took him to work."

"I can't afford to have him keep eating the lines," Ethan complained.

Maeve's grin widened. "Finally found a problem you don't have an easy solution to, huh?"

Ethan bit back the response that *she* had been just such a problem. That answer, even if said in jest, would more than likely land *him* in the dog house. "Why are you so gleeful about it?"

Maeve shrugged and turned back to watching the dog. "You just always seem to glide through life so easily...like one of your surfing sessions. Always smiling, always laughing...everyone loved you and you loved everyone." She turned to him. "It's kind of funny to see something so small finally knock you off your game."

"Glad you're enjoying yourself," Ethan asid, making sure she knew just how annoying that was. "I aim to be entertaining."

Maeve laughed a little before resting her head on his shoulder.

Ethan held his breath. This moment. This. Moment. Life was far from perfect. Ethan, of all people, knew that more than most. But for a split second...it *felt* perfect. The woman he'd been in love with for years was curled up at his side, trusting him enough to lean on him and initiate a touch. He was excited and eager for the business opportunity sitting at the shop. It had such potential to shift his career into the stratosphere that he couldn't help but feel excitement for the future. And even that stupid dog was adding a little fun to his life as he sat there with Maeve on his shoulder, who was laughing at Tox's antics.

What more could he possibly ask for?

"Have you ever thought about trying to surf again?" *What the heck was that?* Ethan mentally punched himself. That was *not* what he had planned to say. Things were good right now. Really good. Why in the world would his brain ruin it by bringing up the very thing that had driven them apart?

Maeve didn't answer him right away and Ethan prepared himself for her anger.

"No," she said softly. "And yes."

Well, now he was curious. "What do you mean?"

"I've thought about that experience almost every day, but not...in a good way and never with the intent of repeating it."

Ethan winced. He knew that was a stupid thing to bring up. How could he ruin their perfect evening with something that reminded her of a traumatic experience?

"But I don't know that it would be a bad thing," she murmured.

His eyes nearly bugged out of his head. "What?"

Maeve shrugged against him. "I'm not saying I want to go. But since you bring it up, I'm starting to wonder if conquering my fear would be better than letting it continue to control me."

Ethan didn't have a response for that. He loved surfing. He loved Maeve. Bringing the two of them together was kind of a natural thing, but he wasn't sure how far he should push something like that. Instead of trying to figure it out, he wrapped his other arm around her and kissed the top of her head. "We'll figure it out as we go along. There's no need to hurry."

CHAPTER 15

Maeve pushed her glasses back up her nose and blinked at the computer screen. "Well, that can't be right." She ran the numbers again and relaxed the tension in her shoulders. "Better."

She'd been a bit distracted lately and was just now catching up on the books for the cafe, which had been woefully neglected. Never in a million years would Maeve have guessed that she would be so caught up in a man that she would neglect her job. And not just any man...Ethan.

She smiled to herself as she continued filling in boxes and making sure everything was up to snuff. She should have done this last week, just to make sure they were completely ready to take on the expense of an employee at the front counter and because they were about ready to break ground for the addition to the house.

It was going to be fairly simple. A single room added onto the side of the house nearest the kitchen, but it would go a long way to helping her dad be able to navigate the house better. He still insisted on working the stairs most of the time himself, but it worried Maeve. He shook intensely most of the time and sometimes his foot could barely manage to lift high enough to go up a step. She was positive that he was going to trip and come crashing down, ending up in the hospital.

And Maeve wasn't the only one worrying. She had seen her mother, more than once, simply staring into space with teary eyes. And Estelle seemed less vibrant than usual, bringing a solemnity to the Harrison household that kept pushing into the edges of Maeve's happiness.

She felt guilty that one part of her life was so wonderful, yet another part was so hard. What was a daughter to do? It had taken her so long to be able to push aside her grudge and hard feelings toward

Ethan that Maeve didn't want to do anything that might mess it all up.

Yet, how could she keep allowing herself to fall further and further in love, when her family was falling further and further into despair?

Maeve leaned back in her seat and pushed her glasses to her head. In a sudden moment of frustration, she tore them off her head and looked at the frames. The pieces of plastic in them held no prescription, but had been sitting on Maeve's nose for a lot of years.

She held onto an ear piece and twisted them back and forth. They had been something safe, something comfortable...and right now Maeve found herself tired of comfortable. Ethan had brought up a good question the other night when he'd asked if she would ever consider trying surfing again.

Logically, she knew hundreds of people who surfed every day and were just fine. But the thought still sent a tremor of fear down her spine.

"I've been letting fear control me for eight years," she whispered to herself. The words tasted...acidic. She hated saying it out loud since it forced her to admit that she was a coward.

Her fingers tightened on the frames. "But no more." She slowly shook her head, determination driving out the fear skittering down her spine. "No. More."

Taking a deep breath, Maeve opened a drawer and shoved the glasses inside, then changed her mind. Taking the glasses in hand once more, she stood and walked to the garbage beside the door. Sticking her nose in the air, she allowed her fingers to open, the glasses landing with a *plink* inside the liner. "No more," she repeated once more to herself.

Sitting back at the desk, Maeve allowed herself to still for a moment. She felt...freer. The longer she focused on the sensation, the more it grew until she felt as if she were floating above her seat.

The last few weeks with Ethan had been slowly building cracks in her carefully built life. The one that kept her safe, from never venturing out or trying something new. The one that kept the man she loved at bay so that she didn't have to face the fears and loss of trust that had hurt her teenage feelings so intensely.

The one that kept her from truly living.

Grabbing a pad of paper and a stubby pencil, Maeve began to write a list.

Swim in the Atlantic Ocean.

She nodded. There. She'd spent her entire life in Oregon and she had always, secretly wanted to see more.

Visit Italy.

Her father's family was there and yet Maeve had never gone. Her relatives had always come to the United States instead of the other way around, until a few months ago when Dad and Mom went so they could see those who were unable to travel.

Try sushi.

Maeve's nose wrinkled even as she wrote it. She loved seafood…as long as it was cooked. But she'd never had the guts to try it raw before, though she had a few friends who thought it was okay. But the new Maeve, the one who was going to live life to the fullest, was going to be brave enough to try. Even if the thought made her want to throw up.

Kiss Ethan on the beach at sunset.

Okay…that one wouldn't be that hard. But she really, *really* enjoyed his kisses and there just seemed to be something so romantic about a sunset on the sand with the waves crashing nearby.

Maeve shifted the pencil in her fingers, the tension in her shoulders tightening again. With very deliberate movements, she forced her hand back to the page.

Learn to surf.

Her heart rate sped up and a light sheen of sweat cooled the back of Maeve's neck. She shook her head, trying to clear all the cobwebs from her head. "No fear," she reminded herself. "No. Fear." The words were ground out through a clenched jaw, but Maeve continued chanting them. "No fear, no fear, no fear."

Gradually, the sensation began to change. Her skin grew less flushed and the bile in her throat retreated. Closing her eyes, Maeve slowed her breathing, which in turn slowed her heart. "No fear," she whispered, the words much easier to say than before.

She wasn't a scared little girl. She was a grown woman. A woman in love. A woman helping a disabled father. A woman who ran her own accounting business. There was nothing about surfing that she couldn't accomplish. She might never be good at it. She might never manage to go more than a few feet before falling off. But she refused to let it continue to have control over her.

Maeve let her pencil drop and leaned back in her seat feeling like she had already won. She could do this. If she could overcome her fears about Ethan, she could do the same for surfing. And then she'd truly be free.

Grabbing her phone, Maeve held back a squeal of excitement. She couldn't wait to share her decision with Ethan. He would be so proud of her.

Want to have dinner with me tonight? I've got something to celebrate.

Maeve chewed the inside of her cheek while she waited impatiently for a reply, her fingers dancing a frantic rhythm on the desktop. When her phone finally chimed, she grabbed the device.

There's nowhere else I'd rather be.

*****

Ethan grumbled as he grabbed his keys, Tox's kennel and rushed out the door. He'd forgotten the time and was now running late...again...for dinner with Maeve. He just couldn't seem to get his head out of working on Ollie's surfboard. Ethan was so determined that this be the best board he'd ever made that his entire day was spent planning and creating.

He was about ready to start the cutting process and was already feeling the pinch of time. It had taken him so long to decide on a design that now he was a few days behind where he wanted to be. Ethan knew that was nothing to be worried about. A couple of days was fine. But he couldn't seem to help but be anxious. His entire business, therefore his future with Maeve, was dependent on this sale. It was the exact miracle he had been hoping for and Ethan was determined to take advantage of it.

"Hey, babe," Ethan said into his phone as he pulled away from the shop. "I'm on my way. Did you have a restaurant in mind tonight?"

"I thought we could grab takeout from the cafe and walk down the beach," Maeve said, her voice slightly high on the phone speaker.

"That sounds perfect. I need to drop Tox off at the house and then I'll come get you."

"Bring him by the house," Maeve insisted. "My parents would love to dog sit for the evening."

"Are you sure? I don't want to add to your mom's stress."

"Yep. Dad has been asking when you'd bring him by again anyway."

"Great. I'll do that. Be there in five." He shut off the phone and put his full focus back on the road. "Okay, bud. You've got a fun evening set up. You want to see Tony? Mama Em?"

A thumping of Tox's tail against the side of the kennel was his only answer.

True to his word, it only took about five minutes to pull into the Harrison driveway. Ethan grabbed the kennel and hurried out of the car. The front door opened before he could knock and Maeve stood there, looking like an angel, her smile wide. "Hey, handsome!" she said cheerily.

Ethan stepped up and stole a short but fierce kiss. He just couldn't help himself. It was just so amazing to have her smiling at him and welcoming his company. He still struggled to believe this was his life now. "Hey, gorgeous."

Maeve laughed softly and tucked a piece of her hair behind her ear.

Ethan reached up and untucked the hair, twisting it around his finger. "Your hair looks nice." She didn't wear it down very often and Ethan loved it. Her hair was heavy and soft and felt great between his fingers.

Her cheeks flushed. "Thanks," she whispered, those brown eyes looking at him adoringly.

It was a look that Ethan wanted in his life forever. *The surfboard,* he reminded himself. *Get that surfboard right and you'll be able to have everything you want.* His hand shook when Tox yipped and Ethan was pulled out of his musings and he set the kennel on the floor.

"Hey, sweetie," Maeve cooed, bending down and opening the door. She laughed when Tox came out, his whole body twitching with excitement as he licked and sniffed everything in sight. "You're acting like you haven't been here before, silly," Maeve said. She stood and patted her thigh. "Come on. Dad's waiting for you."

They ushered the puppy into the sitting room where Tony was sitting on a couch, reading a book. "Is he here?" Tony asked, setting the book to the side.

Ethan tried not to notice how much the book had been shaking when it hit the couch. "Lonely, Tony? I thought you'd figured out how to keep your wife at your side."

Tony laughed. He patted his knees, trying to get Tox's attention. "She decided the grocery store was more interesting." He gave a dramatic sigh. "Guess even a man can't keep up with a place with endless amounts of ice cream."

Ethan grinned. He scooped up Tox and walked over to plop him in Tony's lap. "I hate to break it to you, but the right treat would probably pull Tox away as well. He doesn't seem to be a respecter of persons."

Tony shook his head. "No loyalty anymore." He eyed Maeve. "Even among daughters. She's ditching me tonight for a date and the beach."

Maeve rolled her eyes and put her hands on her hips. "So needy," she teased.

Ethan made a face. "She is, huh?" He rubbed the back of his neck. "Yeah...I'm not sure what kind of daughter you raised, Tony, but that's just wrong. Isn't it her job to—" He chuckled when Maeve punched his arm. "Ouch!" he teased. "Now she's beating me up! What kind of rules did you have in this house when you were a kid?"

Tony tsked his tongue. "It's not my fault! I blame her mother."

"I heard that!" Mama Em shouted as she came in the garage door.

Tony leaned forward, careful not to squish Tox, who was enjoying his belly rub. "She's got ears like a vampire," he said in a mock whisper. "I can't get away with anything."

"Heard that too," Mama Em said wryly. "And if you want dinner tonight, you'll apologize."

"Sorry!" Tony automatically shouted over his shoulder. He opened his eyes wide to Maeve and mouthed, *Help me!*

Maeve shook her head. "Good luck, Dad. You picked her first."

"Have a good time tonight, sweetie," Mama Em said as she walked over, giving Maeve a kiss on the cheek.

"What?" Tony cried in outrage. "She gets a kiss and I get threatened with starving to death? Where's the love?"

Ethan couldn't seem to stop grinning as he took Maeve's hand. "And on that note, I think we better leave before World War III breaks out."

"Good idea." Maeve lengthened her stride and pulled him toward the front door. "Night!" she called back to her parents. She closed the door just as her parents called back. "Whew! We made it out alive."

Ethan brought her hand to his mouth. "Come on. Let's go get our food so I can have you all to myself for a while." He loved how Maeve's cheeks turned pink again and he led her to the car, opening her door and making sure she was settled.

Nearly an hour later, they pulled into a spot along the boardwalk, food containers nestled in Maeve's lap and both of their stomachs growling. "Guess I should have called in our order," she muttered, unbuckling her seat belt.

"It's fine," Ethan assured her, trying to hide his own frustration. He had hoped he might be able to have the time after dinner to keep working on that last little obstacle with the board. He just knew if he had a little more time, he could finally figure it out and the whole thing would flow beautifully. But the line for dinner had been too long and now he was feeling antsy.

Easy... he warned himself. *It'll be fine to let the board go tonight.* The words felt hollow in his mind and his cynical side tried to argue back, but Ethan shut out the words. He hadn't spent any time with Maeve today. He had always been really good at putting work aside and focusing on the present. He could do it again tonight. The board could wait...he hoped.

CHAPTER 16

Ethan seemed distracted. His leg kept bouncing and his smile was slightly more hesitant than usual and it was starting to bother Maeve a little. She'd been so excited to share her breakthrough with him, but now it felt awkward. *He had a busy day,* she told herself. *He was running late and probably just hasn't settled down yet.*

"So..." She hedged, hoping to get a conversation going. "Tell me about work." She took a bite of a breadstick. "Did you have a lot of customers?"

"Hm?" Ethan turned her way, his eyebrows high. "What was that?"

Maeve laughed slightly to cover her annoyance. "Work? Did it go well today?"

"Oh...yeah..." Ethan chuckled and rubbed the back of his neck. "Sorry. I'm a little distracted. That surfboard...the custom one?"

Maeve nodded.

"I've been stuck on a part of the design and I just can't seem to quit thinking about how to fix it."

"Want to tell me about it?" she asked. "Maybe I can help."

Ethan leaned over and left a peck on her cheek. "Thanks, but we can talk about something else. It'll probably do me good to get my mind off it." He picked up his own breadstick and tore it in half. "That's when answers come, right? When we're not looking for them?"

Maeve nodded her agreement. "Yep." She pinched her lips together and toyed with her food. "In fact...I kind of had that happen today."

"Yeah?" Ethan swirled his fork through his pasta. "What happened?"

"I, uh...made some decisions."

He nodded, eyes still on his plate.

A tiny pinprick of hurt nestled against Maeve's sternum. Ethan was the eternal cheerleader. She had really hoped for a little bigger response from him. *He just doesn't understand yet,* she assured herself. *You haven't finished telling him what the decisions are about.*

"I made a life list."

"What exactly is a life list?" he asked, stuffing a large bite into his mouth.

"I feel like..." Maeve made a face and tilted her head back and forth. "I feel like I've been letting fear rule my actions for a really long time." She glanced up from under her eyelashes. Ethan was still watching her, his face open but non-reactive. "And I'm tired of it."

He nodded and swallowed. "Are you talking about us? Like how I hurt you?"

"Yeah...that and more," she clarified. "The example of me being afraid to surf again is just one of several parts of my life that were held back. I was afraid to surf because I didn't want to get hurt. I was afraid to trust you again because I didn't want to get hurt. I was afraid to study something creative in school because I didn't want to fail."

"You didn't want to study accounting?"

Maeve shrugged. "I like accounting. Numbers make sense and I enjoy seeing them all come together, but it's the reason *why* I went into accounting that bugs me."

"And it was fear?"

"Yeah." Maeve nodded. "I'm tired of letting it win." She straightened in her seat. "And today, I decided I want to do better. So I made a list of things that I've always wanted to do and I've decided I'm going to start marking them off."

"Good for you," Ethan said with a smile. "Is there anything I can help you with?"

Maeve's frustration melted. He was such a good guy. He didn't tell her it was dumb to make a list, he didn't try to placate or tell her fear had nothing to do with anything. He simply heard her out and asked to help. Why had she held off being with him for so long?

"Actually..." she flirted. "There is."

"Yeah?" Ethan grinned and leaned forward. "Why does it sound like you had this all planned?"

Maeve glanced down, unable to look him directly in the eye, but enjoying their conversation anyway. "I, uh...have always wanted to..." She blew out a breath. "I love romance movies where the couple takes a walk on the beach and kisses in the sunset, okay? It's always my favorite part."

He laughed. "Do I get the opportunity to recreate this with you? Is that why you wanted to go out to dinner tonight?"

Maeve could feel the heat crawling from her neck to her cheeks. She had to be bright red by now, but she forced herself to nod. If she was going to do this list, she couldn't chicken out on the first one. "Please?"

Ethan took her hand and brought her knuckles to his lips. "I'd love that."

"Thank you," she whispered. "And there's one more."

"Oh? More kissing?"

"I'm all for kissing," she said with a small laugh. "But no. This is something else."

"Hit me with it."

"I want to try to surf again."

Ethan went still and a slow smile spread across his face.

The heat in Maeve's cheeks grew to almost unbearable levels. She was glad he was excited, but the predatory look in his eyes was equal parts delicious and frightening. She might have unleashed something she couldn't quite handle. *And you're going to enjoy every minute of it,* a voice cooed in the back of her head.

She shifted in her seat, then straightened. Yes. She was going to enjoy every minute of it. She loved Ethan. She had for years and she wanted to share not only herself, but parts of his life as well. Surfing was a huge part of Ethan's life and though Maeve had no interest in becoming any kind of a professional, she wanted to enjoy it because *he* enjoyed it. Just like she hoped he would enjoy the fact that she liked numbers and symmetry and building spreadsheets.

"I would love to help you do that," he said in a husky tone.

Maeve smiled back at him. Her stomach fluttered and she knew that her dinner was done. "Maybe we could do at least one of them tonight?"

Ethan glanced out the window. "Then we'll have to hurry. The sun is all but gone." He waved down their waiter and got the check, quickly ushering Maeve outside where he took her hand. "Come on. We'll have to run."

Maeve couldn't help but laugh, feeling young and free in a way that life had kept from her for too long.

Ethan pulled her off the sidewalk and up the sandy rise that separated the ocean from the town. Going down was a little tricky, since her sandals kept slipping, but he was relentless.

"Almost there," he said over his shoulder, winking at her.

In a moment, they reached the edge of the water and Ethan pulled them down far enough that the edges of the waves were brushing over her toes. The water was icy cold and the evening air wasn't far behind, but Maeve barely noticed.

Slowly, Ethan tugged her closer, the distance between them disappearing until they were pressed completely together under the burnt orange sky. "Is this what you had in mind?" he whispered just centimeters from her mouth.

Maeve nodded. She had been so nervous to bring up her wish, but now...she felt only anticipation. The evening was beautiful. A handful of fluffy clouds scattered along the horizon, soaking in the sunset's colors and broadcasting an impressive display of colors. Orange, bright pink and dark lilac spilled across the sky, coming together to create something breathtaking. There was nothing that could have been more picturesque than what she was experiencing right now.

Ethan was warm and his hands held her securely. Her heart was thudding against her chest as his eyes went from hers to her lips and back again several times. She let her hands wander, climbing his muscled arms and wrapping around his neck until she could give him a gentle tug, asking...pleading for him to finally close the distance and give her what she wanted.

His lips twitched just slightly, letting her know he found her eagerness humorous, but the smirk lasted only a split second before he gave in and showed Maeve that her movie-created dreams could never compare with real life.

*****

Ethan tightened his hold on Maeve, pulling her more closely into his chest. He could do this forever. She fit so perfectly, as if she were made exactly for him. He loved it when her hands crept up into his hair and toyed with it. Or when she lightly ran her nails down the back of his neck. She seemed to know exactly what to do to get a reaction out of him and his desire to take things slow before they got married was quickly waning.

All the years that had been wasted between them because of his stupid teenage mistake sat heavily on his shoulders. If he had just paid a little more attention, he could have had her in his arms long before now. He could have fulfilled her kissing wish years ago, maybe on the very night he would have proposed. It would have been the perfect set-up.

Though he wasn't upset to be fulfilling it tonight, it just seemed so...pointless that they'd never done it before. Maeve claimed she had been held back by fear, but Ethan knew better. Maeve hadn't been the problem. *He* had. *He* had been blind to her troubles. *He* had taken the situation and treated it like a game, rather than truly trying to find out what had happened. *He* had failed to take care of her when it mattered most.

But no more. He was going to fix everything. And it all started with the surfboard sitting back at his shop, waiting to become famous and set his shop to buzzing with customers.

Ethan pulled back, breathing heavily. "Did we check it off your list?" he whispered.

Maeve laughed, her voice slightly deeper than normal.

The sound did funny things to his chest and he flexed his palms against her waist.

"And then some," she said with a breathless laugh.

Ethan laughed with her, then tucked a piece of her hair behind her ear. She never used to wear it down, but he'd noticed she did it more often now...and he liked it. The look was so feminine and he found himself constantly wanting to touch the strands. "You're so beautiful," he whispered, letting his fingers linger on her jaw line.

Maeve smiled, but looked away. "The list said to kiss at sunset, it said nothing about being drowned in flattery."

He smiled and kissed her forehead. "I added that for free."

Maeve laughed again, her forehead dropping to his chest. "Ethan, I think you might be the death of me."

"At least we'll go down together."

She shook her head and slapped his shoulder playfully. She leaned back, smiling. "What am I going to do with you?"

Ethan shrugged. "You could give me a repeat performance of a minute ago. That would definitely teach me a lesson."

"Oh yeah? What lesson would that be?"

He brought his nose down to rub against her cheek. "That I never want to let you go."

She let out a shaky breath and Ethan leaned back so he could see the last bit of light on her face. He knew she'd be blushing. She always blushed when he got all mushy with her, but he knew she loved it.

His fingers traced the bit of the light as it played with the angles on her face. Her skin was cool in some spots and warm in others. He paused, something starting to tickle his mind.

A sunset...

The design. The design he'd been working on for the surfboard. He'd been so stuck, nothing unique and noteworthy coming to mind. Flowers, geometric shapes...it had all been done before and Ethan didn't want something to blend in, he wanted something to stand out. Something that would please Ollie, but also catch the attention of every follower he had.

Quickly, the pieces of the puzzle began to snap together in his mind. The orange and purple from the sky, the pink and creamy tone of Maeve's skin, the dark background of her eyes and hair...he had it. He knew exactly what he was going to design.

"Maeve. You're a genius." Cupping her face, Ethan kissed her hard and fierce.

"Wait...what?" Maeve asked when he pulled back. "What just happened?"

"You solved it," Ethan responded. He took her hand and began tugging her toward the parking lot. He had to get this down. Tonight. While it was fresh in his mind. He needed to capture every nuance and line that was swirling in his brain. Tomorrow would be too late.

Maeve would understand. She'd want him to do well at this job. After all, she of all people had to know just how important it was for his dwindling business.

"I solved what?" she persisted when he opened the passenger door for her.

"My block," Ethan reiterated. "The surfboard. You solved the block." He shut her door and walked around, jumping into his seat.

"So we're going to the surf shop?" she asked, still sounding dazed.

Ethan shook his head. That would bore Maeve to tears. "Nah. I'll take you home. I don't want you just sitting around falling asleep on the couch." He grinned at her in the dark interior of the vehicle. "You get some rest. No reason for two of us to have dark rings under our eyes. Yours are far too pretty for that."

Maeve was quiet and Ethan guessed that she was blushing again, though he couldn't see it. He reached over and took her hand, entwining their fingers and resting them on his thigh while he drove.

He was so excited he could barely think straight. The board was going to be magnificent, if only he could make sure his vision came to light. He'd name the design "Maeve" after its muse. But that little tidbit would have to wait to be shared. Wouldn't it be a wonderful surprise to gift to Maeve after Ollie made the board become famous?

Ethan jerked to a halt in the driveway and climbed out, rushing to her side so he could open the door. "Sorry to cut everything short," he said quickly. "But I really want to get it all down while it's fresh in my mind."

"It's fine," she responded. Her voice was a little quieter than usual, but Ethan shook it off in his excitement.

He walked her to the door. "One more for luck." He gently cupped her cheeks, letting his thumbs caress the soft skin of her cheek bones before leaning down for a sweet goodbye. "I love you, Maeve," he whispered.

Forcing himself to let go, he rushed back to the car. He could stay there all night kissing that woman, but then he'd never finish the board and save his way of taking care of her. He wanted Maeve forever, not just for a dinner date and he couldn't do that until he finished Ollie's order.

So tonight he would sacrifice their evening for something greater. Their future.

CHAPTER 17

Maeve stirred the pot of sauce on the stove. The aromatic herbs were heavenly and she took a long sniff. "Ahhhh...why does Grandma's marinara always turn out so good?" she murmured.

"Because she's Italian?"

Maeve jumped with a squeal. "Michael! You dork," she scolded her cousin. "What do you think you're doing?" Maeve grabbed a towel and wiped her hands. "And how did I not hear you knock?"

Michael grinned. He had the same easy going grin as her other cousin, Jayden. But Michael's looks were tempered by glasses and well trimmed hair, where Jayden liked to leave himself slightly disheveled. It more than likely came from his sassy and spunky mother, Belle, where Michael's mom, Grace, was much quieter in demeanor and deportment.

"Sorry," he said, still smiling. "I haven't knocked on your door since I was five years old. Did you want me to start now?"

Maeve rolled her eyes. "Whatever." She turned back to the stove, grabbing the spoon and stirring. "What brings you by tonight?"

Michael jabbed a thumb over his shoulder. "These two wanted to say hello."

"Maeve!" Michael's mother, Grace, came sweeping into the room. Quiet as she was, she was elegance personified. Light hair that was slowly growing lighter with age, a serene face and classic clothes that never went out of style, Aunt Grace was extremely near and dear to Maeve's heart. "I feel like I haven't seen you in forever," Grace murmured as she hugged Maeve tightly.

"I know the feeling," Maeve whispered back. She gripped her aunt fiercely. Maeve's mother had always said that Maeve's studious demeanor came from Grace's side of the family. When the more Italian side of her family got crazy, it always made Maeve feel as if she still belonged somewhere. "How is it we live in the same small town and still manage to go weeks without talking?"

Grace stepped back and smoothed down Maeve's curls. "I don't know, but I don't like it." Her smile dropped. "Speaking of not talking...Emory has been pretty closed-lipped about your dad. How's he doing?"

Maeve opened her mouth, but her father beat her to it.

"He's fine, Grace," he hollered from the couch where the television was quietly showing a basketball game rerun. "At least he would be if all the mother hens in this family would leave him alone."

"Tony..." Grace scolded as she walked toward him. "You can't blame us for caring."

While her aunt and dad bickered good naturedly, Uncle Enoch walked up and slung his arm around Maeve's shoulders. "Heya, kiddo. How's life?"

Uncle Enoch was everything an uncle should be. He was the world's best handyman, knew how to fix anything, and could always be found hanging out with the kids instead of the adults. He'd never stopped calling Maeve "kiddo," even though she was far from resembling a child anymore. Of course, he called everyone some type of nickname, so Maeve didn't feel too frustrated with him.

"Fine," she said with an easy shrug. She knew Enoch was really asking about her father as well, but with her dad in the room, it wasn't really her place to tell. Her dad was losing his body, not his mind.

Uncle Enoch raised an eyebrow. "Yeah?"

Maeve smiled. "Yeah."

"So the rumor I heard about you and a certain surfer...?"

Maeve tilted her head into his shoulder. "You never listen to rumors, do you, Uncle Enoch?"

He chuckled and kissed the top of her head before letting go and starting to walk away. "Don't be planning any weddings without talking to us first, huh? At least one of you girls needs to use the inn for your vows."

Maeve's cheeks grew hot and she shook her head, causing her uncle to laugh even more. She would absolutely love to get married at the Gingerbread Inn...but she and Ethan hadn't even come close to talking about that. She'd barely worked past forgiving him for hurting her, she definitely wasn't quite ready to commit to a lifetime...yet.

Maeve loved him, she did. But she wasn't a speedy worker and this was a big decision. Only time would tell if it would all work out between them.

Michael's chuckle sounded exactly like his father's when he sidled up to Maeve's side. "I see the rumors are true, then."

She smacked her cousin's arm. "Geez. Is there no privacy in this family?"

"None," he said with a shake of his head. His blond hair was styled neatly back, away from his face and he tucked his hands in his pockets, giving him a boyish look. "There can't be when you have a family as big as ours."

"So true," Maeve muttered. She turned to stir the pot one more time before turning off the heat. "Mom ran to the grocery store. She should be back in a few minutes for dinner. You're all welcome to stay, of course."

"Why do you think we chose right now to come by?"

Maeve laughed as intended. "And everyone thinks you're so straight laced." Maeve narrowed her eyes and leaned in. "You're just as sneaky as Jayden, but you're quiet about it."

Michael groaned. "I guess someone was bound to figure out my secret. Can't believe it took you a quarter of a century to figure it out."

"Quarter of a century," Maeve repeated. "Who talks like that?" She opened her eyes dramatically wide. "Oh, yes. Middle school literature teachers, that's who." She shook her head and tsked her tongue.

"Do you quote Shakespeare for all the students too? Are you teaching the boys how to flirt with the girls?"

Michael put a hand to his heart. "Would you like to hear a little *Romeo and Juliet*? I've always loved a good story where everybody dies."

Maeve's laughter grew, drawing the attention of the older adults in the adjoining room. "Yeah...Shakespeare was always too depressing for me."

Michael nudged her arm. "Well, he got a few things right."

"What's that?"

"I'm pretty sure he said something about love and food," Michael mused, though his smile wasn't as genuine as before. He glanced at the stove. "In that case, I think we should do exactly as he said and 'eat on.'"

"That was bad," Maeve teased. "Even I know that's not how the quote goes." She lifted the pot from the stove and walked toward the counter. "What is it with you men and your stomachs? It seems like the only time I see Ethan anymore is when he's hungry."

"A guy knows a good thing when he sees it," Michael offered. He began pulling down plates. "Do you need me to drain the pasta?"

"That'd be great," she responded. "Set an extra. Ethan said he'd be by later."

Michael chuckled. "Are you going to fill him with food? Or something else?"

"Are you serious?" Maeve hissed. "My dad is right there."

"He's sick," Michael whispered back. "Not blind. In fact, I heard from Jayden, and no, I don't know who he heard it from, that your dad gave Ethan permission to kiss you."

Maeve groaned and smacked her forehead. "Men. You drive me nuts."

Michael's laughter never seemed to end. "Don't worry. I don't see that changing anytime soon."

*****

Ethan pulled into his driveway, eyeing the one next door. He was supposed to stop by for dinner with Maeve and her family, but there were a bunch of cars already there. "I'm pretty sure that one's Michael's," he told Tox, who was yipping in his crate. Ethan looked over his shoulder. "Do we interrupt the family gathering?"

Tox yipped again and wagged his tail.

"Okay...but if we end up in the hot seat, I'm totally throwing you under the bus," Ethan said, pointing a finger at his puppy.

Tox whined and Ethan chuckled.

"Alright, alright. No buses. Besides, Mama Em won't let anything happen to you." Ethan made a face as he got out. "Pretty sure Tony feels the same way." Walking around, Ethan opened the kennel, rather than carrying it, and picked Tox up. The tiny body wiggled and Ethan had to adjust his grip. "I think you're growing, dude. Better watch it, or you'll be too big to sit on the lady's laps."

The closer they got to the Harrisons' front door, the more Tox moved. His excitement was palpable and Ethan couldn't help but laugh. While he, himself, was excited to see Maeve, as always, he was also exhausted. The last few nights had been spent working on that board and Ethan was wearing out. The design hadn't been as easy as he had planned, but he wasn't giving up either.

The computer image was slowly coming together in order for Ethan to put it on the board, but he wasn't quite ready for the print yet. The board was still under construction and truthfully, Ethan was a little behind schedule. He was working so hard to make things perfect that he was having a hard time moving on to the next step.

I'll get it, he told himself. *But it's gotta be perfect. Nothing else will do.*

He knocked, nearly dropping Tox when he began barking excitedly. "Dude, quiet."

Maeve was laughing when she opened the door. "I thought I heard the little punk." She reached out and grabbed the puppy. "Were you excited to see us?" she cooed, nuzzling the dog's fur.

Ethan put his hands on his hips and made a sad face. "What does a guy have to do to get a little love around here?"

Maeve's grin never faltered. "Bring a dog."

"I did."

"Well, sorry." She stepped closer and kissed his cheek. "Hi," she whispered, staying close.

"Hi, yourself." Ethan wrapped an arm around her waist and tugged her into his chest. This. This was why he'd been working so hard. This was why he was pulling late nights. This was why he needed that board to be perfect. It was his ticket to having this woman in his life for more than a couple of hours in the evening. He couldn't accept defeat. Maeve was worth every bit of his weariness and frustration. He bent down and took a much more satisfying greeting.

"Mom! Ethan and Maeve are kissing in the doorway," Estelle called from the top of the stairs.

"What?" another voice called. Ethan was pretty sure it was Michael. "Hasn't the guy learned to sneak around back? Everyone can see you in the front."

Maeve groaned and ducked her head. "My family is crazy."

Laughter was growing as Ethan took Maeve's hand and they walked farther inside. Slowly, Ethan felt his spirits lift. He loved the Harrison family. Even the extended part. His household was so quiet and though his parents had been wonderful, he'd always been jealous of Maeve, her sisters and all their cousins growing up together. He enjoyed people and this family gave him everything he needed.

"Ethan, Ethan, Ethan," Tony said, clucking his tongue. "Have you learned nothing?" His hand waved toward Michael, who was grinning like a Cheshire cat from a recliner. "At least one of you boys listened to my lessons on wooing women."

"Dad…stop," Maeve begged.

Tox barked and she set him on the ground. His tiny legs spun out for a moment before racing for the couch and doing his best to jump up.

"Oh my goodness," Grace cooed. "How cute you are." She picked up the puppy, but had to set him down in order to allow Tox to say hello to Tony. Grace laughed. "I think you have an admirer," she said with a laugh.

"The man has too many admirers," Enoch muttered.

Ethan chuckled and tucked Maeve farther into his side. "Any chance you have an extra dinner lying around somewhere?" he whispered.

"Of course," Maeve told him. They walked toward the kitchen. "I dished you up and put it in the oven, so it should still be warm."

"You're heaven sent." Ethan moaned as he smelled the pasta. "Please tell me this is your grandma's spaghetti sauce."

"Marinara," Maeve corrected. "She'd beat you with her rolling pin if you called it spaghetti sauce."

Ethan stuffed in a mouthful. "Good thing she'll never know," he said around his too-big bite.

"You mean as long as nobody tells her," Michael said, easing into the seat across from Ethan. He smiled. "I'd shake your hand, but it looks like it's busy."

Ethan shrugged. "What's up, man? Long time no see."

Michael nodded. "Yeah. Work and all that. The fall has been a bit rough."

Ethan huffed. "Tell me about it." He wiped his mouth. "What grade are you teaching this year?"

"Seventh and eighth honors English."

Ethan nodded, impressed. "Wow. So you get the good kids, right?" He took another large bite, he couldn't help it. Mama Em might not have been raised Italian, like her husband, but she'd certainly taken to the recipes like a native.

Michael laughed and pushed a hand through his hair. "You'd think." He didn't elaborate and Ethan, though curious, let it drop. His smile grew as his eyes darted between Ethan and Maeve. "So…"

Ethan braced himself. Here it was.

"Maeve doesn't have an older brother at home…"

"And you're not about to be one now," Maeve ordered, glaring her cousin down. "Do you really think Dad hasn't already pulled out the gun and shovel routine?"

Michael chuckled. "Still…a guy needs to know where he stands."

"Right next to her," Ethan responded, winking at Maeve. Her cheeks turned bright red again and he wished he could caress the skin. That blush was his undoing.

"Stop," she said half heartedly, slapping his upper arm. "You're making me blush."

"I think, dear cousin," Michael said with a huff, "that was the point."

Ethan tapped the side of his nose. "Someone gets it."

Michael shook his head, still smiling. He tapped the table. "Good too see you. I'll let you eat and we can chat later."

Ethan nodded his thanks and kept shoveling the food in his mouth. As his belly grew satiated, he found his spirit doing the same. Ethan had planned to go back and work on the board tonight, but…the Harrison home was full of happiness, laughter and the woman he loved. The longer he sat at that table, the more he didn't want to leave.

One more night won't hurt…right? I'll just do extra work tomorrow.

Shoving aside his concerns, Ethan let himself relax. His solitary life had broken wide open lately and he was loving it. He'd never felt so light, so cared for and so…wanted. Maeve was a miracle worker and he was more and more grateful that they had found their way past the eight-year hiccup that had kept them apart.

Tonight, he was going to just enjoy. After so many years, the future could wait one more day.

CHAPTER 18

Maeve woke up the next morning feeling much more hopeful than she had for several days. Ethan had seemed...distant for the past week. Ever since she'd shared her life list with him, he'd been distracted and only rushing into the house late at night for dinner, then leaving immediately.

Last night, however, he'd stayed. He hadn't run off, he had stayed by her side and laughed late into the evening with her family. Everyone in her family loved Ethan, and had since he was a young boy. Ethan had always been around, had grown up with Maeve and her sisters, was friends with Antonio and all Maeve's guy cousins and was, generally speaking, already part of the family.

Last night it struck Maeve how natural it was to have him in the group and how easy it would be to imagine him there as a permanent fixture. Michael had teased her about marriage, and the thought had been lingering on the side of her brain ever since.

No, she and Ethan weren't serious enough to consider marriage, but he'd said he loved her. In a quick *I'm leaving* type of way, and Maeve felt strongly enough about him to want to say it back...if she ever got the chance anyway.

Last night, in front of her family hadn't been the right venue and then he'd been half asleep when he'd walked across the grass, so she hadn't wanted to say it then either. *Soon*, she promised herself. "Soon I'll tell him exactly how I feel. Especially if he keeps hanging around like last night."

Giving her hair one last brush, Maeve glanced in the mirror. She looked...different. Her eyes were brighter and her cheeks flushed. *You look like someone in love.*

The thought made Maeve blush even harder and she covered her cheeks with her hands. It was exactly the look she'd seen on Aspen when Aspen had been dating Austin. What was it about love that made a woman seem so different? The world was brighter, the smiles were easier and laughter bubbled up as if it were her first language. It was just so silly and yet so wonderful.

Shaking her head at her musings, Maeve put away her makeup, which had never seen so much use as it had the last few weeks, and headed downstairs to go to work. Before backing out of the driveway, she sent off a text.

Hey! Thanks for hanging out last night, my family loved it. Are you coming for dinner tonight?

Throwing the phone in the side seat, she put the car in reverse and drove to the shop. It was already buzzing with people by the time Maeve pulled in. A line was running down the sidewalk, waiting for Estelle to unlock the front door.

Though it was a wonderful thing to see how many loyal followers the shop was gaining, Maeve had to wonder what made today so special.

"Lemon poppy-seed pound cake," Aspen announced as Maeve walked in the back door. Aspen put her hands on her hips and grinned like a maniac. "Have you seen the reaction?"

"I'm lost," Maeve said, raising her eyebrows. "Do you mean the people out front?"

Aspen nodded. "I had Estelle advertise in advance that today I would be trying a new flavor. Lemon poppy-seed pound cake." She clapped her hands in glee. "And now we've got a line up halfway down the block. It worked!"

Maeve laughed softly, enjoying her sister's enthusiasm. It made her slightly jealous, however. While Maeve enjoyed her work, she wished she had something she was as passionate about as Aspen. Baking cakes infiltrated every part of Aspen's life. Her brain never stopped thinking of flavors and no matter how many hours the baker spent in the kitchen, she never seemed to tire of her work.

By the end of the day, Maeve was definitely ready to leave her trusty calculator behind. What would it be like to feel so deeply about what she did? In her mind, Aspen was saving the world, one cake at a time.

And what do you do?

Maeve forced the thoughts aside. "That's great. What a perfect marketing strategy."

Aspen's cheeks were glowing bright red. "Totally. It was Austin's idea, but Estelle put it into action."

"You have the cakes ready...right?"

Aspen rolled her eyes. "Oh ye of little faith. They're in the walk out."

Maeve nodded. "Perfect. Good luck! And save me a slice."

"Just one?" Aspen sang as Maeve walked toward her office.

Maeve grinned over her shoulder, pausing at the door with her hand on the handle. "I'm sure Ethan would love one," she agreed. "Thanks."

Aspen gave a teasing salute, wiped her hands on her apron and went back to work.

Maeve walked into her office feeling slightly dejected. Ethan hadn't answered her text, she'd had another moment of realization in understanding just how much her fears had held her back, and Aspen had remembered that Maeve would need two slices, but Maeve herself hadn't thought about it.

Her mind latched onto the concern and began racing with it. Would she ever think of herself as a twosome instead of single? Was there something in her life she would yet discover that she would love as much as Aspen loved cakes? Did Maeve *want* to find something like that? Or was it easier to simply flow through life trying to create as few bumps as possible? Did Ethan have his phone on him? Why wasn't he answering her? Was he ignoring her? Maybe he hadn't gotten her text...

"Oh my word…" she breathed, pressing her hands against her cheeks. "Stop it!" She'd spent too many years having fears just like this and it had kept her from something wonderful.

Ethan.

He *was* wonderful. Even if he wasn't answering her as quickly as she'd hoped. Life happened. She could be patient. He'd get to her when he had time. After all…he also had something he was passionate about. His surfing was his life and his enthusiasm for building this board was almost contagious.

Maeve threw back her shoulders, sat down at her computer and began to pull up all the files she needed. There was no need to worry. He was simply caught up in something else. Someday, when she had a hobby she adored, she'd understand exactly how Ethan, and even Aspen, felt when they got caught up in the creativity of a new project.

Still, as the next two hours passed and Ethan didn't respond, Maeve couldn't seem to quiet the voice that wondered, *Why can't I be the thing he's so passionate about?*

*****

I need to answer her back, Ethan reminded himself as he pushed his hand through his hair. He'd been working on that stupid board all day and when Maeve's text had come through, Ethan had told himself he'd take care of it in a minute.

Well, a minute had been several hours ago and he knew he needed to answer or she would think he was ignoring her. He blew out a breath and grabbed his phone. Last night had been great, but now Ethan felt like he was a day behind. It wasn't anyone's fault but his own. He was the one who'd chosen to take last night off, and now he was suffering the consequences.

Hey, baby. Dinner sounds great. Maybe around seven?

"I'll need to eat anyway," Ethan reminded himself. He could take a break for dinner. Especially if he made good progress this afternoon. He was basically closed for the winter for his daily surfing lessons. He'd give it just a couple more weeks, but then the doors would be shut for the season, though his online store would still be available.

That sounds perfect, she texted back. **I'll see you then.**

Ethan set the phone aside and scrubbed his hands over his face. He was so tired. How was he going to do it all? The deadline for the board was looming, he still had so much work to do, but he also wanted to be with Maeve. It had taken him so long to get to this point with her that he didn't want to lose it now.

I'm having dinner with her, he told himself. *It'll be enough.* "I can still get some work done afterwards," he muttered.

Sighing, Ethan went back to work. As much as he wanted a rest, he simply couldn't take it. The board had to be just right. Without that, there'd be no future for him and Maeve and the work he'd done on that relationship would all be for nothing. He wouldn't ask to take their relationship into something more permanent until he had a way of taking care of her. He couldn't. She was successful and beautiful and he wouldn't ask her to tie her life to his if he brought nothing to the relationship.

Tox growled and something crashed.

Groaning, Ethan forced himself to walk away from the project and go over and see what his dog had destroyed now. "Ah, man...really?" he asked the tiny dog.

Tox looked up, tail wagging and tongue lolling. He looked inordinately pleased with himself.

Ethan, on the other hand, felt as if another two ton weight had been added to his shoulders. He'd thought a miracle had landed in his lap when Maeve finally began to welcome his attentions, but now it seemed as if everything was going wrong.

Ethan squatted down. "I kind of need those, buddy," he said in a low tone. Slowly, Ethan began putting the snorkeling fins back on the rack. Somehow, Tox had managed to pull one down, causing an avalanche of rubber to cascade to the floor. "At least you didn't take a bite out of one this time." Ethan shook his head. This dog was becoming a menace. He needed training. But how in the world was Ethan supposed to add that to his list? He could barely fit in a meal, let alone several hours a week to keep the puppy from destroying the entire shop.

Ethan glanced at the clock and sighed again. "Riley owes me big time," he muttered. Hurrying through the chore, he grabbed Tox, put him in the playpen area, then went back to work. He only had a couple of hours before he needed to be at Maeve's and Ethan needed to get through about eight hours' worth of work.

When he glanced at the clock again, somehow it had shifted much faster than he'd expected. How did time move so fast? He'd helped a couple of customers, but mostly just been caught up in creating Ollie's surfboard and yet it seemed like Ethan had merely blinked and the day was gone.

Grumbling under his breath, he grabbed Tox and hurried to his car. He was already a few minutes late for dinner with Maeve. It was a good thing they didn't live very far from each other.

The streets were a little busier than usual, making Ethan's commute seem like eternity before he pulled into her driveway. Snatching the kennel out of the backseat, with a yippy, happy dog, Ethan skipped up the front porch steps and pushed straight through the front door without knocking.

He used to do that as a kid. Hopefully no one minded if he reinstated the tradition.

"Ethan?" Maeve called from the kitchen area. Her head popped into view and a small smile appeared.

"Hey, sweetheart," Ethan responded, making sure his own smile was extra wide. He knew he'd been late a lot lately, but luckily, Maeve had been patient with him. She understood he was under a lot of stress and he appreciated her willingness to work with the situation.

"Hi." Maeve's smile still looked slightly sad as he kissed her cheek. "Long day?"

Ethan shrugged. "You could say that."

Tox yipped again, eager to be set free.

Maeve's smile widened. "I think you better let him out."

Ethan rolled his eyes. "Calm down, punk. No one's running away." Ethan set down the kennel and opened the door. The tiny ball of fluff was off like a rocket, racing straight past Maeve and jumping near the couch.

Maeve laughed. "He's not there. Poor Tox will be disappointed."

"Where is Dear Old Dad tonight?" Ethan yawned and used his hand to cover it up. He really needed sleep. *No. You need to finish that board. You can sleep later.*

Maeve's face fell. "He, uh...wasn't feeling well tonight. He's in bed."

"How are things going with the reno?"

She shrugged. "See for yourself." She led him over to the window closest to the construction. The foundation appeared to have been laid and the beams in the walls put up.

"Looks like they're off to a good start," Ethan murmured. He closed his eyes and rubbed them. They were stinging from so much work today. "I'll try to check in with Matt later and see what the full plan is."

"I'm sure Dad would appreciate that," Maeve said softly.

Ethan opened his eyes to look at her and found her golden orbs staring. She narrowed her gaze and tilted her head. It was almost as if she were seeing into his very soul. It made him want to squirm, though Ethan held still. Just what was she seeing? Or maybe the question should be, what was she *hoping* to see?

"You look like you could use a good meal," Maeve said softly. "Come on."

Ethan followed, feeling slightly off kilter. The rapport between them felt slightly awkward, though he wasn't sure why. Yeah, he'd been a little late, but he was here. He was making her a priority even though he was itching to get back to the shop.

He walked behind her into the kitchen and wrapped his arms around her waist. Settling his chin against her shoulder, he asked, "Are you okay? Are *we* okay?" He held his breath as he waited for her response.

"Of course."

Ethan closed his eyes and relaxed. Yeah, he could tell she wasn't her usual happy self, but her dad wasn't doing well and their house was under construction. Anyone would be stressed during that. It made sense that she probably needed a little more attention than he was able to give her at the moment.

I'll make it all up to her, he promised himself. When this project was over and he'd saved his business, he would make sure she got all the attention she needed and wanted.

Giving her one last squeeze, he straightened and let go. "Glad to hear it. How can I help with dinner?"

CHAPTER 19

Maeve sat next to Ethan, waiting and watching while he ate. He'd been late again and her family had ended up eating without him since her dad hadn't been feeling well. Now Maeve was feeling a bit bad about that. "Next time I'll wait for you," she assured him.

Ethan chuckled and wiped his mouth. "Don't worry about it. It was my fault. You don't need to wait."

Maeve nodded, but still wasn't convinced. There was something about his behavior lately that made her feel like he wasn't as involved in their relationship as she was. Truthfully, Maeve was feeling sort of neglected. She'd thought last night was better, but now they were right back where they were.

Ethan didn't respond to her, was late for everything, and always seemed in a hurry when they were together.

Easy, she tried to tell herself. *It's probably just your own paranoia. You've spent so long stuck behind fear that now you're letting it color your thoughts in regards to everything.*

"So...when are you going to climb back on that surfboard?" Ethan asked between bites.

Maeve tapped her fingers on the table as she considered her answer. "Um...I'm not sure. It's getting a little late in the season. Should I wait until next spring?"

"I suppose you can," he responded. "But it's not too late. We can surf year round here, if you're willing to get cold."

Maeve wrinkled her nose and fake shivered. "I'm not a fan of cold."

He chuckled. "I think that's a universal female thing."

Maeve rolled her eyes.

"But I'd hate to see you have all winter to chicken out of it."

She stiffened. "What?" One side of Ethan's mouth was twitching and Maeve knew he was baiting her, but she was so ticked off, she didn't care.

"Waiting. It just seems like something someone would do if they were trying to wiggle out of their promise."

She scowled. "I'm not wiggling out. I told you. It's part of my life list."

"So prove it." He shoved a large bite in, smiling while he chewed.

"Fine. I will."

Ethan nodded and swallowed. "Great. When are you going to do it?"

"When can you take me?"

His eyes grew distant and he scratched the side of his head. "That's a good question. My schedule has been a bit full lately..."

"Too full to take your girlfriend surfing?" Maeve teased. She tsked her tongue. "Maybe I need to rethink this whole relationship if you don't even have time to share your favorite pastime with me."

Ethan reached over and squeezed her knee, making Maeve squeal. "Fine, Ms. Impatient. How about Saturday? I'll close down the shop for the morning and we can take as long as you need to figure it out."

Maeve pinched her lips between her teeth. Saturday seemed so soon. Was she sure she really wanted to do this? At the time she'd made the list, she'd been desperate to push out of her comfort zone and live life to the fullest. Surfing had seemed like a natural extension of that. She wanted to share something with Ethan and she wanted to prove that fear wasn't going to hold her back any longer. But now that the opportunity was staring her in the face...it was making her resolve twitchy.

"Maeve?"

She blinked, coming out of her thoughts. "Sorry. Uh...yeah. Saturday sounds great."

Ethan beamed. "Perfect. Want to ride with me? Or do you want to meet there?"

Maeve swallowed, trying to bring moisture to her dry mouth. "I'll meet you there. That way I can pick up my board from the storage unit."

"Just get one from the shop. I don't mind."

"I know," she assured him. "But it'll be fine."

Ethan nodded. "Okay. Saturday at six it is."

"Six? That early?"

Ethan rolled his eyes. "That's when the surfing crowd goes out. Did you want to wait until the waves were gone?"

Maeve slumped in her seat. She hated waking up early. "Fine," she grumbled like a petulant teenager. "But don't expect this to become a habit."

He chuckled and leaned over to kiss her cheek. "So noted." He went back to finishing his dinner. "You never were a morning person when we were younger. I guess you didn't outgrow that, huh?"

"Guess not." Maeve straightened in her seat. She heard footsteps overhead and glanced up, her stomach starting to churn again. Her dad had really been having a tough time lately and though Mom tried to act like everything was fine, Maeve knew it wasn't. She wasn't a kid who didn't notice things anymore, she was an adult who saw more than she wanted to.

The addition couldn't come fast enough. Getting him up the stairs this evening had been a miracle and Maeve kept hoping Ethan would show up to help, but he'd been late...again.

Her doubts and questions about whether dating him was a good idea seemed to grow a little stronger each time something went awry and she hated it. *No relationship is perfect,* she scolded herself. *Give him some slack. He runs his own business and he's definitely been worried about the board for the famous guy. It'll be okay.*

The words felt slightly hollow, but Maeve held onto them with everything she had. It *had* to be okay. Her father *had* to be okay. Her relationship with Ethan *had* to be okay. Her ability to conquer her fears *had* to be okay.

She felt as if she were juggling a dozen balls in the air at all times and they were all glass. She couldn't afford to let any drop or it would be a disaster. She couldn't imagine losing her dad, she desperately wanted to leave her fear behind her and she wasn't sure she'd survive a second heartbreak from Ethan.

The pressure for everything to work out was heavy and Maeve felt she had no choice but to keep pushing forward.

"So...that board you've been working on?" she asked.

Ethan raised his eyebrows. "Yeah?"

"How's that coming? I feel like we haven't talked about it in a while." Maybe the problem wasn't that Ethan was pulling away. Maybe it was that she wasn't showing him she was as interested as she should be. Just now she'd been complaining about meeting him early for surfing. What was he supposed to think about that? *Idiot,* she grumbled in her head. *No wonder he's just been taking care of business without you. All you do is whine and complain. You need to show him you want to be involved.*

Ethan nodded. "It's...been fine. Not going as quickly as I'd like, but okay." He smiled, though it looked a little strained. "I'm working on it though." He glanced at his watch. "Speaking of...I didn't get quite as far as I needed to on it today. I hate to eat and run, but do you mind if I hurry back to the office to get a bit more done? That way I won't have anything standing between us and our date on Saturday."

That churning was back. He was leaving. She didn't care that he wasn't sticking around for dishes or anything, but she had at least hoped for a little of his time. More than just the time necessary to shovel food in his mouth. "It's fine," she said, trying to make herself sound peppy. "I understand."

It's not fine. It's not fine.

"You're so amazing." Ethan scooted back his chair and leaned over for a quick peck. "Thanks for being so patient." He grinned and left.

Maeve didn't move. She didn't see him to the door and didn't bother turning around to watch him leave. Instead, she sat like a lump, fighting back tears. *What am I doing wrong?* she wondered. *And how can I fix it?*

Math...math made sense. If an answer wasn't right, she simply retraced her steps and solved it again. But relationships weren't quite as easy and Maeve was definitely feeling out of her depths. Numbers were logical, people were not and right now the man she loved was being the least logical of all. He'd spent eight years chasing her and now that he had her, he was pulling away.

"Saturday," she whispered. "He's meeting you Saturday." She blinked rapidly, refusing to let the tears fall. "It'll have to be enough."

*****

Ethan knew Maeve hadn't been happy with him leaving, but he was so grateful she hadn't given him a hard time. After all, he was doing this for them. For *her*. He hadn't spoken to her about his plans for their future yet. They'd only been dating a few weeks, though he'd been in love with her for years. But it was far too early in their relationship for him to bring it up. Right now, he would focus on saving his business so that when the time was right, he'd be ready.

"It'll all work out," he muttered in the car. "She'll understand in the end. Besides," he reasoned, "I'm taking time off to help her Saturday. That should tide her over until I finish the board."

His head was still trying to wrap around the fact that he was taking time off. He honestly wasn't sure how he was going to do it. The board really needed all his time and focus. His deadline was coming up in just a couple weeks and if he didn't have it done, he was going to lose everything, not just the contract.

Ethan pulled into his parking spot and paused. Something was missing. "Crap," he muttered, grabbing his phone. He waited impatiently for Maeve to answer.

"You left your dog," she said by way of greeting.

"Yeah, I'm sorry," he hurried to respond. "I totally spaced it when I headed out. Do you need me to come get him? Will he be in the way?" His fingers tapped impatiently against his steering wheel. He needed to get to work.

"No. Actually, I was thinking about taking Tox upstairs to Dad. I'm sure he's still awake and the company would probably be appreciated. Go ahead and take care of what you need to."

"You're so amazing," Ethan gushed. He closed his eyes and rested his forehead against the steering wheel. He didn't deserve this woman and his resolve to take care of her grew. If she was going to offer him the opportunity to work without interruptions, then he was going to make the most of it. "Thanks. I owe you big time. I can come grab him when I head home."

"It's fine. No rush. Like I said, Dad'll be grateful for the company."

"Okay, then. I'm at the office, so I better run, but I'll see you soon." He hung up and leapt out of the car. Instead of going through the front door, he ran around to the back, which led straight to his office and workspace. Tonight he would go back to sanding. He wanted that board as silky smooth as Maeve's hair and needed to fix a few areas. After that, he could go home and sleep.

He walked inside and flipped on the light, glancing at his computer. Grinding his teeth, he realized he hadn't checked his email all day. He probably should do that. Ethan had sent the initial designs to Ollie, but had yet to hear back.

His office chair skidded a little when he sat down and Ethan quickly clicked to where he needed to be. "Bingo," he murmured when he noticed a new message from his client.

His heart pounded in his chest. The design was good–Ethan knew it was–but Ollie had to agree or it would all be for naught. His foot bounced as he waited for the message to load and those few seconds felt like eternity until the small paragraph showed up.

Ethan scanned the message, a wide smile spreading across his face when Ollie mentioned how sleek the design was. But as soon as the smile had appeared, it fell and Ethan felt as if his world had just crashed.

The colors are on point and I really like the shading. But I'm gonna need it sooner than we thought. Nicholas Wagner got hurt and I snagged a spot in the Ventura Open next week Saturday. I'll need the board by Wednesday.

Thanks!

Ollie

Ethan felt like he couldn't breathe. He was supposed to have two more weeks. Two. More. Weeks. Now his timeline had been cut to six days, if he was going to be able to ship it in time. His chest rose and fell in an erratic pattern and Ethan actually put his hand against his sternum, trying to regulate his heart rate, but it was no use.

How in the world was he going to pull this off? He still needed to finish sanding, then there was the time needed for the resin to cure and the sealing to harden.

Ethan rubbed his aching forehead. It would be fine if that was the only thing he was doing, but between the shop, Maeve, and life in general, he simply was going to have a hard time getting it done.

"Guess who's getting no sleep tonight," he muttered. Ethan shook his head. This wasn't what he signed up for.

He grabbed his phone and called Maeve.

"Hey," she greeted.

"Hi," Ethan said quickly. He hated to do it, but he was going to have to cancel their date on Saturday. "I..uh..." He hesitated, guilt welling up in his stomach like a tsunami.

"Did you forget something else?" she teased. "Is there a cat hiding here that I don't know about?"

Ethan could visualize her smile. Her sweet, gorgeous, welcoming smile. Her golden eyes would be twinkling with humor as she teased him and he could just imagine the twitching of her perfect lips. Lips he loved to kiss and was so grateful to call his.

I can't do it.

"Yeah," he said with a forced laugh. "I got off so quick last time that I forgot to tell you that I love you." His eyes opened wide. That wasn't exactly what he had planned to say. He knew he'd said it once before, but it had been quick and more of a testing of the waters. This was...a little more blunt. And there was no squiggling out of it now.

"I love you too," she whispered after a moment's hesitation.

Ethan fell back in his seat. It was amazing how four little words were the best pep talk he could have ever received. His energy levels skyrocketed as if he'd consumed a gallon of coffee.

He could do this. He *would* do this. She was worth every minute of sleep he lost in order to get this done.

"Well, now that's the best thing I've heard in a long time," Ethan said in a low tone. "I'm looking forward to celebrating that on Saturday morning."

A soft, breathless laugh came through the line. "Me too."

"Okay. See you then. Bye." Ethan waited until she responded before hanging up. He slowly set down the phone. That wasn't what he'd planned the conversation to be, but now he knew it was the exact thing he needed. Maeve was exactly what he needed and he would spend tonight working to bring her everything she deserved.

"Time to get to work."

CHAPTER 20

Maeve tapped her fingernails against the desk. It had been two days since she'd seen Ethan. He'd texted a couple times and picked up Tox, but otherwise he'd claimed being too busy. Maeve had moved past the feeling depressed stage and was starting to get angry.

It wasn't right for him to chase her so hard and then simply stop showing up. They'd said "I love you" and then never seen each other again. Weren't couples supposed to celebrate that milestone? Even if it was only with a small kiss?

"No," she whispered to herself. "That's not fair. Give him the benefit of the doubt. He's working on a big project." Maeve shook her head. Keeping the fear and frustration at bay was getting harder each day. What was she supposed to do? Ignore it? Accuse him of ignoring her? Follow him to see if he was actually busy? All of the above?

"Hey, Little Mae," Estelle said as she walked into the office. Sighing, Maeve's older sister slumped down into a chair. "Geez, my feet are killing me today."

"You're too young for your feet to be killing you," Maeve said wryly.

Estelle glared. "Don't tell me what my body knows."

Maeve grinned. "Well, you obviously can't read the signs, so someone has to."

"You've been spending too much time with Ethan." Estelle groaned. "His sarcasm is rubbing off on you."

"I wish," Maeve muttered, turning away from her sister.

"What was that?"

Maeve shook her head, keeping her attention on the computer screen. She wasn't actually reading anything there, but she didn't want Estelle to read anything on her face either. Maeve knew full well she had a terrible poker face.

"Spill it, little sis," Estelle said sharply. "What's wrong?"

"Nothing," Maeve argued. "Why do you think anything would be wrong?"

"Because you're avoiding eye contact and you aren't gushing over Ethan."

Now it was Maeve's turn to glare. "I don't gush."

Estelle smirked, one perfectly shaped eyebrow arching high. "Until lately."

Maeve pinched her lips.

Estelle continued to study her sister, her head tilting to the side. "Do you love him?"

Maeve sat still. She wasn't sure how to answer. Did she love Ethan? Yes. But she was also upset at him. Not to mention hurt that he seemed to be ignoring her. And worried that he had changed his mind.

Estelle's expression softened. "Did you break up?"

Maeve shook her head, though the movement was stiff and jerky. "No."

"But...?"

Maeve shrugged. "But things are complicated right now."

"Then it's a good thing I've got Anna running the front at the moment."

Maeve huffed. "I'm not spilling my heart to you again, Stell."

"Why not?" Estelle spread her hands to the side. "I'm your sister and we've got a few minutes before I need to go back to work."

Maeve made a face. "Isn't there supposed to be chocolate and a sappy movie playing before anyone has a discussion like this?"

"You hate sappy movies," Estelle pointed out. "And you prefer fruity desserts over chocolate."

Maeve plastered on a triumphant grin. "Then it looks like our sister to sister chat can't happen."

"Mae…" Estelle pressed. "What's going on? You've looked down for several days now."

Maeve slumped in her seat. "I don't think I want to talk about it."

"But you'll feel better if you do."

"Who made you my mother?"

Estelle grinned. "You did when you first started using me as a confidant."

"I was an idiot," Maeve grumbled.

"Come on. Let's get this figured out."

Estelle looked so earnest and Maeve's defenses were crumbling. Would it hurt to talk to Estelle? It wasn't like Estelle didn't understand most of what was going on. It was the newest problems that Maeve had kept hidden.

"Mae," Estelle said softly. "Come on. I'm here."

Maeve nodded. "You're right. I just…gah!" She pushed her hands through her hair. "I'm not sure how to handle the situation. I feel like I'm between a rock and a hard place." The next twenty mintues were spent hashing over everything that had happened. Ethan's attention, Ethan declaring his love, Ethan leaving their dates early, Ethan not answering her texts, and finally Ethan going MIA for several days in a row. By the time she'd finished it all, Maeve felt exhausted and she leaned her head back against her chair. "Well?"

Estelle's lips were pursed. "I can see how that would all be frustrating."

Maeve nodded. "Yep."

"And honestly, I don't think your anger is unfounded…but…"

Maeve raised her eyebrows. "But?"

Estelle shrugged. "But I find it odd that you haven't simply asked Ethan about it. You're a black and white type of gal. If you don't understand, why not just ask?"

Maeve sat still for a moment. Why hadn't she bothered to ask? It was a simple enough question, but the answer seemed more complicated. "Because I'm afraid of the answer," she said softly.

Estelle gave her a sympathetic look. "And I get that as well. But wouldn't it be better to know and eventually move on than to wonder and be miserable?"

Maeve closed her eyes. "Why does it all have to hurt so much?" Maeve could hear Estelle rise from her chair and walk across the floor. She opened her eyes to see her older sister squatting down next to the chair.

Estelle grabbed Maeve's hand. "Matters of the heart always carry the possibility for hurt because they also carry the possibility for joy. You can't have one without the other. If Ethan has lost interest, we'll all mourn with you. You're not alone. But if he simply has something else taking up his time, then at least you'll have a chance to be patient and not lose one of the best things to ever happen to you."

Maeve huffed a laugh. "One of the best things, huh? What makes you say that?"

"The fact that I've seen you smile and laugh more in the few weeks you've been together than I've seen you do those things the rest of your life." Estelle leaned in. "He's helping you learn to *live*, Mae. Don't throw that away until you really understand what's going on."

The words were like a sledgehammer to her chest. How did Estelle know that Maeve was trying to learn how to truly live? To experience life at its fullest? No one in her family knew about her Life List. Maeve had only shared it with Ethan.

The realization made her pause. Why had she told Ethan, but no one else? She took a moment to ponder. She had wanted to share that part of herself with him, something no one else knew. She wanted that kind of connection that only came from two devoted people who clung to each other and gave everything.

And that kind of connection is worth fighting for.

Maeve nodded, then leaned forward and hugged her sister. "Thanks, Stell. You're amazing."

Estelle laughed and hugged her back. "Not yet. But I'm working on it."

Maeve leaned back with a smile. "I can't wait to meet the guy who eventually catches your eye. He's going to be pretty incredible as well."

Estelle cleared her throat and stood up. "You and me both, sista." She smiled, though Maeve could tell it was tight. "Let me know how it goes." Without another word, Estelle slipped out.

Choosing not to examine why Estelle had acted a little off for the last few seconds, Maeve grabbed her phone and keys and headed to her car. She needed to talk to Ethan, and she needed to do it now.

*****

Ethan's eyes were stinging so badly, he was sure someone was poking needles in when he wasn't looking. Squeezing them tight, he rubbed his fingers over his eyelids, trying to bring a little moisture to the area. He'd been working nonstop and it was getting difficult to keep going.

Tox had been his only companion, save a few texts from Maeve, and Ethan was starting to feel the separation. He couldn't wait for the opportunity to go surfing with her on Saturday. He was working on timing things just right so that the board would be curing that morning, leaving him completely free to surf without restraint.

Opening his eyes, he smoothed his hand over the board. It was coming along wonderfully and he was excited to be able to share it with Ollie next week. The hope that everything would work out was within his reach and Ethan clung to it like a fisherman with the catch of the year. He'd finish the board, get it sent off, then have Maeve all to himself.

"But first..." he muttered. "I gotta get through these next couple of days."

The bell on the front of the shop rang and Ethan groaned. With the end of the season so close, his shop had been slow and it had been a blessing, since it allowed him more time to work on the board. Each interruption was a curse...and a blessing.

Walking to the front of the shop, he stopped short. "Maeve!" Holding out his arms, Ethan walked forward. He hadn't seen her for several days and was missing their time together. *Just a few more days,* he reminded himself. A little sacrifice now would mean he'd have an entire lifetime with her later.

"Hey, Eeks," she said softly, allowing him to pull her in for a hug.

Ethan noticed immediately that she was stiffer than normal and he frowned. "Is something wrong?" A sudden thought hit. "Is it your dad? Is Tony okay?"

Maeve pulled away from his hold. "Yeah. Dad's fine...well, as fine as he can be." She took in a long breath. "I, uh...need to talk to you about something."

The frown didn't leave Ethan's face, though the worries about Tony subsided. Something was still wrong and he was struggling to feel like he had the mental capacity to handle it. How many things could go wrong in one week? He was already losing precious time working on the board by talking to her at all. Couldn't this wait until they were surfing tomorrow? "Okay..."

Maeve looked around the quiet shop. "Do you want to talk out here? Or take it in the back?"

Ethan rubbed the back of his suddenly hot neck. "There's no one here but us and Tox." He made a face. "Who's probably chewing something to smithereens at the moment."

She gave him a smile. "Okay, well...I need to know if you still care for me."

Ethan was stunned. Did he still care for her? How could she not know he cared for her? Hadn't he told her he loved her? Hadn't he been showing her his love as he sacrificed sleep and time to get this board up to snuff so he could save his business and build a future for them? He folded his arms over his chest, feeling more than a little defensive. "You're really asking me that?"

Maeve threw her arms out to the side, the quietness she'd entered with obviously gone. "Yeah, I'm asking," she snapped. "Why else would I be here?"

"I don't know," Ethan snapped back. "I actually can't believe you're here at all. How can you question how I feel about you? Everything I've done has been for you."

Her eyes widened and her jaw dropped. "Everything has been for me? Are you serious?"

He took a step back at the accusation in her words. "Yes, I'm serious." Maybe he was tired, maybe he was overworked and overstressed, or maybe he was just plain in a bad mood, but without warning all the anger and frustration he'd felt over Maeve's treatment of him from that stupid teenage mistake came rushing back and straight out of his mouth. "Why can't you just trust me?" he demanded. "All these years, you've held one little mistake against me. Eight years, Mae! Eight years I've been punished for being a teenager and I'm tired of it. I thought we were past this. I thought you had changed and wanted to support what I was doing."

Her olive toned skin continued to flush bright red the longer he talked, but it didn't phase Ethan.

"I know I haven't been around as much lately, but I'm working. I'm trying to save my business and secure our—" He cut himself off. He wasn't ready to talk marriage with her yet. Their relationship was too new, even if he was thinking about it. "Why can't you just trust me?"

Maeve's jaw was clenched. "It's a little hard to trust when you spend those eight years I *held against you* trying to break down my barriers and as soon as I open up, you disappear. Was it all just a game to you?" she cried. "Once you got what you wanted, you split?"

"You've got to be kidding," Ethan muttered. He stepped back, putting some distance between them. "That's really what you think of me? That I'm some playboy, out for only one thing?"

Maeve wiped at her wet cheeks. "I don't know what to think, Ethan. I thought things were good between us, but then..." She shrugged and put her hands on her hips. "Then you just quit answering my texts and you don't come over anymore. I haven't seen you in two days." She blew out a breath. "I came over here to give you the benefit of the doubt and try to talk it out." A harsh laugh burst through her lips. "Turns out that was a great idea."

The pain in Ethan's chest was still pulsing. He was doing all this for *her.* All of it. The lack of sleep, the tired, burning eyes, the skipping of meals. And instead of being grateful, she was accusing him of playing her. He shook his head. "I don't know what to think either."

Maeve huffed. "You don't have any explanation for it? Why've you been so busy?"

"I've been working on the board."

"Okay..." Maeve paused, as if to let him offer more insight. "It's one surfboard. How is it that it's taking up so much of your time?"

She didn't get it. She simply didn't get it. All this time Ethan was sure that she understood and was supporting him in his work. He had hoped she had similar dreams to him of turning his business into something full time that could support a family, but it turned out she didn't understand at all.

And I'm not in the right frame of mind to explain it to her.

If she didn't view him as marriage material, then he would simply have to show her. And that meant doing exactly what he'd already been doing. Once the board was off and his business showed the results, he'd be able to present himself as something worthwhile and someone she could trust.

"I don't have time for this conversation right now," he said bluntly. Pushing a hand through his hair, he turned when he heard a crash in the back. *Dang dog.* Even the puppy was driving him crazy today. "Look, I gotta go see what Tox has messed up and then I need to get back to work. Just..." He tried to find the right words. "Just hang tight and we can discuss this soon. Maybe when we're both in better moods, huh?"

Maeve just stood there, staring at him.

Ethan raised his eyebrows. "So, I'll see you in the morning?" Another crash came from the back. "Crap," he muttered. Stepping forward, he kissed Maeve's forehead. "Just give me a little more time, okay? We'll get this figured out."

Not waiting to see what she did, Ethan rushed to the store room. He needed to take care of the pup and then get back to work, especially if he was taking the morning off. If the coating wasn't done at just the right time, it would throw everything off and he wouldn't be able to go in the morning. And it sounded like he needed to go. He needed to show Maeve that he was sincere and worthwhile. That he was worth giving her heart to.

CHAPTER 21

Maeve blinked against the dark room. She'd barely slept last night and was seriously considering canceling this morning. Nothing had gone right yesterday and she wasn't sure just how eager she was to keep pushing.

She'd tried to stand up to Ethan about how she was feeling and instead had started a fight. He didn't seem to understand why she was feeling neglected, instead saying she didn't trust him.

Maeve threw her arm over her eyes. How in the world could he accuse her of not trusting him? She'd forgiven him, pushed past her fears and had put her heart in his hands, but it was currently being trampled on.

What she'd wanted was to be held and told it would all work out. What she'd gotten was a pat on the head and told to let Ethan handle it.

"Men," she grumbled. Pushing herself upright, Maeve had a debate with herself. To go surfing? Or not to go surfing? What did she really want?

As she sat in the darkness, listening to her own breathing and feeling her heart beating against her chest, Maeve's mind churned. "What do I really want?" she asked herself. The question sat on repeat in her mind. Instead of just pushing past the painful thoughts, she truly let them simmer. She thought about her life without Ethan. Her life with Ethan. Her current struggles with Ethan. She thought about her business, her fears, her buried emotions and worries. And just like the day she'd finally thrown away her glasses, Maeve came to a decision.

"I want to live," she whispered into the room. "I want to truly live and if at all possible, I want to do it with Ethan." Despite their current fight and how hurt she was at being brushed off yesterday, she loved him. This current behavior wasn't normal for Ethan. He usually took great care to be attentive and in the moment, which was part of why his disappearing act was hurting so badly. It felt as if it were her fault that he was suddenly gone all the time.

"He asked for time," she reminded herself. "Time and trust." Maeve blew out a breath. "I can give that to him. I can *choose* to give that to him." She threw off the covers, determination pushing her to her feet.

Fumbling her way across the room, she flipped on the light switch, then shuffled to the dresser to find her swimsuit. Next came her wetsuit in the back of her closet. It was a little tighter than when she was younger, but with a lot of grunting and wiggling, Maeve managed to get it over her hips.

Deciding that cursing her shape wasn't the best way to start her morning, Maeve slipped on her shoes, then headed downstairs for a quick bite of breakfast before driving to the beach.

The sun was just starting to come over the horizon as she pulled into the parking lot next to Ethan's shop. Stepping out of the car, Maeve stood still. It was so beautiful! Mist rose off the water, hitting her directly in the face, making her feel alive and eager to accomplish her goals.

She hurried up to Ethan's shop, but it was dark inside. In her excitement, she hadn't bothered to grab the key for the storage unit and would have to take Ethan up on his offer of a board. Glancing at her watch, Maeve realized she was five minutes early. Crossing her arms over her chest, she turned and rested her back against the door. Five minutes passed, then ten, then fifteen. Maeve tapped her foot. *Where is he?* She walked back to the car and pulled out her phone. No texts.

Are you coming?

She waited another ten minutes, but there was no answer. The same hurt and frustration that Maeve had been feeling yesterday began to simmer in her stomach. She had half a mind to drive back to his house and give him a piece of her mind, but she forced herself to pause.

"He asked for time and trust," she reminded herself. Closing her eyes, she took in a deep breath of the salty sea air. "I chose to distrust him once, and it wasn't right. This time I'll choose differently. This time I'll choose to move forward."

Throwing her cell back in the car, she locked it and headed to the back entrance. She knew where Ethan kept a spare key and she used it to get inside. Going up to his rental boards, she wracked her brain to remember how exactly to find a board for her size and did the best she could, considering the circumstances.

Lugging the board outside, she locked the door, replaced the key and faced the ocean. The board was awkward under her arm, but she made her way to the waves, stopping twenty feet from getting wet. Slowly, she took off her shoes and shoved her arms into her wetsuit, zipping it all the way up. Bending over, she attached the ankle strap to her leg and straightened.

Her heart rate skyrocketed. She was really going to do this. She was going to go back out on the water just like she had when she was sixteen. Memories of that day tried to surface and Maeve ruthlessly shoved them aside. "No fear," she reminded herself. "No fear. I choose life."

She watched the couple of other surfers out on the water, reminding herself of how it was done. Swimming out, paddling on her belly until she caught a wave, then rising to her feet to ride it in. Easy peasy. She could totally do this.

"It'll all come back. Just like riding a bike," she murmured.

Her legs felt stiff as she walked to the water and the temperature bit into her toes, making her wish she'd worn booties. *Next time,* she told herself. And there would be a next time. She was determined to win this battle. There would be no more nightmares, no more reliving her almost drowning in the night, no more waking up gasping for breath.

She was choosing to trust Ethan. She was choosing to trust herself.

Hiking up the board, she waded deeper, then laid it down and climbed on, wobbling only a little bit. Paddling out was harder than she remembered, but the workout felt good on her muscles. It got her blood pumping and she began to feel eager and alive, just like she had when watching the sun rise only a few minutes before.

Wanting to make sure she was being as safe as possible, Maeve swam out near another surfer waiting for a wave.

"Morning!" he shouted, waving.

Maeve smiled and waved back.

"Ready to catch a ride?"

She nodded. "I'm gonna try anyway. Still pretty new."

"Eh...all it takes is practice," he assured her. Glancing over his shoulder, he grinned. "Get ready. It looks like a good one's coming."

Maeve noticed the wave he was speaking of and felt a swell of nausea in her stomach. *I can do this. I can do this.* Positioning herself just right, she watched the other surfer, hoping to catch her timing from him.

"Here we go!" The young man began moving his arms and Maeve joined in.

She cupped her hands, tugging at the water and ignoring the freezing sting against her palms. Anticipation fueled her movements and her breathing grew erratic. It was as if the wave behind her were a living, breathing thing and she could feel it bearing down.

The water beneath her shifted and Maeve felt a slight jolt before her board began to pick up speed. She'd done it! She'd caught it! Gripping the sides of the board, she held her breath, watching the wave begin to rise higher, the white water starting to curl.

It's now or never.

Tightening her hold, she locked her muscles and did her best to remember Ethan's instructions so many years before. Her legs came under her and Maeve used her muscles to push upward, throwing out her arms for balance.

For one fleeting moment, she felt as if she were flying on top of the world. The rush of the water, the spray against her skin and the wind stealing her breath, but when her weight shifted too far to one side, Maeve flailed and the sense of euphoria came crashing down in tandem with her forehead, aiming straight for the board.

*****

A loud bark woke Ethan from a heavy slumber. He coughed and rubbed his sore neck. "What the heck?" Groaning, he realized he had fallen asleep on his desk. "Idiot," he muttered.

Standing on shaky legs, he twisted his body every which way, trying to work out all the kinks he had developed while sleeping in such an awkward position. "I'm getting so old."

He had spent most of the night working on the board and he was proud to say there was only one step left. Yawning, he made his way to the kitchen, feeling desperate for a drink to hydrate his dry mouth and throat.

Grabbing a glass of orange juice, Ethan went to stand at the window, smiling at the bright, rising sun. His eyes strayed to the driveway next door and he froze. Maeve's car wasn't in the driveway. He jerked around, looking for the time on the microwave, and nearly dropped his glass as he began running.

Every curse word he had ever heard began to play through his mind, but he didn't waste the air in his lungs bringing them to light. Instead, he saved it to help him move faster, but it still didn't feel fast enough.

Tox barked again and Ethan pinched his lips together. Shoving his feet into his flip flops, he ran over, scooped up Tox, who had never been kennelled last night, grabbed his keys and ran to the garage.

Wetsuits and boards were easily found at the shop, so Ethan didn't waste precious time grabbing the ones in his closet. It took a great deal of effort to set the dog down nicely, rather than throwing him across the seat in his haste, but Ethan forced himself to slow down enough to be safe. Crashing before he could get to the shop wouldn't help anyone.

The ten minutes down Main had never felt so long. "Please say she waited, please say she waited," he muttered under his breath. The more he chanted it, the more he worried she had simply gone home and would never speak to him again.

He blinked several times, trying to clear the sleep from his eyes and head. He still felt groggy. While he'd accomplished his work last night, he was a little worried that the price wasn't going to be worth the cost. Maeve was already upset that he was spending so much time on the project. How would she feel now that he was late...really, really late...to their surfing lesson?

A large crowd of cars were gathered around the parking lot at his shop and Ethan's heart dropped to his stomach. Blue and red flashed through the early morning air. "No..."

Bile rose in his throat and Ethan threw the car into park, not caring that he was stopped in an illegal parking zone. Tucking Tox under one arm, Ethan tore through the crowd, pushing the gawkers aside. "Who got hurt? Who was it?"

Call it premonition, call it intuition, but when Ethan saw Maeve sitting on the step of the ambulance, shock was not among the multitude of emotions that burst into his system like a tsunami.

"MAEVE!" he bellowed. Shoving through the last of the crowd, he stumbled toward the emergency vehicles.

"Whoa, sir," one of the responders said. "I'm going to need you to stay back."

"That's my girlfriend," Ethan argued. Tox yipped several times. "Hush," Ethan told the dog.

"Sir, just calm down," the responder said, holding up his hands.

"I'm telling you, that's my girlfriend," Ethan argued. His voice grew louder as Tox's barking increased and the man continued to try and hold him back.

"Hang on," another voice shouted.

Ethan sighed in relief when Gavin walked up in his fire uniform. "Gav. Tell this guy to let me through."

"I've got him," Gavin said to the emergency worker.

Scowling, but nodding, the man let Gavin take over.

"Man, you can't just jump in like that," Gavin said in a much lower tone.

"Sorry, but I need to see Maeve. Here." Ethan shoved Tox into Gavin's chest and then rushed over. "Sweetheart, what happened?"

Maeve winced when the worker dabbed at the large cut on her forehead.

"You'll need to come in for stitches," the female emergency worker said. She glanced toward Ethan. "Do you want a minute before we go?"

Maeve looked at Ethan and he couldn't quite interpret the look in her eyes. "No," Maeve said, her voice flat. "Let's go."

"I'll go with you."

"No."

Ethan stilled. "You don't want me to come?"

Maeve didn't answer for several heartbeats. "No."

Ethan turned to the worker. "I promise not to keep her long, but I do think we need a moment, please." He had to work to keep his words in a civil tone. Why was Maeve being like this? Yes, he'd been late, but he'd come as soon as he'd woken up. It was an honest mistake. One made while he was trying to secure their future together.

The woman looked back to Maeve, who sighed and nodded.

"Thank you," Ethan said as the responder left. "Mae, what happened?" He reached for her, but she pulled back.

"I went surfing," Maeve said bluntly.

"Did you hit the board?"

She blinked, not offering any verbal confirmation.

Ethan shoved a hand through his hair. "I'm so sorry I was late. I fell asleep in my office and didn't have my alarm. I came as soon as I woke up."

"You weren't here."

Ethan opened his mouth to defend himself, but she plowed on.

"Every single time I give you my trust...you aren't there."

"That's not fair," Ethan said fiercely. "I'm only one man, Mae. I can't do it all."

She stood up. "Maybe not," she snapped. "But I'm not asking you to do it all. I'm asking you to be here when you say you're going to be here. You said you would be there eight years ago and I nearly died." Her tone had dropped to a low, steely sound. "I asked you to be more present for our relationship these last couple weeks and I got brushed off. And today you said you would be here...where it all started...to help me start over." She pointed a finger at him. "You. Weren't. Here."

He groaned and threw his head back. "I know!" He brought his volume down when Gavin glared. "I know, Mae. I know I wasn't here. I know I made a stupid mistake eight years ago. I know I've been absent this last week and *I know* that I missed our date this morning. But has it ever occurred to you that I might have a reason?" His chest was heaving and his emotions were pinging through him with reckless abandon. It made Ethan feel out of control, a sensation he wasn't used to and didn't appreciate, but how could she not see his side?

"I'm all ears," she said sarcastically. "Tell me what was more important than being with the woman you claim to love?"

Ethan pinched his lips, doing his best to ignore the accusation in her words. "I was trying to save my business," he whispered harshly. "I was trying to make sure that when it was time to propose, I actually had a way to support the only woman I've ever wanted to spend my life with." He leaned in. "So don't accuse me of lying about my feelings. I've spent years trying to prove how I felt and all you've done is hold onto a grudge about a mistake made when I was a teenager. Well, guess what?" He slapped a hand to his chest. "I'm not perfect, Mae. I'm just a guy, trying his best to be worth something."

Tears trickled down her cheeks, but Maeve didn't budge. She didn't seem moved by his words at all and Ethan realized everything he'd been working for had just been lost.

He took a step back. "But you know what? You don't have to understand. That's fine. If you can't see that what I've been doing was for you, then I suppose you were the wrong person to set my dreams on." Spinning on his heel, Ethan grabbed Tox and marched back to his car.

Once inside, he couldn't bring himself to pull away until the ambulance had left with Maeve in the back. Despite their breakup, he didn't want to see her hurt. Yes, he knew he'd screwed up, he wouldn't deny that. But her refusal to understand his side wasn't right either, and right now...Ethan was far too tired to keep fighting for it. If Maeve didn't trust him and didn't want to be a part of his life, then fine. He'd save his business for himself instead. He'd get that board finished early and send it off to Ollie and if everything took off as planned, then maybe he'd consider moving his shop to somewhere else. Somewhere he could forget all about golden-eyed Italian women who made him feel whole.

CHAPTER 22

Maeve's head felt like someone had hit her with a...well...a surfboard. She'd been so proud of herself for getting a wave so quickly and scrambling to her feet, but it had all been in vain. Her lack of experience had swiftly pulled her feet out from under her and her head had taken the brunt of the fall, clipping the board as she went down.

She sighed and rested her head back. She had a mild concussion and wasn't allowed to drive home, so now she was waiting for Estelle to come get her and it was the longest hour of Maeve's life.

No, the five minute fight at the beach felt longer.

Immediately, Maeve's chest began to ache, almost worse than her head, and tears trickled down her cheeks. She hated crying. She rarely ever showed her emotions, but Ethan had brought her to tears twice now and Maeve was sick of it.

Every doubt and fear that she had worked so hard to get rid of, every part of her past that she was running from, had come barreling back to her with the force of a hurricane.

Now, however, instead of the incident from her teen years, the vision she couldn't get out of her head was the sight of the board coming to meet her and not being able to stop it. Over and over again, the dark blue came rushing toward her and Maeve felt helpless to do anything.

"Maeve." A hand shook her knee.

Maeve opened her eyes and she tried to smile. "Oh, look. It's my favorite oldest sister to the rescue."

Estelle chuckled softly. "Well, someone has to take care of the baby of the family. It's a wonder you lived this long with how much you like to live on the edge." She patted Maeve's leg again. "Come on. The paperwork's done and I'm breaking you free."

Maeve stood on shaky legs and numbly followed Estelle out of the waiting room. By the time they made it to the car, which was practically sitting at the entrance, she was already feeling overtired again. Flopping into the seat with a groan, Maeve gave a half hearted apology. "Sorry about being wet."

"That's the least of my concerns," Estelle said wryly. She pulled out and began maneuvering the streets toward the highway. There were several minutes of silence as Estelle began the hour long drive home, but once the cruise control was on, the questions began. "What happened?"

Maeve blew out a breath. "I'm sure you can guess." She rubbed the spot on her sternum again. How was it that breaking up with Ethan could hurt so much? She should have seen this coming. She had never been more important to him than that stupid board. And why in the world did he think he needed to prove himself with his business? When had Maeve ever told him that the amount of money he was making made her feel differently about him? All she'd ever wanted was to be able to trust him. To have him be there when she needed him...when he *promised*. And he'd broken that trust over and over again.

"I'd like to hear it from you," Estelle responded easily.

Maeve turned to look out the car window. "I'm not sure it's worth telling."

"Maeve," Estelle snapped. "I'm going to be really blunt right now."

Maeve frowned and turned to look at her sister.

"You can hate me if you want, but someone has to say something." Estelle glanced over, then took her focus back to the road. "Wake up and stop being a victim."

Another slap of pain hit Maeve. First the injury, then Ethan, and now Estelle? What was this? Were they out to kill her? "Victim?" Maeve cried, then brought a hand to her forehead and brought her volume down. "I'm not a victim," she said through gritted teeth.

"Well, you're certainly good at acting like one," Estelle shot back.

Maeve turned back to the window. They still had a long ride home, but she wasn't going to sit here and let herself be insulted by her sister, who didn't even know what was going on.

"I know you were hurt," Estelle continued, her tone softer this time. "But have you listened to Ethan's side of the story?"

"As a matter of fact, I have," Maeve shot back. "He was working late on that stupid board and fell asleep in his office, which meant there was no alarm to wake him up."

"So it was an honest mistake."

"No," Maeve argued. "It was a man who has promised me multiple times now that he would be there and he wasn't. It was a man who claims to love me but keeps putting work and other things first. It was a man who said he was working for our future, but is doing it by sacrificing me!" She was shouting by the time she finished, despite her headache, and her breathing was shallow and erratic. Maeve didn't even know where the level of hostility was coming from. Inside she was hurting, but she hadn't meant to become a screaming machine. It was rare for her to raise her voice and she loathed confrontation, so the amount of vitriol in her tone surprised even herself.

Estelle didn't respond right away and Maeve folded her arms over her chest, trying to keep herself together. She felt wild and reckless and like she would fly apart at any moment. In truth, she didn't even recognize who she was at that moment and it frightened her a little.

"Feel better?" Estelle asked.

Maeve grunted. No, she didn't feel better. She felt worse. Physically and emotionally.

"I'm sorry he let you down," Estelle continued. "But you still need to own your own pain. It's not Ethan's job to make you feel safe and secure in the relationship...it's yours."

"So, what?" Maeve whispered, losing the energy for the fight. She'd had too many of them lately. "I'm just supposed to let him walk all over me?"

Estelle shook her head. "No. You're supposed to be in charge of your choices. If you're hurting, it's because you choose to hurt. And honestly, sometimes we need to hurt. Sometimes we need to feel pain so that when the good times come, we enjoy them all the more. But sometimes pain becomes a distraction. It keeps us from enjoying the people around us and seeing all the wonderful things life has to offer." She hesitated. "Including boyfriends who make mistakes, but are doing their best. But I have to wonder...you might..." Estelle sighed. "You might need professional help, Mae. How deeply this is hurting you might be more than you can handle on your own."

Maeve shook her head and turned away. She didn't need to hear this. She was the one who had been hurt, no one else. And she didn't need therapy. She needed people to keep their promises. Why her sister wasn't willing to see Maeve's side was a mystery, but there was one thing Estelle was right about.

Maeve was able to make her own choices. And in this case, those choices included tuning out her sister, stepping away from the man who couldn't be trusted, and nursing her wounds in private.

A deep and heavy loneliness, one more familiar than Maeve wanted to admit, settled on her shoulders. It was the same weight she'd dealt with the first time she'd been through this with Ethan.

And yet you survived, she reminded herself. And she could survive this time as well. It might not always be pretty and it definitely wasn't as exciting as she would have hoped, but survival wasn't about feeling happy. It was about enduring when hope was lost. And right now, that was all she had left.

*****

Ethan pulled into his driveway and threw open his car door, storming into the house and slamming the front door behind him. He only slowed himself long enough to drop Tox to the ground without hurting the small creature before hurrying through the house, into the backyard and into his workshop.

The surfboard, in all its glory, was sitting on the sawhorses, glinting in the sun pouring through the side window.

Ethan took a moment to study his work of art. It was nearly perfect, just like he'd hoped it would be. He only had one more coating to put on it and after curing for several hours, it would be ready for shipping on Monday, just like he had hoped.

But looking at it now was painful. The picturesque sunrise he'd created reminded him of one person and it wasn't the soon-to-be owner of the board.

Maeve.

Everything he'd done had been with her in mind. With their future in mind. And because of one...alright...*two* mistakes, she was willing to throw it all away.

A sudden burst of righteous anger made him want to grab a tool and destroy the board, but instead of giving into the impulse, Ethan held back, clenching and unclenching his fist. He didn't like anger. In fact, he avoided it like the plague.

His shoulders slumped and his chin fell to his chest. He hadn't avoided it this morning. He'd given into it, in a way that was out of character for him. He rubbed his aching forehead and shuffled to a chair. He was so tired. His head hurt, his entire body ached and his heart felt as if it would never beat normally again.

Rubbing the area did no good, but Ethan couldn't seem to stop himself from trying. This was why anger was so horrible. It caused people to say and do things they didn't mean. Maeve was angry, he was angry and now they'd separated and lost something Ethan had hoped to hold onto for the rest of his life.

He jumped when someone pounded at his door. Frowning, Ethan tried to figure out who would be coming to his work area this early on a Saturday morning. "Come in."

The latch turned and Gavin poked his head inside. "Hey."

Ethan fell back into his seat, suddenly feeling idiotic and vulnerable. Gavin had seen too much this morning and Ethan wasn't sure how to address it. "Hey."

Gavin walked farther inside, leaving the door open behind him. "I, uh...wanted to check on you."

Ethan gave a dark chuckle and spread his hands to the side. "As you can see, I'm just fine. It's Maeve who was injured."

Gavin rolled his eyes. "She might have been the one to go to the hospital, but she wasn't the only one hurt this morning."

Ethan groaned. "What do you want from me, Gavin? Are we having a girl chat here?"

Gavin's jaw clenched. "I'm sorry. I was under the impression we were friends."

Ethan blew out a breath, then leaned forward onto his knees, covering his face with his hands. "No...I'm sorry. We are friends."

A creaking stool let Ethan know his large friend had sat down. Gavin was a firefighter and looked the part with his large frame and defined muscles. The guys used to tease that he needed to model for romance novel covers, but Gavin paid them no mind. He was a simple guy, but very focused when he wanted something. He of all people would understand Ethan's dilemma.

"Do you want the short version or the long version?" Ethan asked wryly.

Gavin smirked. "What do you want to share?"

Ethan shrugged. "None of it. But misery loves company...or so they say."

"Then lay it on me."

Ethan spent the next twenty minutes spilling the whole story. All of it. He didn't hold anything back, including his frustration with how Maeve was reacting to the whole situation. "I thought we'd gotten over the trust thing," Ethan said as he wound up. "She said she was willing to wait and yet..." He splayed his hands to the side. "Look where that got us."

Gavin didn't speak for several moments. "She has a point."

Ethan jerked back. "Whoa, whoa, whoa. Aren't you supposed to be on my side?"

Gavin shrugged. "I'm friends with both of you," he said easily. "I'm not on anyone's side. I'm just telling you how I see it."

"And that is?"

"That you made a promise and broke it."

"Nice." Ethan leaned back, crossing one leg over the other. "So you're also going to hold my teenage years against me."

"I'm not talking about when you were young," Gavin said. "But I think you've let the board blindside you. I heard what you and Maeve said to each other this morning. Honestly, I think you're both being idiots."

"But you still think it's all my fault."

Gavin sighed and tilted his head. "No, Ethan. I'm not saying it's all your fault. I'm simply saying she wasn't wrong in accusing you of breaking a promise. You promised you'd be there this morning. You weren't. That means you broke your word. So can you really blame her for being hurt?"

"But what about my business? My board? Would you be willing to ask a woman to marry you if you had nothing to your name but an old house your parents left you in their will?"

Gavin scratched at his chin. "I think you're missing the point." Standing up, he walked back to the door. "I'm sorry you two are fighting. But if you want to have any chance of getting back together, one of you needs to be humble enough to actually apologize and own up to what you did."

The giant was gone before Ethan could come up with a response. Shaking his head, Ethan snorted. Gavin had no idea what he was talking about. The man had never been in love. Had never been planning to ask a woman to marry him. He was just a guy who put out fires.

"Well, he can't put this one out," Ethan grumbled. Standing up, he checked on Tox, who was digging up a spot in the backyard, and walked back over to the surfboard. As of this point in time, it was all he had left. "You'll live," he told himself. "You did before and you can do it again."

Only this time...I won't follow her around like a lovesick puppy dog, waiting for any crumbs she sends my way.

Grabbing the can of resin, Ethan put on his gloves and mask and got to work. The sooner he finished, the sooner he would see his business take off. And the sooner his business took off, the sooner he could leave Seagull Cove behind. There was nothing left for him here.

CHAPTER 23

Maeve finished putting the last of her numbers into the spreadsheet, then leaned back with a sigh. She wanted to bang her head against the desk, but considering the bruising that was already there, it would do far more harm than good.

Something had to give. She'd been dragging herself around for a week since the latest surfing incident and she knew she was getting on her family's nerves. She was getting on her own nerves! But she didn't know how to break free of the depression that had enveloped her.

It was like life had lost its color. For the first time ever, Maeve hated going to work. She didn't want to be in the office. She didn't want to be stuck behind a computer. And even the joy of how well the numbers came together meant nothing to her. She'd been spending enough time alone that at some point, she'd begun naming the dust bunnies in the corner of the office.

She felt like a volcano ready to erupt and knew that if she didn't snap out of it soon, she'd do something stupid.

Yeah...like go crawling back to Ethan. The man who hasn't bothered to call or text or apologize!

"That's it." Slamming her laptop shut, she stuffed all her things in her bag, grabbed her keys and headed out. Aspen was singing and dancing while she worked on her latest creations and it made it easy for Maeve to disappear out the back door with no one being the wiser.

The wind was whipping today and she pulled her jacket closer around her body, trying to shield it, but the cold seemed to go straight through the fabric. Fall was truly here and she was going to have to pull out the winter clothes.

The thought of a long, gray winter only made Maeve more depressed. She didn't want endless cold and wet. She wanted sunshine and happiness. Two things that seemed completely out of reach in her life.

The ride home was short, but Maeve was still ready to be out of the car by the time she got there. Maybe she would get a heavier coat and take a walk on the beach. Anything that might help her shake the incessant dreariness that was following her every footstep.

"Who's home?" her mother called when she came in the front door.

"It's me, Mom," Maeve answered.

Mom came out from the kitchen, wiping her hands on a towel. "What brings you home so early?"

"I finished," Maeve said bluntly.

Mom put her hands on her hips. "When are you going to forgive that boy and move on?"

Maeve rolled her eyes. The last thing she needed was to hear another lecture from her mother. "He's not a boy, Mom." It was the only thing she could think to say that wouldn't get her in trouble. Every single person in her family was on Ethan's side and it was ticking Maeve off. When was she going to be important enough to care about?

Ethan cared more about his surfboards and everyone else cared more about Ethan. She was the one who had been hurt! Twice! But no one cared about her side of the story. They all just thought she was holding onto a grudge and it wasn't fair.

"Little Mae?" her father called out. "Why don't you come sit with me."

Maeve pressed her lips together. "I thought I might take a walk."

There was a creaking sound and her dad shuffled into the front entry room. "I'll go with you."

"No...Dad, you don't have to do that," Maeve argued. She knew her father wouldn't handle a walk well. At least not a long one. Plus, she didn't want to keep discussing the situation with Ethan.

"I know I don't have to," he said with a grin. "I want to."

Hammering rang through the house, shaking the walls a little. Maeve hadn't even been paying attention to the construction going on, she was so focused on how angry she was.

"I need a break from the noise," her dad continued.

"Anthony," Mom said softly. "I don't know if that's a good idea."

Dad kissed Mom's cheek. "We'll be back soon." He turned to his daughter. "How's the weather out there?"

"Cold."

"Good. It'll get the heart pumping." Heading toward the front closet, he pulled out a coat and offered it to Maeve before getting his own.

Maeve didn't know what to say, so she followed along, pouting but compliant.

"You be careful with him," Mom whispered, grabbing Maeve's arm.

Maeve nodded. She knew exactly what her mother meant, but the pain of watching her strong dad breaking down was more than her fragile emotions could handle at the moment. "We won't go far."

"Thank you." Mom kissed her cheek and went back to the kitchen.

Maeve walked beside her father, her hands stuffed in her pockets to stay warm, as they worked their way down the sidewalk. She wasn't going to be the first one to break the silence. If he wanted to talk, he'd have to take charge.

Unfortunately, her father had never been one to back down from a hard issue.

"Do you love him?"

"Dad..."

"It's a simple question, Little Mae."

Maeve sighed. "It doesn't matter if I love him. I can't trust him."

"Because he wasn't there to save you."

She kicked at a rock, but didn't answer.

"Well, if you're kicking liars out of your life, are you going to stop talking to me as well?"

Maeve's head jerked in his direction. "What are you talking about?"

"When you had strep throat as a child, I told you the medicine tasted like candy."

Maeve chuckled. "I hardly think that counts, Dad."

"And when you did your hair for the first time as a teenager, I told you it looked just like the woman in the magazine you were trying to copy." He leaned over. "Spoiler alert...it didn't."

Maeve huffed. "It's not the same."

Dad stopped walking and Maeve had to turn to face him. "I also promised you that I would be around to walk you down the aisle and teach your children how to mold chocolate into shapes."

The words fell like an atomic bomb between them. They hurt. Far worse than the cut on Maeve's forehead, and yet she had no way to argue. He *had* promised those things, and yet life had a funny way of changing things. The odds of him having that opportunity were growing slimmer every day and it was slowly eating the Harrison family alive.

"He's human, Little Mae," her dad whispered. "He's good and strong and yet he's flawed. He made those promises with every intention of keeping them, but fate had other plans." He stepped forward, bringing them toe to toe. Using his knuckle, he raised her chin until she met his eyes. "Despite what I said when you were younger, I won't always be here and there's no one else I would trust with your heart than Ethan Markle. A man who will love a woman from a distance, for as long as he has, is worth fighting for."

Maeve's eyes were filled with tears. She'd cried more than her fair share in the last week. "He hurt me," she whispered thickly.

Dad nodded. "And you hurt him. I'm hurting my whole family, including the woman I pledged my life to and yet no one has cast me aside."

Maeve stepped back and wiped at her eyes. "No one blames you."

"Ethan messed up, Mae. I'm not condoning what he did, but if what you've told us is the truth, then he had good intentions, but terrible execution. We're all learning as we go, don't blame him for needing a few lessons now and then."

Maeve didn't have a response for that. Her father turned back toward the house.

"I think we earned some hot chocolate, huh?"

She laughed softly, despite the tears and pain. "Don't you ever get tired of chocolate?"

Reaching out, he took his daughter's hand, cradling it with shaking fingers as he led her back. "Not yet, though there might come that day. But one thing I'll never get tired of or regret is spending time with those I love. They will always be my greatest source of joy."

*****

Ethan sat at his desk, staring at the blank computer screen. It had gone to sleep several minutes before and he hadn't bothered to wake it back up. He knew what he would see. Surfing competition updates that would let him keep track of how Ollie was doing.

The kid was proving his worth and apparently Ethan's board wasn't too shabby either, since every single interviewer had asked about the unique design.

Ethan knew he was watching the very beginnings of his dreams come true. Within the next few days, he'd be able to see his website hits and social media views skyrocket.

And yet I'm sitting here feeling sorry for myself.

He looked around his office, noting all the awards and pictures he'd surrounded himself by. At one point in his life, he'd been proud of those accomplishments. They were the reason he'd started his surfing business. He loved it. He loved everything about it. He'd spent his youth learning how to surf and his adulthood teaching others. He should, by all accounts, be elated.

So why did he feel dead inside? Why was his mind on the one thing that slipped through his fingers, rather than the thousand things that already had or were about to go right?

Someone knocked on the front door of the shop and Ethan forced himself to stand up. He had officially closed for the season, but every once in a while, someone would drop by for a particular item.

Michael, Maeve's cousin, was standing outside the glass door, peering in. "Ethan? You in there?" he shouted.

Ethan paused in the shadows. Michael didn't surf. He definitely wasn't there to grab some more wax or to repair an ankle strap.

Michael pounded again. "Ethan?"

Tox came snuffling up to Ethan's feet. Upon seeing Michael, he barked, racing toward the glass.

"Guess the cat's out of the bag now." Ethan pushed his feet into action. He waved when Michael spotted him, and unlocked the door. "Michael," Ethan said by way of greeting.

"Hey, thanks for letting me in," Michael said, rubbing his arms. He was wearing a long sleeved, button down dress shirt and it did little to combat the cool fall breeze of the ocean.

"Of course." Ethan stepped back and put his hands on his hips. "What's up?"

Michael took a deep breath, paused, then took another breath.

Ethan rolled his eyes. "Did Maeve send you?"

"Are you kidding? She'd kill me if she knew I was here."

"Then why did you come?" Ethan narrowed his eyes as a thought came to mind. "You've been talking to Gavin." Like Ethan, Michael and Gavin had both grown up in Seagull Cove and had been friends for a long time. This was the problem with a large group of friends...they always passed news down the grapevine.

Michael shrugged. "I heard a few things."

Shaking his head, Ethan turned and walked away.

"Hey, wait up."

Tox growled and Ethan glanced back to see Michael glaring at the dog. "Watch out," Ethan joked. "He bites."

"I'll bet he does," Michael muttered before following Ethan to the back.

"Should I be expecting a cousin beat-down?" Ethan asked as he flung himself into his seat. "Since Antonio isn't here, you're going to beat me up instead?"

Michael chuckled and took the seat across the desk. "Yeah...I think we both know that's not happening." Michael's lean, runner-style build was quite a bit different from Ethan's broader muscles. While neither of them could compete with Mason or Gavin, Michael definitely wasn't built to take on Ethan's athletic frame.

Ethan shrugged. "With the way I'm feeling, I might just let you do it."

Michael tapped his fingers on the arm of his chair.

"Why are you looking at me like I'm one of your students?" Ethan asked.

Michael shook his head. "I'm just trying to understand what's going on in that hard noggin of yours."

"Noggin? Really?"

Michael grinned. "Sorry. A hazard of the job."

Ethan snorted. "Well, very little is going on in this *noggin,* as you put it. It's too full of misery and despair." He raised an eyebrow. "How was that?"

"Not bad. Let's write it down and I'll add it to next year's curriculum."

That made Ethan grin. It had been a long time since he'd done that and it felt sort of foreign. "What do you want from me, Michael?"

"Nothing," Michael assured him. "I want to see if I can help."

"How would you help?" Ethan asked. "Your cousin hates my guts."

"And why is that?"

Ethan huffed. "You know why. I let her down...again." He shoved his finger toward the back workspace. "I spent every waking minute, and more than a few of the ones that I should have been sleeping, trying to build a surfboard for a client that would change the course of this shop. And do you know why?"

Michael waited patiently.

"Because with every moment of sleep I lost, every bite of food I didn't take, every minute I didn't get to hold Maeve, I told myself it would be worth it. It would be worth it because when all was said and done, that board was going to be the jumping point for this shop and never again would I be barely paying the bills. I couldn't afford to barely pay the bills because my hope had been to take on the responsibility of another person." He leaned back. "I was planning for our future," he said hoarsely. "And when all that sacrifice caught up to me, Maeve threw me to the sharks."

Michael still didn't say anything and Ethan began to feel that anger he'd been struggling with for the week build again. "Well?" he demanded. "Aren't you going to tell me how stupid I was? How I shouldn't have put the shop before Maeve? How I shouldn't have pinned everything on one single moment in time?"

"Why?" Michael asked. "It seems like you're already doing that yourself."

Ethan blew out a disgusted huff.

"Did your client like the board?"

Ethan frowned. What was Michael getting at? Why wasn't he lecturing or trying to convince Ethan of how stupid he'd been? "Yeah. He's using it in the Ventura Open today."

"And how's he doing?"

"Good."

Michael nodded. "Glad to hear it. So, I'm guessing that'll mean more business for you."

Ethan shrugged. "By all accounts...yeah."

Michael smiled. "Congrats! Maybe this means you can finally stop strapping on a construction hat during the cold months."

Ethan didn't respond. He still couldn't figure out what Michael was trying to do.

Michael slapped his arm rests. "Well, I better get back. School got out early today, but I have a huge stack of papers to grade this weekend."

"I don't get it," Ethan muttered.

Michael paused at the office door and raised his eyebrows.

"I don't get why you came. You haven't offered any condolences or arguments or advice or anything else."

Michael hesitated and shifted his weight. "I guess I just wanted to see if you were the same."

Ethan's eyebrows furrowed. "The same?"

Michael nodded. "The same as Maeve. She's just as defensive and miserable as you are, and while I've got some pretty good ideas about why you're both acting so dramatically, the more I listen, the more I figure you probably need to come to the answer on your own." He nodded. "See ya. Oh! And good luck with the board. I hope it works out exactly the way you wanted."

CHAPTER 24

Maeve dropped her father off at the house, passed on the hot chocolate, then left again almost immediately. She couldn't seem to get her dad's words out of her head and the implication behind them.

He's not going to be around.

He's going to die.

And all he wants is to spend time with those he loves.

This time her feet took her toward the boardwalk and she sat down on a bench. Only a few days ago she had been nearby, crashing her head against a surfboard in a weird attempt to live life at its fullest.

Leaning forward, elbows on her knees, Maeve shook her head at her stupidity. How had she ever thought that surfing was going to be the key to it all? Why had she settled on that moment in time over another?

Because it was something you were afraid of.

"Hey, Maeve!"

Maeve jerked her head up. "Oh, hi Riley." This was the problem with living in a small town. No place was safe. No matter where a person went, they ran into someone they knew. In this case, Riley had obviously decided the boardwalk was the perfect place to walk the dogs for the afternoon, since she had at least six leashes in her hands.

The dogs yipped and barked, a couple of them coming over to get in Maeve's face for a hello. Smiling a little, Maeve tried to pet each of them, but the wriggling mass made it difficult.

"Ignore them," Riley said. "They're all a bunch of needy animals."

Maeve's laughter grew. "At least they go after what they want," she said without thinking of the underlying meaning in those words.

"As opposed to people?" Riley offered.

Maeve stiffened. "Does everybody know?"

Riley shrugged, adjusting the leashes as the dogs tugged at her. "Probably. I mean, Gavin was there, your sister's cake shop is the hot spot in town and everybody knows everybody. How could they not?"

Maeve groaned and let her head fall back. "What am I supposed to do, Ri? It's all such a mess."

"First, you can stand up and take half of these dogs. They're driving me crazy."

Reluctantly, Maeve stood up and helped. She really wasn't in the mood for it, but what was she supposed to say?

"Now we walk," Riley continued.

There was silence for several minutes between the two women and Maeve thought maybe the subject wouldn't come up again, something which made her feel equal parts grateful and frustrated. She really had no idea what to do. Her family said forgive him, her heart said take him back, but her mind said he had his chance. How many chances were too many? Yes, they all made mistakes, but were all mistakes created equal? Weren't his fairly big ones?

"The real question is...what do you *want* to do?" Riley offered, as if she'd been reading Maeve's thoughts.

Maeve glanced over at her friend. "What if what I want and what's right are two different things?"

Riley shrugged. "Are they?"

Maeve thought about it. "I don't know," she answered honestly. "I'm torn between a couple of...emotions? Ideas? Principles?"

Riley nodded. "Sounds hard."

Maeve snorted. "You could say that."

"But seriously...forget what everyone else has said," Riley pressed. "Forget what you think is right or what you think your Sunday School teacher would say. What do you *want*? Like, deep in your heart. What do you want?"

It took Maeve longer this time. Riley was trying to help her without simply telling her to take Ethan back, which Maeve appreciated. And since Maeve couldn't seem to find her footing on her own, she found herself wanting to follow through. She thought of her emotional struggles, of Ethan's excuses, of her father's lesson. What did she want? Deep down in the very depths of her soul?

"I want Ethan," she whispered hoarsely.

"Well, then," Riley said breezily, as if it were no big deal. "Go get him."

Maeve chuckled darkly. "It's not that easy. I can't just...I mean...even if I can forgive him, I said some horrible things. He'll never take me back."

"Maybe he feels the same way."

"And maybe he doesn't."

"There's only one way to find out," Riley continued.

Maeve rolled her eyes. "Riley, you know I love you, but it's easy to tell me to go get him back when it's not your heart involved."

Riley smiled. "I know. But how much worse can it hurt than it does now? If he says no, you're not out anything but your time. If he says yes, then...well..." Riley shrugged. "All's well that ends well."

Maeve contemplated that. It was true. She was already hurting. Would it really hurt worse to have him turn her down? That little voice in the back of her head that had guided her for the last eight years had a very eager answer.

Yes.

"I...I think I'm afraid," Maeve whispered.

Riley stopped, tugging on the dogs to do the same. When Maeve stopped as well, Riley stepped forward and wrapped her arms around Maeve. "Fear is a cold bedfellow," Riley whispered in Maeve's ear. "Don't let it win."

With one arm stretched out against the leashes, Maeve gripped her friend in the other. Riley was tall and thin, a direct contrast to

Maeve's own short build, but the willowy woman felt strong and solid. Her hug was exactly what Maeve needed and her words were even better.

For the second time in her life, she began to feel a determination to overcome her fears. She'd done it once before. Back when she threw away her glasses and planned a life list. But this was different. Maeve didn't want to stay in the shadows being safe anymore, but she also didn't need a list.

She needed her people.

She needed her dad's advice. She needed her mother's baking. She needed Aspen's cakes. She needed Estelle's blunt scoldings. She needed her friends' support. But most importantly, she needed Ethan. She needed his kisses and his touch and the opportunity to learn together what they needed as a couple. He didn't know how much she needed his time. She hadn't known how much he needed his business.

They had so much to learn and it would never happen if she kept running when things got hard.

Maeve pulled back and sniffed. Her mind felt much lighter and her direction more clear. She wasn't sure how she was going to get Ethan to forgive her, but there had to be a way. "Thanks," she said to Riley. "I think I needed that."

Riley grinned. "Are you ready to get your man back?"

Maeve nodded.

"Then let's drop the pooches off and meet at the shop. Sugar always does wonders for my brainstorming."

Maeve laughed softly. "Sounds like a plan."

*****

Ethan sat in his chair as Michael left, his mind churning over everything his friend had shared. Maeve was still upset. Michael had said she was *miserable*.

Tox came over, sniffing at the chair, and Ethan absentmindedly picked up the dog, setting him in his lap and scratching behind the pup's ears.

"She's miserable, Tox," Ethan muttered. "By all accounts, I should be happy she's having a hard time. So why does it make me feel worse?"

He didn't like the idea of Maeve hurting. Logically, he'd known she had been physically hurt. But she'd been so angry that Ethan hadn't truly considered that their breakup would leave her feeling bad. After all, it was Maeve who initiated it. Didn't that mean she'd be relieved? Or grateful, even, to be rid of him?

Tox settled into a ball of fluff and began to snore, causing Ethan to smile. It was funny how everything in his life, the dog included, came back to Maeve. The design on the board. The puppy's name. Ethan had done a wonderful job of surrounding himself with all things Maeve.

"Dude!"

Ethan's head jerked toward the door. Tox barked, the sound having woken him up. "Back here, Jayden."

The sound of flip flops against the wood floors could be heard getting closer as Jayden came to the back. He poked his head inside. "Hiding?"

Ethan chuckled. "I just narrowly avoided getting beat up by your cousin. What makes you think I was hiding?"

Jayden grinned and pounded one fist against the other. "Ready for round two?"

"Bring it on."

Jayden chuckled as he walked to seat and plopped down. "So I guess I don't have to give you any kind of a lecture about hurting my family, then, huh? Michael did it for me?"

"How did you know it was Michael?"

"Lucky guess."

Ethan shook his head. "You can deliver the speech if you want. Michael didn't give me much of one. Mostly he listened to me bawl my guts out like a baby."

Jayden rubbed his chin. "Yeah...he has this weird ability to listen. I have no idea what that's like."

Ethan smiled, but didn't respond.

"So...what are you going to do to win my other cousin back?"

Ethan's eyebrows went up. "You want me to get her back?"

"Don't you want to?" Jayden asked. "I would think this whole brooding routine is a clear sign that you want her."

"I'm not brooding."

"Man, you are so brooding."

Ethan scowled and Jayden pointed at his face.

"See? Point made."

Ethan rolled his eyes. "Not. Brooding."

Jayden put up his hands. "Fine. Call it what you want. But it still looks to me like you want her back." He leaned forward. "Funny thing is though, I'm wondering why none of us ever saw you two together. The family grapevine said you were dating, but not once have I seen you two around."

Ethan's eyes dropped to his suddenly very fascinating desk. "Yeah, well..."

"Oh, this oughta be good."

Ethan gave Jayden a severe look. "You're right. Michael was better at listening."

Jayden grinned unrepentantly. "But I'm better at problem solving."

"And what problem are we solving?"

"Dude, you're thick in the head or something." Jayden opened his eyes wide. "How. To. Get. Her. Back."

Ethan slumped in his seat. "She won't take me, Jay. I've let her down twice now."

He shrugged, not the least bit concerned. "I've let her down more than that and she still loves me, so it stands to reason she loves you too."

Ethan snorted. "If only it were that easy."

"Do you love her?"

Ethan nodded.

"Is your business more important to you than her?"

Ethan wanted to be offended at the accusation, but he knew where the question was coming from, so he chose to shake his head. "You know me better than that."

"I know that you've wanted this business since we were kids, but you didn't see Maeve as a viable girlfriend until we were teenagers," Jayden said in an uncharacteristically serious tone. "Since Tone isn't here, I'll ask again. Is your business more important?"

"I was sacrificing our time to save my business so that I could propose to her and have something worthwhile behind me," Ethan said in a steely tone. "I was never trying to put it first. I was trying to secure our future."

Jayden relaxed and nodded. "I had hoped it was something like that, but no one was really sure."

"That's because you're all on Mae's side," Ethan muttered.

"Wrong!" Jayden shouted, causing Tox to bark again. "From what I understand, her whole family is rooting for her to quit being an idiot and take you back."

"She's not an idiot," Ethan shot back. "I hurt her. She has every right to be upset."

"And now you're going to apologize and we'll get that wedding back on track."

Ethan pushed a hand through his hair, then set Tox on the ground. "She thinks she can't trust me."

"So show her she can."

"How?"

Jayden pursed his lips and tilted his head. "Good question." He slapped his knees. "This might require a little food for thought." Standing, he made his way to the door before pausing. "Coming?"

Ethan was so confused. Jayden seemed to jump around in his thoughts without worrying about the fact that everyone else couldn't follow. "Where're we going?"

"The cake shop," he replied. "I need food if I'm going to have to think this hard." He winked. "Don't they say the way to a man's heart is through his stomach?"

"I'm not trying to win your heart," Ethan muttered, shoving Jayden playfully.

"Good thing." Jayden shivered dramatically. "You're so not my type. I don't go for brooders." Laughing, he raced through the shop, making sure to stay out of Ethan's reach. "Come on. I think Aspen has a new flavor this week."

"Aspen always has a new flavor."

"Which is why we should go there more often."

Ethan shook his head, but he was smiling. Jayden was a good guy, and Ethan appreciated the help, but he seriously had his doubts about whether or not there was any hope of getting Maeve back. It had taken her eight years last time to forgive him. Could he wait another eight?

He scooped up Tox and locked up the shop. He didn't have the answer to his questions, but sitting around...*brooding*...wasn't helping either. At least he'd get a good slice of cake out of the trip, even if the one thing he really wanted was out of reach.

CHAPTER 25

"Riley," Maeve muttered as she looked at the crowd. "I really don't want to be here."

Riley waved a dismissive hand in the air. "They'll clear out soon. Don't worry about it. We can sit in the Double A corner, or we can go in the back if it's too much for you."

Maeve kept her head ducked. She knew all too well that she and Ethan were the hot topic throughout the town right now. Her family couldn't talk about anything else, and they were far too prominent in town for the breakup to go unnoticed, not to mention Ethan was a pet favorite of old ladies and the envy of every teenage boy in town.

She was sure she could feel everyone's eyes on her and it made Maeve want to run.

Because you're scared.

She sighed at the words. She really didn't want to examine just how many habits in her life were because of fear. The more she understood how heavy it had been, the more she knew she'd discover. She wanted to shake it off and move on, but Maeve was sure that at some point in time, she was going to have to come to grips with it.

She led a structured life. A safe life. And honestly, Maeve didn't truly want to turn a one-eighty, she simply didn't want to keep running from the people most important to her. She had finally figured out what her dad meant in his little chat that wasn't a lecture, but was kind of a lecture. He'd been telling her she would regret losing Ethan. Life is short. Anthony Harrison was a prime example. A man who should be in the very best years of his life was instead slowly wasting away. But of everything he'd built, his lesson to her had been that the people were the most important. They would be his regret, not the loss of his career or his fame. Not the inability to work with chocolate or travel the world. But the kids he'd helped raise and the grandchildren he would probably never see.

Estelle's words came back to her and Maeve was starting to think her older sister's harsh words were right. She needed help. Professional help. It wasn't right for her to be so frightened and struggle so much to trust and grow. Her little incident as a teen had scarred her and she wasn't going to be able to overcome it on her own.

If Maeve threw away her opportunity to be with the man who held her heart, she would also have regrets, but it would be at her own hand, instead of a cruel twist of fate. Dad couldn't help his disease, but Maeve could fix her situation with Ethan.

As long as he's willing, she reminded herself. She'd been pretty horrible to him and had put her own wants above his needs. If only she'd been willing to be a little patient. If she'd waited for him to surf. Or waited for him to finish the board before demanding more of his time.

Her eyes stung slightly, but Maeve blinked it away. She needed to make a plan to move forward. The past would be addressed in its own time.

"What do you want?" Riley asked, her eyes on the bakery case.

Maeve shrugged. "Whatever."

"I've heard the lemon poppy seed is to die for," Riley gushed.

Maeve gave her friend a look. "They're all to die for, Ri. This is Aspen's shop."

Riley cackled and rubbed her hands together. "I know. Isn't it awesome?"

Maeve finally focused on Riley, who looked like a kid in a candy store, which she sort of was. "Why are you so excited about this? You've eaten your body weight in Aspen's desserts."

Riley shrugged. "Can't I get excited once in a while? About something that doesn't need to be walked twice a day, or fed constantly?"

Maeve laughed. "You're describing men and dogs."

Riley joined in. "That's probably a little too true. Ooh, look. It's our turn." Riley stepped up to the counter and smiled at the teenager.

Maeve waited until it was her turn. Apparently, Estelle wasn't working today. Maeve hadn't been paying attention to her sister's work schedule as of late. "I'll have the Chocolate Tsunami," Maeve said to Anna.

"That's my fav," Anna gushed. She tilted her head. "You look a lot like Estelle..."

Maeve gave her a tight smile. "We're sisters."

"Oh! You must be the one who works in the back office. The accountant?"

Maeve nodded. "That's me."

"Do you still want me to ring up the purchase?" Anna asked with a frown. "Don't you get your cake for free?"

"It's okay to ring it up," Maeve told her. "It'll make the numbers easier. If I'd taken it straight from the back, I wouldn't have worried about it."

"Gotcha." The young helper finished the transactions and Maeve took her plate and followed Riley, who was busy texting. "Now where? This place is a madhouse today."

"It always is in the afternoons," Riley muttered, her eyes still on the phone screen. "You just don't see it because you're in the back."

"Which is where I'm going now," Maeve responded. "There's no way I'm sitting out in this crowd when there's a nice, quiet office in the back."

"Just...a...sec..." Riley finished whatever she was working on and stuffed the phone back in her pocket. "Great. Let's go."

Maeve guided them around the counter and into the kitchen area.

"Maeve!" Aspen hollered. "You coming to help?"

Maeve shook her head. "Nope. We're gonna eat in the office."

Aspen waved at Riley. "I'll stop by later," Aspen said. "When I finish frosting this red velvet."

Maeve headed to her office and stepped inside, sighing in relief at the decrease in chaos. The kitchen hadn't been much better than the front, since Aspen often listened to loud music while she worked. "So much better."

"Oh, shoot," Riley muttered, looking around. "I forgot napkins. Be right back."

Maeve headed to her chair, relaxing in it as she waited for Riley. After a minute, she started to nibble on her cake. "Geez, she's taking a long time." Five more minutes went by and Riley still hadn't returned.

Standing up, Maeve headed to the door to check on her friend, but when she tugged on the handle, it wouldn't budge. "What?" Maeve jerked it again, but the door wouldn't move. "Hello?" Maeve pounded on the door. She checked her pockets and then groaned when she realized she hadn't brought her keys. The office had originally been a store room which locked from the outside when their father had used the building. During the renovation, the girls hadn't bothered to change the knob, assuming it wouldn't matter.

Well, it matters now, Maeve thought angrily. She pounded on the door. "Aspen? Riley? Can anyone hear me?"

Several more minutes of pounding yielded no results and Maeve finally gave up. She stormed back to her seat, sat down and stuffed some cake in her mouth. She was definitely going to give Riley what-for when she got back. Locking Maeve in her own office was a low blow. "But the real question is...why?" Maeve muttered around a mouthful of cake.

Stabbing another piece, she tried to drown her frustration in sugar and chocolate and ignore the fact that yet another person in her life had betrayed her.

*****

"Have you tried the lemon poppy seed yet?" Jayden asked as they stepped inside the crowded shop. He put the phone he'd been fiddling with in his back pocket.

Ethan shook his head and eyed the interior. "Geez, it's crowded today."

"You're just spoiled because Maeve usually brings it home to you."

Ethan punched Jay's arm good naturedly. "Like you're one to talk. You get way more cake than I do."

Jayden just grinned and shrugged. "Family privilege."

"Hey, guys."

"Riley," Ethan said with a smile. He nodded at Tox in his arms. "Any chance you've found a home for the little guy here?"

"I have," Riley said with a too-wide grin.

"Not happening, Ri," Ethan warned her.

Riley clasped her hands at her chin, her blue eyes extra wide. "You need him! He needs you! Would you really want me to take him back so he can live his life in a cage and someday be euthanized?"

Ethan rolled his eyes. "You don't euthanize."

"But what if I have to? What if the government takes over and I don't have control anymore?"

"Riley," Ethan said firmly. "I'm a bachelor and a business owner. A long term commitment isn't what we talked about."

She pouted like a champ. "Just a little longer?"

Ethan pointed a finger at her. "Two weeks. That's it. Find him a home in two weeks."

She waved him off and turned back to Jayden. "I just came from the kitchen. It's a lot quieter back there. I'll bet Aspen would let you sit in the office if you want."

"Sweet." Jayden gave Riley a fist bump. "Dude, let's get out orders and go back."

Ethan handed Tox to Riley. "Here. You can handle him for a bit. I probably shouldn't have brought him inside at all."

"Hey, baby," Riley cooed, holding the panting dog up to her face. "Wanna go for a run in the park?" Her voice was high and excited as if she were talking to a baby.

Ethan just shook his head as he watched her walk out of the shop, still talking to the dog. "Sometimes I think she's got it right," he said in an aside to Jayden. "Dogs are easier than people." He paused. "And other times I think she's crazy."

Jayden snorted a laugh. "Sounds about right. Come on. Let's get in line."

It took fifteen minutes to get up to the counter and order their desserts.

"To the office!" Jayden said, leading the way into the back. "Hey, Aspen!"

Aspen smiled widely and waved. Her hands and arms and apron were covered with green frosting. "Enjoy!"

Jayden gave her a salute and Ethan smiled. He'd been a little nervous about coming back. He hadn't spoken to a single member of the Harrison family since his and Maeve's breakup. Though Jay had said they were on his side, Ethan had worried Aspen would say something to the contrary.

They made it to the office without any snarky comments, however, and Jayden waved Ethan forward. "After you."

Ethan shook his head. "How chivalrous."

"I try."

He pushed open the door and stepped inside, only to come to a screeching halt.

"Don't let it close!" Maeve shouted, practically jumping over her desk.

"What? Oof!" He stumbled and almost dropped his cake when Maeve pushed him to the side.

Maeve pounded on the door. "Jayden Gordon. You traitor! Open this door right now!"

"Work it out, Maeve!" Jayden shouted back. "For everyone's sake. Work it out."

Maeve let her forehead fall against the door. "Ow."

"I'm so lost."

Turning, she shot him a glare. "Our friends...AND FAMILY!" she shouted toward the door. "Have locked us in here."

Ethan stared until the words penetrated. He couldn't have heard her right. "Locked us in? From the outside?"

She pinched her lips and folded her arms over her chest. "It used to be a storeroom."

Lunging forward to set his plate on the desk, Ethan came back and tried the knob. Cursing under his breath, he turned back to Maeve. "I have the distinct feeling we've been had."

"To say the least." Maeve went back to her chair and fell into it.

Ethan hesitantly sat across from her.

"Now what?"

He put an ankle on his knee. "Now what what? What do you want to do?"

Maeve opened her mouth, but hesitated. "I...I guess I need to talk to you, but I don't like being forced into it."

"Do you *want* to talk to me? Or just need to?"

"Aren't they the same thing?"

Ethan shook his head. "Nope. I won't force you to talk to me. I would never do that." *I would think you'd know that by now.* Why did it feel like Maeve was undercutting his worth at every turn?

She closed her eyes and hung her head. "I'm sorry, Ethan." Those golden eyes finally met his and the heaviness of the remorse immediately caught his attention. "That wasn't fair of me. I know you won't force me to do anything and I shouldn't have acted like you will. I'm just…" She blew out a breath. "The truth is, I was planning what I was going to do in order to get you to talk to me, but being locked in this room was definitely not part of the plan."

Ethan put one ankle over the opposite knee. "You wanted to talk to me?"

She nodded. "I wanted to ask forgiveness."

"I thought you just did."

"Not for that," she grumbled. "I wanted to say I'm sorry that I was so horrible at the beach."

Ethan just stared. Here he'd been blaming it all on himself, but now it sounded like Maeve was doing the same thing. He began to chuckle and the sound grew, causing Maeve to furrow her brows.

"So…that's funny? That I was a jerk?"

Ethan shook his head. "No…it just made me realize that sometimes we're more alike than we are different."

"How so?"

He leaned onto his elbow. "Little Mae…I was actually coming to the shop to work out with Jayden how I was going to win you back and apologize for everything I did that drove you away."

"So we were both coming to do the same thing?"

"Sounds like it."

"But my stupid cousin and ex-friend locked us in together."

"About sums it up."

Maeve shook her head and whistled low. "I guess they didn't want us to waste any more time." She frowned. "I wonder how long they've been planning this?"

Ethan shrugged. "I don't know. But I'm starting to think maybe we should take advantage of it."

Her eyes lit up. "You want to make up?"

He nodded slowly. "Yes. And I'll start by saying just how sorry I am."

CHAPTER 26

Too many emotions were bubbling just under the surface as Ethan talked. Maeve could barely distinguish one from another, but the strongest ones were love and hope. Of that she was certain.

Seeing him had been a bit of a slap in the face, especially after she realized he'd been tricked into being locked into the room as well. When she got out, she would have words with Jayden and his meddling ways.

And if Riley thinks I'll ever consider fostering a dog for her, she's dead wrong.

But the fact that both she and Ethan had come to the same conclusion about reconciling...well, it sent her dreams through the roof. Somehow, he must have missed her the same way she missed him, even though she'd been an absolute shrew. And she still needed to give him a proper apology, but she also didn't want to interrupt his own. It seemed they both had things to get off their chests.

"I'm sorry I wasn't there that morning," he continued. "I'm sorry I was oblivious eight years ago. I'm sorry I blew you off to go work on the board and that when you tried to tell me how you were feeling, I brushed it aside." He sighed and slumped in his seat. "I'm sorry it took you getting hurt and leaving me to make me realize just how stupid I'd been." He rubbed his chin, where several days' worth of whiskers were visible, even with their blond color. "I've lived by myself for quite a few years now, but I don't think I ever truly realized what it meant to be alone."

Maeve felt the sting of tears when his hazel eyes latched onto hers.

"I finally had a glimpse of what heaven was like," he said hoarsely. "And I blew it by working too hard to try to keep it."

Maeve blinked several times, opening and closing her mouth as she tried to figure out how to ask the right question before finally admitting, "I...I don't understand what you meant by that last part."

Ethan stood up and came around the desk. He offered his hand and Maeve prayed he wouldn't see how much hers was shaking when she reached out, closing their fingers around each other.

She stood and craned her neck to look up at him. Dropping her hand, he cupped her cheeks.

"I realized, after we started dating, just how little I had to offer this relationship," he said softly.

Maeve started to shake her head, but he cut off the movement.

"No. Hear me out." Ethan swallowed. "You're so beautiful. You're well educated, you're logical and you're a fantastic businesswoman. I'm..." He shrugged. "A surfer bum. I keep my business afloat, but I've never tried for more because I enjoy the pace at which it all moves. And this year it caught up to me. I flirt so much with the line that with one bad season, I nearly lost the shop."

"That's alright," Maeve assured him. "We can save it."

He chuckled and kissed the tip of her nose. "We did save it, but the prize wasn't worth the cost."

Maeve frowned. "I'm still lost."

"That board? You heard me at the beach about it being my ticket for success?"

She nodded.

"I pushed so hard and sacrificed our relationship because I knew that if the board got attention at the competition, my sales would go through the roof. And when my shop was a success, I could finally stand up to you as an equal, not some lazy surfer who couldn't support his family."

Her eyes widened. "Family?" she croaked.

Ethan smirked. "Eventually. But I knew I needed to have everything in place so that when the time was right, I'd be ready to go. So that board was more than a board." He brought their foreheads together. "It was my ticket to you."

"Ethan," she whispered thickly, a fat tear running down her cheek. "I've never cared that you enjoy a more laid back lifestyle. I wanted to help you save your shop because it was *yours*. It was important to you and that made it important to me, even though I hated to admit it in the beginning." She hiccuped a laugh and wiped at her face. "But I love my work and could easily expand without it being too much of a hassle. If we got married, you wouldn't have to change yourself or your business. If I married you, it'd be because I wanted *you*, the beach bum who adores his work, not this other person you think is more worthwhile."

"And that's why I love you," he said before sneaking a quick peck. "But it's not a matter of if," he corrected her with his signature cocky grin. "It's a matter of when."

Maeve playfully smacked his chest. "That's a bold claim. We've only been dating for a few weeks and as of five minutes ago, we were still broken up."

"But we've known each other for years," he corrected her. "Our get-to-know-you round is long gone. We can jump straight into can-this-work-for-the-long-term."

Maeve rolled her eyes. "You're ridiculous."

"And that's why you love me."

Maeve laughed softly and wrapped her arms around his torso, resting her head against his chest. "Maybe," she admitted. "But we can't move into any stage at all until I apologize as well."

Ethan squeezed her tight. "You don't need to apologize, sweetheart. I understand that I hurt you."

Maeve shook her head. "No. You didn't hurt me." She leaned her head back. "I hurt myself."

He frowned. "What?'

She pulled away completely, needing to stand on her own two feet in order to get the words out. "I...I've let fear win for so long," she admitted. "First, when I almost drowned back when we were teenagers. I let it ruin my life for years, convincing myself that if I gave in to my feelings for you, I would get hurt. I would regret it. I would be letting you get away with something horrible."

He pushed his hand through his hair and blew out a breath. "You weren't wrong," he said in a low tone.

"I was dead wrong," Maeve said fiercely, drawing his attention back. "You made a mistake, Ethan. You were young, I was young and we both made mistakes that day. But the biggest mistake of all was that I was unwilling to let go of it. My mistake became a festering wound and it's only grown heavier and more infected over the years."

Her legs were shaking and Maeve leaned back against her desk. She hadn't realized just how much it would take out of her to admit to all of this. She'd made a few first steps when she'd made that life list and thrown away her security glasses and started dating Ethan in the first place, but she hadn't truly cleansed the wound. She'd simply wiped at it, making it better for a few days, or weeks, but with the infection still simmering below the surface, it hadn't taken much for the worries and pain to come racing back, eager to take over their standard place as her default decision makers.

"The more I talk about it and realize just how deep it all goes," she said, her tone dropping into a whisper, "the more I think that I might actually need professional help. I think I'm broken." The words stung, but the ring of truth to them felt freeing. For the most part, Maeve knew she was a healthy, normal woman. But this situation, the memory of her near drowning, had traumatized her and she was tired of it. She wanted freedom, and her break up with Ethan had shown her that she couldn't do it on her own.

*****

Ethan tucked Maeve under his chin, resting against her hair. "You're not broken," he assured her. "You're just a little bent. We can fix that." He leaned back just enough to look in her face. "We can totally fix that, together, with a therapist, or whatever you want." He wiped a tear with his thumb. His heart was about to break in half as he saw the anguish on her face. "If you'll have me, I'll be with you through it all, sweetheart. There's nowhere else I'd rather be."

"Even if I struggle for a while? Even if I get scared and don't want to do things?"

He shrugged. "Why would that matter? You said you loved the easy-going, non-ambitious me. Why can't I love the working-on-getting-better you?"

Maeve's face crumpled and she began to cry in earnest.

Ethan wrapped his arms fully around her and held on. She shook against his chest and her hands clung to his shirt, gripping tightly. He had no idea how much time had passed before her crying subsided, but the moment was so potent that when she pulled back, Ethan almost didn't let go.

He knew they'd just taken a step in their relationship, one that was much different than the others. They'd been attracted to each other for years, but misunderstandings and trauma had kept them apart. A topic they'd barely breached during their few weeks together.

This was something different. Both of them had just shared their deepest heartaches and pains and neither had gone screaming to the door, demanding to be let out. She'd stayed. She'd stayed and assured him that it didn't matter. He knew his business would be just fine. He already had proof of that with the hits on his social media during the surfing competition that afternoon.

But to know that she would have taken him, accepted him, *loved* him even without the business? Even without a way to take care of their future family? It meant more to him than he could say. And so when words failed him, Ethan had only one other way to express himself.

Reaching out, he grabbed the back of her neck and pulled their lips together. Maeve squeaked slightly, caught off guard, but didn't resist in the slightest. In fact, she stepped closer, reaching up on her tiptoes, and hung on his neck as if he were her lifeline.

Oh, how he'd missed this. Missed holding her and kissing her. A week was too long to go without his favorite activity. He couldn't get enough. His hand slid down her back and he pulled her in until there was no space between them. Tilting his head, he deepened the kiss, loving how she seemed just as eager as him to reconnect the bond they had broken.

"Knock, knock...oops." Jayden's deep voice chuckled.

Ethan pulled back, fighting with the desire to glare at Jayden. "What do you want, Jay?" he asked, his voice lower than normal. He couldn't take his eyes off Maeve. She was staring at him in wide-eyed wonder, as if she'd felt everything he'd been trying to convey through their kiss. Every ounce of love and support and gratefulness had apparently been received the way it had been intended.

"Uh..." Jayden chuckled again, the sound slightly uncomfortable. "Well, we were going to check to make sure you hadn't killed each other, but I didn't expect to find you practically eating my cousin. It's a bit disconcerting, actually."

Maeve rolled her eyes, finally turning to her family member. "Then close the door."

Jayden scrunched his nose. "I don't think I should. Your mom would boil me with her pasta if I left you two alone any longer."

Ethan sighed. Jay was right, but Ethan would never say it out loud. He was running high on adrenaline and hormones. It was probably best they weren't alone. "We'll have more of that later," he assured Maeve, who gave him a commiserating smile.

"I'll hold you to it."

"I won't let you down."

"Stop whispering sweet nothings and get out here," Jayden whined. "My ears can't handle it."

Ethan looked over to see his friend covering his ears like a child.

"You're a dork," Maeve said, though there was no bite in her tone.

"And you're an accountant," Jayden shot back.

Maeve paused at the doorway, frowning. "Since when is that an insult?"

Jayden shrugged. "Sitting behind a desk counting all day? Sounds like punishment to me."

She smacked his chest and Jayden rubbed the spot as if he'd actually been hurt. "Dude," he said to Ethan as he walked through the threshold. "Are you sure she's the one you want? Seems a bit violent to me."

"Not as violent as I'm gonna be in a second," Ethan threatened with a grin. "You locked us inside."

Jayden backed up with his hands up. "Someone had to take a stand. You were both miserable and nice talks from friends and family weren't working. So...drastic measures it was."

Maeve put her hands on her hips. "You wait until you fall for a girl. I'm so using this against you."

Jayden scratched his chin, his cheeks slightly pink. "Guess I'll have to be grateful that day'll never come, huh?"

Ethan flung his arm around Jayden's neck and gave him a half headlock, half hug. "Thanks, man."

Jayden straightened and smirked. "You're welcome." He looked around. "Where's your cake?"

"In the office, on the desk."

"Didn't you eat it?" Jayden asked, his jaw dropping.

"Uh...no?" Ethan's eyebrows shot up. "I was a little busy."

"Again! Not for my ears!" Jayden put his hands over his ears again and ran for the office, retrieving the uneaten cake. Smiling, he shoved a large bite in his mouth. "Never let a good piece of cake go to waste."

Ethan wrapped an arm around Maeve's waist. "Have it. I have something better."

"Awww..." Maeve said dramatically.

"Ewww," Jayden grumbled. He looked at his plate. "Don't worry. I think you're the superior specimen here."

"Talking to cake again, Jay?" Aspen asked as she walked in from the front of the shop. "We talked about that, right? It's not healthy."

"Don't listen to her," Jayden continued to his half eaten slice. "She doesn't know what she's talking about."

Aspen laughed, then turned to Ethan and Maeve. "So...we all better?"

Maeve huffed. "Pass it down the gossip chain. We're fine."

Aspen put her hands on her hips. "We were worried because we love you both. Don't be snarky. That's my job." She smiled, softening her scold, and walked over with her arms out, hugging her younger sister. "I'm happy for the two of you. You belong together."

Ethan accepted the hug when it came his way as well. "Thanks."

Pulling back, Aspen took a deep breath. "This calls for cake." She narrowed her gaze. "But something...different." Muttering to herself, she walked to the pantry.

"Better leave her be," Maeve said, tugging on Ethan's hand. "She's going to be testing things out until she figures out what she wants."

"Does this mean we're free to take a walk on the beach together?" She smiled and Ethan hurried his steps. Maeve and the ocean. Two of his favorite things. He glanced back at Jayden. "Coming?"

Jayden shook his head. "No way. Aspen's in a creative mood." He rubbed his hands together. "I'm sticking around for samples."

"He'll need an antacid after he's done," Maeve muttered.

"Then I suppose his punishment is just." Ethan entwined their fingers and took the lead, guiding Maeve out of the shop and into the partly sunny day. With his shop closed, the competition still in swing and his heart mending, Ethan knew there was no better way for him to spend his time than soaking up all that Maeve had to offer. He'd sacrificed too much of their time together and now he'd start to give back. And when the time was right, he'd give her all the time in the world.

CHAPTER 27

Maeve blinked her eyes, trying to get rid of the sand blast they'd experienced during their walk. She rubbed at them, grumbling under her breath. "Stupid wind."

"I don't know," Ethan quipped. "I always enjoy getting my skin exfoliated. I'm pretty sure it took three years off my face."

Maeve glared at him, but couldn't seem to stop from smiling. "You're ridiculous."

"And you're stuck with me."

She shook her head, that dang smile still splitting her face. "Come on. I'm sure Mom and Dad will want to say hi."

Barking met the couple as they came into the house and a small ball of fluff careened around the corner, jumping up to greet them.

"Hey, cutie," Maeve cooed. She picked up the small dog. "What're you doing here?"

"Surprise!" Riley said from the family room doorway.

"Oh...it's the traitor," Maeve said wryly.

Ethan coughed to cover a laugh, then tried to school his face when Maeve looked at him.

Riley put her hands on her hips. "I"ll have you know, I was taking care of very important business. I couldn't leave you in the office all by yourself."

"Really..." Maeve responded with no small amount of sarcasm. "Then tell me, what was so important that you had to lock me in, then shove Ethan in against his will?"

"I was finding a home for him." Riley beamed and pointed to the dog.

Maeve stilled as realization dawned. "You're kidding."

Riley shook her head. "Ethan said he couldn't take him forever, so I found another home."

Maeve looked at the panting bundle. "My parents actually agreed to you?"

"Bring him back, would you?" Dad called from his usual spot on the couch. "I'm trying to teach him a trick."

Maeve continued shaking her head as they walked farther in. "Dad...you *never* let us have a dog. Said they were too much work."

Dad shrugged and grinned. "And now I have no kids to take care of. Your mother's going crazy. Not enough people to spoil."

"Don't listen," Mom called from the kitchen. "This was all his idea."

Maeve set the puppy on her father's lap. "This is so unfair."

"Why? You live here. You can enjoy him." Tox had climbed into Dad's lap and was turning circles.

"Seriously, Dad. I just...can't believe you said yes."

"Maybe I'm just really good at being persuasive," Riley quipped from behind Maeve and Ethan.

"Somehow, I'm doubting your charm is the culprit here," Maeve said with a raised eyebrow.

Riley grinned. "I don't know...it got you locked in an office with Ethan."

"What?" Mom came over, a dishtowel flung over her shoulder, as usual. "Who was locked in an office with Ethan?"

Maeve waved an arm at Riley. "You started it. Go right ahead."

Riley shrugged. "Someone had to do something, Mrs. Harrison. They were both being idiots."

"Ain't that the truth," Dad muttered.

"Antony," Mom warned. She pointed a finger at Riley. "No one said anything about locking them in a room."

"How else were we going to get them to talk?" Riley defended herself. "Every time the subject was brought up, they ran screaming in the other direction. The only option left to us was to lure them with cake and force them into compliance." She waved a hand at the couple. "It worked, didn't it?"

Mom tsked her tongue, but Dad laughed.

"If the blush on Ethan's ears is anything to go by, it worked too well."

Maeve groaned and pressed her eyelids. "Dad...please don't."

"Maybe we need to turn on a few more lights and check for beard burn," Riley mused.

"Okay!" Maeve put her hands up. "I don't know why I bothered coming back to the house. Here is your one warning. Ethan and I have worked out our differences. We're together again. And the next person who makes some kind of inappropriate joke is gonna be sleeping with Tox. Got it?"

"Do you know how he got his name?" Dad asked.

Ethan choked.

Maeve looked back, frowning. "Are you okay?"

His face was red and he kept coughing, but nodded. "Yeah," he wheezed. "Just fine."

She turned back to her father. "What are you talking about?"

Dad was smiling a little too wide for comfort. She had a feeling he was about to continue pushing boundaries. "Tox. The name Tox. I have a theory about where it came from."

Maeve shrugged. "Why does it matter?"

"Because it has to do with you."

"Aaaand on that note, I think maybe we need to go visit the workshop," Ethan said loudly. "Come on, Maeve. If you're nice, I'll let you go over my accounting books."

Riley laughed, while Mom clucked her tongue again.

Maeve held up her hand to Ethan. "Wait a second. What's going on here? What do you not want me to know?"

Ethan widened his eyes and shook his head.

"Have you ever wondered where we got your name, Little Mae?" Dad continued. His smirk was driving Maeve crazy.

"Just spit it out, Dad."

His eyes darted to Ethan, then back to Maeve. "Maeve is an old Irish name."

"Irish?" She scrunched her nose. "I didn't know that."

Dad nodded. "And it means 'Intoxicating'." He paused, as if waiting for Maeve to figure it out.

She frowned. Intoxicating...Her eyes widened and she looked to Ethan. "You named the dog...after the meaning of my name?"

He glanced up from under his lashes before dropping his gaze back to the floor. "Maybe..."

Maeve's heart lurched. She walked over. "You really were thinking about me before we got together."

He shrugged and nodded. "Maybe."

Maeve laughed softly. "Thank you. For not giving up."

Ethan smiled, his shoulders relaxing. "What if I told you you were my muse for the board I built for Ollie?"

Maeve's jaw dropped. "What?"

Ethan walked over to Dad. "Hey, Tony. Where's the remote?"

*****

Ethan hoped this was going to be a good idea. He hadn't really planned to share all of it with Maeve. But Tony, being Tony, had somehow figured it all out.

"I'll get you for this," Ethan whispered when Tony winked.

"You can thank me in grandbabies," Tony whispered back.

"You did *not* just say that," Maeve shouted.

Ethan felt as if his cheeks were going to melt off. "Careful, Tony. That might backfire on you."

"I'll take my chances."

"I'm going to move to Italy." Maeve groaned. "I'm living with Grandma."

Mama Em laughed. "Are you really telling me that you think your Italian grandmother is going to be less embarrassing and invasive than your father?" She snorted. "Please. I once watched her accuse your Aunt Grace of being a thief."

Maeve huffed and folded her arms over her chest. "Okay. Fair point. But seriously? Bargaining for grandchildren? Too far, too fast, Dad."

Ethan skimmed the channels as fast as he could. This was going downhill fast. "Okay...here we are." He held back a sigh of relief when the room quieted down. He could just imagine how Riley was never going to let him live this down and every person in their friend group would probably hear about the conversation by the end of the day. The gossip chain among their friends was alive and well, but it was even better amongst the town. Ethan was pretty sure Mr. Theon over at the hardware store would never look at him the same way again.

Maeve stepped up next to him. "Is this a surfing competition?"

Ethan nodded and pointed. "See that guy? That's the one I built the board for."

Maeve's eyes went up. "He's...winning."

"I told you he was the next up and coming thing."

She leaned her head against his shoulder. "I know, but it's kind of surreal to watch it happening in front of us."

"Will they show your board?" Mama Em asked.

"Probably. They were earlier this morning."

The room grew silent, other than Tox's light snores as they watched the coverage. After a couple minutes, the reporters flashed back to an interview earlier in the day and there, front and center, was Ethan's board.

He tuned out the interview, opting to watch Maeve instead, since Ethan had already seen it live earlier that morning.

Her eyes widened, began to glisten with tears and shaking fingers came over her mouth when Ollie talked about where he'd gotten the beautifully painted surfboard. "Ethan," Maeve whispered thickly. "You're famous."

He chuckled. "Uh...no. Ollie's famous. But using my board should mean that my shop is safe from going under. I created the paint job from the night we were on the beach at sunset. You were my inspiration."

With a quick lunge, Maeve wrapped her arms around his neck, a second bout of crying causing her to shake in his arms.

Ethan held on again. Maeve wasn't one to cry much, but she'd done a lot of it in the last few hours and he was starting to wonder if he was the problem.

"Sorry," she hiccuped, pulling back and wiping at her eyes. "I'm just so excited for you."

"We all are," Mama Em said softly.

When Ethan turned back, she smiled at him.

"Your parents would be so proud."

Ethan felt his own tears well up. He didn't spend a lot of time wondering if his parents were watching or what they thought of his life choices, but hearing those words struck a chord nonetheless.

Ethan's surfing obsession had come from his father, though it hadn't been a career for the man. But it was a pastime they'd enjoyed many times together. Thinking about them as he had a moment of triumph built a fire inside of Ethan. He wrapped an arm around Maeve's waist. "Dad might be excited," he quipped. "But I'm betting Mom is more worried about what happened with Maeve and me."

Tony chuckled. "That's a true statement. She was forever telling Emory that our families would be related someday."

"Oh, you," Mama Em scolded. She smacked her husband's shoulder with the towel. "Quit putting the cart before the horse. Let them figure it out for themselves."

"Yes, dear," Tony said automatically. When his wife turned around, he faced Ethan again. "Remember. Payment in grandbabies," he mouthed.

"And we're going out," Maeve announced loudly.

"Uh..." Riley raised her eyebrows. "You might wanna..." She pointed a finger to her own face. "You're a little flushed," she whispered loudly.

Maeve huffed. "Fine. Be right back." Still sniffling, she stomped up the stairs, apparently headed to the bathroom with Riley on her heels.

Her mascara had been a little smeared and her cheeks flushed, but Ethan hadn't minded. She still looked beautiful to him.

"Can I buy all of Tox's equipment from you?" Tony asked once his daughter was out of earshot.

Ethan smiled. "I'm sure we can work something out." He didn't want to admit it, but he was going to miss the pipsqueak. Still, it was better to let Tony have the pup. Ethan could look into getting one later, after everything was settled with Maeve.

Tony scowled. "I have a feeling I'm not going to like your terms."

Ethan shoved his hands in his pockets and shrugged. "Guess we're even, then." His smile grew when Tony grumbled some more. "How's the addition coming? Did Matt say when they were going to be done?"

"A few more weeks," Tony said on a sigh. He glanced hurriedly over his shoulder, then dropped his voice. "I have to admit, it'll help. Those stairs are the bane of my existence."

Ethan sat down on the coffee table so they could talk. "How bad is it, Tony?" He'd been so excited for his reunion with Maeve, and before that, too caught up in the board and his business to have a serious discussion with his neighbor. Ethan had spoken to Maeve, but he had a feeling that Tony kept some of the more serious problems from his kids. He'd never been one to enjoy worrying others.

Tony's shoulders slumped, then shrugged. "Bad enough." He glanced up. "Bad enough I'm not sure how many of those grandchildren I'll get to meet."

Ethan swallowed hard. "Have the doctor's given you any indication....?" He couldn't quite finish the sentence. This discussion was more uncomfortable than being teased about Maeve. No one wanted to talk about death, especially if the person they were talking with was the person dying.

Tony shrugged again. "Less than most," he said softly. "My case seems to be more aggressive and progressing faster than average. Two years? Two months? If we're lucky, another five? I really don't know."

Ethan nodded, his knee bouncing. "You know I'll take care of them, right?" He didn't want Tony to worry about any of it. He needed to focus on enjoying what time he had left, not worrying about how his family would survive when he was gone.

Ethan wasn't going anywhere. Now that he had Maeve back, he would pursue their relationship right up to the chapel and white dress like he'd planned from the beginning. They'd live next door and when Tony's disease finally won, Ethan would make sure Mama Em and any other children left would have everything they needed. He wouldn't let the Harrison family down ever again.

Tony gave him a half smile and a nod. "I know. Thank you. You're a good man, Ethan. And I'll be honored to call you my son officially when it all comes together. Between you and Austin, I'm not worried at all." He leaned forward. "Just don't take too long, got it?"

Ethan smiled back. "I don't plan to."

CHAPTER 28

This time, getting out of her car in the early morning sunshine, Maeve was feeling a little less hesitant than she had a couple months ago. Back then, she'd been determined to conquer her fears and show Ethan that she had everything under control.

This time, she was already working her way through her emotional struggles and the surfing lesson was merely an activity that she was going to enjoy with her boyfriend.

"Morning, beautiful," Ethan said, jogging up to her side. He gave her a kiss on the cheek, his smile wide. "Ready to tackle a few waves?"

"As long as they don't tackle me back," Maeve muttered, rubbing the tiny white scar she had from her stitches.

"Bad luck, is all," Ethan said breezily. He took her hand and began guiding her toward the shop. The shop which had gone through a major renovation in the last few months. The front retail area was basically the same, but the amount of board orders Ethan was getting were keeping him booked months in advance.

Maeve was so proud of him, but this morning her nerves were getting the best of her.

Ethan squeezed her shaking hand as he led her inside. "Let's grab you a board and then I'll show you my world."

Maeve fought the urge to make a sarcastic comment. She wanted to be a part of the world he was offering. She really did. But oh-for-two was terrible odds and even with the help of a therapist over the last few months, she was struggling to keep her composure.

Without warning, Ethan tugged on her hand and gave her a searing kiss. Maeve felt some of the tension leave her shoulders and she returned the affection whole heartedly. Oh, yeah...this was definitely something she could get behind. It was way better than trying to surf.

To her disappointment, Ethan pulled back. "Better?" he whispered.

Maeve stuck her tongue out at him. "Yes, but I don't like admitting it."

He chuckled and tugged her farther back. "I'll be with you every step of the way." He stopped and glanced over his shoulder. "I promise." The words were said with a heavy conviction and Maeve almost felt bad that he needed to reiterate the power behind them

"I know," she responded. "You've proven yourself over and over again. It's myself I'm worried about. Maybe I'm just not coordinated enough to be a surfer. Maybe I'll just always cheer from the beach."

"No can do, sweetheart," he said, his eyes going to a rack of surfboards. "If I can sit through you showing me all the ins and outs of my retail taxes, you can certainly give this another try."

"Taxes are safe, though," Maeve muttered.

"That's one opinion," he quipped.

Maeve rolled her eyes. "Fine. They say the third time's the charm, right? Guess we'll see if we can prove it." They'd already proved it with their relationship. Hopefully the same luck would work out for surfing.

Ethan pulled out the board he wanted and presented it to her. "What do you think?"

Maeve hesitated. "It looks like..." Her eyes widened. "Ethan...did you make me a 'Maeve' board?"

"I couldn't let the muse surf without the real deal."

Another chunk of her anxiety dissipated and she reached out, letting her fingers glide along the fiery sunrise of colors. "It's perfect," she whispered.

"Just like you." He handed her the board, then kissed her cheek again. "Come on. Daylight's wasting."

Nerves still danced in her belly, but Maeve knew she couldn't back down now. Reason after reason just kept piling up as to why she needed to see this through. But first and foremost was because she desperately wanted to give something back to Ethan.

He'd worked his tail off to show her he was trustworthy as she got professional help for her long-held trauma. He was adapting to his booming business and spoiled her every step of the way, excitedly sharing milestones with her like a little boy with his favorite toy.

Maeve felt like she'd had so little to offer. She cheered him on, and she taught him about his taxes, numbers and growth potential. She helped out everywhere she could, but none of it felt like enough. She wanted to show him that she *trusted* him. That she was overcoming the incident that had led to their original separation.

That she was healing.

And how better than to share in the very thing that brought Ethan to life? The activity that had once been a source of contention could now be a way to come together. So though Maeve was doing a bit of grumbling, she really did want to conquer this. And even better, this time she wouldn't have to try to conquer it alone.

He held the door of the shop open for her. "Here we go."

Maeve tucked the board under her arm and walked into the light. Her flip flops quickly became filled with sand as they marched across the beach to the point of the ocean.

Pausing just long enough to zip up wetsuits and talk a little about rules, Maeve all too soon found herself wading out into the icy waters.

"Geez." she gasped. "Maybe we should come back in June."

Ethan laughed. "A full-body wetsuit isn't enough for you? Where are the booties?"

"Forgot them." Maeve shook her head, trying to block out the freezing cold water. "Besides, I should be able to grip the board better, right? Toe to wood?"

He shrugged. "Booties help prevent cold and any possible cuts or bruises. We really should make sure you have some next time." He paused. "But we won't stay too long today. Just a short lesson and we'll go get you some hot chocolate. I have some in the back of the shop."

"I'll hold you to that," she muttered, her teeth beginning to chatter.

"Alright, cold lady. Climb on and let's start swimming. It'll warm you up in no time."

Maeve took a deep fortifying breath. This was it. This was the moment she'd been dreading and waiting for all at the same time. This time it wasn't about her...it was for him.

Swallowing down her desire to throw up, she clambered onto the board and began swinging her arms. It was time to give Ethan a gift he wouldn't forget.

*****

Ethan was going to throw up. He just knew it. "You're amazing!" he gushed, trying to hide his nervousness.

Maeve laughed and shook out her hair, flinging water droplets all over him.

The icy cold water felt good on his heated skin.

"Well, I managed to stay on my feet for a whole thirty seconds. We'll count that as a win."

He flung an arm around her neck and kissed her wet temple. "It'll only get better from here. Thank you for being willing to try again." He'd been so excited to share this with her. She'd had such bad experiences with one of his favorite parts of life and he'd been praying for weeks that he'd manage to change all that.

From the smile on her face, Ethan was guessing it hadn't turned out too bad.

She shivered. "I think you promised me hot chocolate."

"It's in the shop. Come on." Stepping back so they could walk better, he took her hand and led the way. The closer they got, the more his nerves began to dance. Life had been so good lately. Christmas had been the best year ever, having spent it with the Harrisons. The addition to the house had proved to be a huge blessing to Tony and the tension at the house had lessened some with the improvements. Ethan's business was better than ever and for the first winter ever, he hadn't gone to work construction, except to help resign and extend his workshop on the back of the surf shop.

But all of those life wins paled in comparison to the one he was hoping to win today. Right now. Just as soon as they got inside...

"Here. Let's let the boards dry off." Ethan set aside the equipment, leaning them against the shop. He'd gather them later.

His stiff hand could barely grip the door handle, but somehow Ethan managed to pull it open. He stepped back, allowing Maeve to go inside first.

"Thanks," she said, beaming at him. Her caramel eyes flashed his way before she walked over the threshold.

Warily, Ethan came in behind her, the door bouncing against his back. Maeve had stopped and he barely had enough room to stand inside.

"What's...going on?" Maeve asked.

A massive crowd stood in the shop, and every friend and relative they had in the small town of Seagull Cove was smiling like lunatics as they watched Ethan and Maeve.

Tox, who was being held by Mama Em, barked, causing a chuckle to go throughout the room.

Maeve shook her head, then turned, looking questioningly at Ethan. "Eeks?"

Taking her arms, Ethan pushed her back ever so slightly. They were too close for him to do this properly. His heart was beating against his sternum so hard, he was sure it would escape any minute. Despite the icy chill of the water they'd just emerged from, sweat trickled down his spine, giving further evidence to his nerves.

As soon as Maeve had stepped back enough, Ethan dropped to one knee.

Maeve gasped, her hands covering her mouth.

Reaching out, he took her arms and brought her hands down so he could clutch them in his own. "Maeve Linlee Harrison," he croaked, then cleared his throat. "Maeve...we've known each other...a long time."

More chuckles resounded.

"For the first few years of our life, you were simply another girl next door. Then you became my best friend's little sister. But eventually, we grew up a little and your beauty captured me in a way very few things ever have."

Her bottom lip began to tremble.

"But being confident and stupid, like most teenage boys, I tried to take the leap from neighbor to boyfriend and I went about it all wrong."

She shook her head. "No...it wasn't wrong."

He held up a hand. "It was wrong because I was more concerned with showing off than taking care of you and fulfilling my promises." He squeezed her hands and smiled. "But luckily, we don't stay teenagers and I like to think that for the most part, I've matured."

A couple of coughs made the group laugh as some of Ethan's friends disputed his claim.

"Our relationship has been," he ticked his head back and forth, "rocky."

She laughed softly.

"And I've made more stupid mistakes, but I'm still learning and I'm still becoming. And now, I've figured out that I'd only like to continue to become more, if you're by my side."

Tears began trickling down her cheeks.

"I love you. So much more than I could ever have imagined. Would you do me the greatest honor I could ever imagine by shifting from being my neighbor, my sweet, beautiful neighbor...to becoming my wife? My stunning, gorgeous, brilliant wife, who surfs with me on the weekends and does my taxes in the evenings? Will you let me hold you when the sun rises on the ocean, forever and always reminding me of the design that provided me with the opportunity to even have a life to share with you at all?" He held his breath as she took a couple of shuddering ones of her own.

"Ethan, you have always been so much more than a neighbor to me. Even when I was hurting and struggling, I could never keep you in that neat little category. I always wanted you to be more, and if moving from the title of boyfriend to fiance and surf partner is a possibility, then I'm all in. Even on cold, early mornings when you're teaching me how to share in the activity that makes you who you are." She pulled loose of his hands and cupped his face, leaning down for a soft, lingering kiss. "Thank you for not giving up and for helping me see all the world had to offer. I'm the luckiest girl alive to get to experience it with you at my side," she whispered thickly.

Ethan was done waiting. He jumped to his feet and gathered Maeve close, kissing her soundly as family and friends shouted their congratulations. When her arms wrapped around his neck, he realized he'd made a tactical error in inviting anyone to join with them at all. He'd thought it would be nice to have them there since so many of them had been instrumental in helping get them back together. *Rookie mistake.*

"Alright, son," Tony said with a laugh, slapping Ethan on the shoulder. "There'll be enough time for that later."

Ethan reluctantly pulled back, but he was amused at the disappointment echoed in Maeve's face. She apparently would have been fine with a quiet proposal as well.

"Is it our turn?"

Ethan turned. "Oh, yeah. Guess we better do this right." He held out his hand and Riley dropped a ring box into it. He couldn't very well have held onto it in his wetsuit, so he'd assigned Riley the job, promising to finally forgive her for all her teasing and snarky comments during his time with Maeve. "This is for you, sweetheart," Ethan whispered, gently pushing the three-diamond ring onto her finger. "One diamond for every chance until we got it right."

Maeve gasped at it. "It's so beautiful."

He kissed her forehead. "Just like you," he murmured against her skin.

Riley cleared her throat, then raised her eyebrows when Ethan looked her way.

"Go ahead," he instructed.

Rubbing her hands in glee, Riley turned and grabbed something off the ground.

"What in the world?" Maeve asked, holding out her arms.

"We can't name her Tox," Ethan said as Maeve cuddled the fluffball Riley had brought. "But I thought it would be good if we had someone to play with Tox when we go visit your parents."

Maeve laughed. "She's perfect." Looking at her dad, she teased, "Want to meet your grandpuppy?"

Tony pointed a shaky finger at Ethan. "That doesn't count."

Ethan shrugged. "Guess we'll see, huh?"

Mama Em pushed her way up and wrapped her arms around Maeve and the puppy. "He's right," she said to Ethan over Maeve's shoulder. "It doesn't count." She pulled back and scratched the dog's head. "Though she is darling."

"We're not even married yet, Mom," Maeve whined. "You can't complain about kids yet."

"Watch me," Tony argued, causing yet more laughter and chatter through the room.

"What about Aspen? She's been married for a while. Talk to her about it," Maeve said, waving her arm toward her sister.

Austin's face drained of all color when the eyes of the room landed on him and he stepped behind his wife.

Aspen rolled her eyes at his dramatics. "Come on, everyone. I made an engagement cake." She grinned. "Who wants the giant chocolate surfboard decorating the top?"

As the mass of bodies began moving toward the back, Ethan held Maeve behind, wanting just a moment alone with her.

"Well?" he asked when it had quieted down. "Is this going to be an okay start to our lives?"

Maeve tucked the puppy to one side and reached up with her other hand, letting her fingers sift through his wet hair. "It's more than I could have ever imagined. It was perfect." She glanced down with a laugh. "Though I have to admit the puppy was a surprise."

Ethan chuckled. "You always seemed to have a good time with Tox and Riley had another litter she was struggling to get rid of."

Maeve laughed. "You're such a sucker."

He leaned in. "I was a sucker for you back when we were only neighbors."

Maeve rose up to meet him. "You were never 'only the neighbor'. But calling you husband is going to be the best thing ever."

Being a husband was going to be great, but Ethan knew the best thing ever was the woman in his arms. They'd finally gotten it right. With a little help, a lot of luck and the interference of far too many family members, they'd managed to figure out exactly what would bring them the most happiness in life. He made a vow then and there to never take it for granted again. They'd worked too hard to get to this point and Ethan had promises to keep. Promises that would keep the love of his life by his side forever and always.

EPILOGUE

Michael leaned his shoulder against the wall, a soft smile playing on his lips. He was happy for Maeve. She and Ethan would be very happy together. Anyone with a lick of sense knew that and had known it since they were all kids together.

Ethan's extroverted carefreeness and Maeve's more watchful and reserved personalities would keep their relationship balanced. She would pull him down from the clouds and he would push her out of her comfort zone.

As witnessed by this morning's surf lesson, he thought with a chuckle.

"Cake?"

He nodded as Gavin handed him a plate, then leaned against the wall himself. "Thanks," Michael murmured, taking a large bite. Geez, his cousin could cook. It paid to be related to the Harrisons. World class food for free. No one could top that.

"What's got that smoke coming out of your ears?" Gavin questioned.

Michael snorted. "Smoke? The wheels aren't turning that hard."

Gavin shrugged. "Something's churning in there. Figuring out your lesson plans for tomorrow?"

Michael chuckled. "Nah. They're set for the year. Though how to keep the kids engaged is another story. This is the time of year when they start feeling like it'll all last forever and they get antsy."

"I thought that was only the little guys," Gavin said. "In middle school they have sports and other activities. Doesn't that help?"

Michael shook his head. "Nope. They still can't sit still."

"I'm so glad I don't have your job."

"I don't know...putting out fires and teaching literature to tweens and teens carries about the same amount of danger."

Gavin's laughter was heavy and low. He was a large guy and his voice, though usually quiet, had a depth to it that few others could pull off. "I'll stick with the fires."

"And the weight benches." Michael frowned. "Is it my imagination, or are you getting bigger?"

Gavin smirked. "It's the off season," he said. "Gotta do something to keep busy."

Michael nodded. "Understandable. Wildfires are a lot less frequent during the winter and I don't usually hear of too many house or business fires around here."

Gavin shook his head. "Nope. Not too many. Which is a blessing...and a curse." He gave a jerk of his chin. "I'm gonna go get a drink. Want anything?"

"Nah. I'm fine here in my little corner, thanks."

Shaking his head good naturedly, Gavin weaved through the crowd.

Michael sighed and set himself back into people watching. Slowly, his group of friends was starting to pair off. First Aspen, followed by Mason and Harper. Now it was Ethan and Maeve. What was interesting was how long they'd all known each other and the last two engagements were people finding love within their group.

He tilted his head, letting his eyes linger on the other women he was friends with. There was Riley, of course. She was close with his cousins. She was peppy and fun and her light blue eyes would attract any man's attention.

Michael blew out a breath. *Nope. Not that one.* She was his friend and he never found himself wanting to push those boundaries.

A flash of red caught his attention and Michael watched Brielle throw her head back and laugh at something Jayden was saying. Brielle was also beautiful, in her own way. Long, wavy hair and brown eyes. She was spunky, said what was on her mind and loved to try and keep up with the boys," as she put it.

Michael shook his head again. That wasn't for him. He liked his quiet life and time spent with Brielle was anything but quiet.

He let his eyes wander again. His mother would be so disappointed in his lack of interest. He was one of the oldest of the cousins and now that there were two getting married, she would be pushing him to find his significant other. But single females seemed to be getting thin on the ground, at least amongst those he was familiar with.

For the umpteenth time, he debated whether he should look to start next fall in a bigger city. There was something to be said for the peaceful familiarity of a small town. Michael had his students for multiple years and got to be good friends with a few. He enjoyed knowing all the parents and being able to work one-on-one with children in a way that larger schools and areas couldn't handle.

But knowing everyone since birth also makes for a hard social life.

"We're so glad you made it!" Aspen gushed, jerking Michael's attention away from his musing. Aspen was hugging someone at the front door and Michael frowned, unable to figure out who had been missing.

Dark, nearly black corkscrew curls were pulled up into a bun with a few straw spirals framing an oval face.

Quinn, Michael said to himself. He'd forgotten about her. She was fairly new to Seagull Cove and Michael had yet to be introduced, though they'd attended a couple of events with the group. Quinn had opened an antique shop in town, which was a perfect addition to every small coastal city along the Pacific coastline.

He watched her smile shyly and tuck back a curl, only for it to spring right back where it wanted to be.

Michael laughed softly to himself. He couldn't see her eye color from his corner, but they looked much lighter than her hair, creating an interesting contrast. Her skin was a study in porcelain, giving her a slightly paranormal look. She could easily pull off a vampire anytime she wanted with a simple swipe of red lipstick.

She was taller than his cousin and willowy in a way the Italian Harrisons lacked. While no one would ever mistake Quinn for anything but a woman, her curves were much more subtle.

He found himself slowing down in his cake consumption as he watched her. Something about the line of her jaw and the tenderness of her smile kept his attention. Her movements were fluid and elegant and when she finally spoke, it seemed that her hands were an active part of the conversation.

There were scores of poems and ballads written about women just like Quinn. Her ethereal beauty was the kind that Medieval men went to war over and Michael could just see some soldier declaring his undying love to her before shipping across seas.

"There's that smoke again."

Michael blinked, finally wrenching his mind out of his too wild imagination. His love of stories and fantasy didn't always serve him well in social situations. "Are you feeling more hydrated now?" Michael asked, hoping no one had noticed his staring.

Gavin huffed. "Yeah. But I'm about ready to blow this joint. The cake's gone and no one will stop talking about dates and dresses." He raised an eyebrow. "Do school teachers ever play hooky?"

Michael cleared his throat, still trying to force his brain into an appropriate line of thought. "Uh, yeah. Sure. I'm done here." His eyes flashed to those dark curls one more time and his curiosity went up yet another notch. Maybe he hadn't quite ruled out all the possibilities in this town.

He'd muse on it for a while, but he was starting to think that a trip to the newest shop in town just might be in his future.

DON'T MISS MICHAEL AND QUINN'S JOURNEY TO LOVE
IN "THE SWEETEST DISCOVERY"